PRAISE
MONSTER HUN

"A crackling good read. Annelise Ryan brings us to a fascinating location with a complex, edgy plot and an intelligent, fearless protagonist. Be prepared to read *A Death in Door County* in one sitting!"

—Terrie Farley Moran, award-winning coauthor of the Murder, She Wrote novels

"An adventuresome page-turner for anyone who's ever gotten goose bumps wondering what creatures might lurk in deep, dark waters. . . . You'll turn the last page of *A Death in Door County* feeling spine-tinglingly satisfied—and raring for the next installment."

—Alicia Bessette, bestselling author of *Murder on Mustang Beach*

"A satisfying adventure cozy."   —*Kirkus Reviews*

"Full of fascinating history and lore, as well as the underwater geography of these fearsome waterways, this new mystery from Mattie Winston series author Ryan is a tour de force featuring a plucky and [eminently] likable sleuth. A deliciously clever and entertaining puzzle, highly recommended."

—*Library Journal* (starred review)

"Ryan conjures a wonderfully spooky atmosphere as Carter risks her life in search of the truth, and expertly keeps readers in the dark about the perpetrator's identity for most of the narrative. With a strong premise and smart characterizations, this series is well suited to a long run."   —*Publishers Weekly*

"This monster-hunting cozy series keeps delivering the chills as Bigfoot stalks the deep dark woods.... Filled with great characters, fast-paced plotting, and scary situations, this cryptid-based cozy is a nice break from the usual and provides readers with a great escape."   —*Fresh Fiction*

BERKLEY PRIME CRIME TITLES
BY ANNELISE RYAN

Death in Door County
Death in the Dark Woods

DEATH
in the
DARK WOODS

⌐

ANNELISE RYAN

BERKLEY PRIME CRIME · NEW YORK

BERKLEY PRIME CRIME
Published by Berkley
An imprint of Penguin Random House LLC
penguinrandomhouse.com

Copyright © 2023 by Beth Amos
Excerpt from *Beast of the North Woods* by Annelise Ryan copyright © 2024 by Beth Amos
Penguin Random House values and supports copyright. Copyright fuels creativity,
encourages diverse voices, promotes free speech, and creates a vibrant culture. Thank
you for buying an authorized edition of this book and for complying with copyright
laws by not reproducing, scanning, or distributing any part of it in any form without
permission. You are supporting writers and allowing Penguin Random House
to continue to publish books for every reader. Please note that no part of
this book may be used or reproduced in any manner for the purpose
of training artificial intelligence technologies or systems.

BERKLEY and the BERKLEY & B colophon are registered trademarks
and BERKLEY PRIME CRIME is a trademark of Penguin Random House LLC.

Book design by Elke Sigal

Berkley Prime Crime paperback ISBN: 9780593441626

The Library of Congress has cataloged the Berkley
Prime Crime hardcover edition of this book as follows:

Names: Ryan, Annelise, author.
Title: Death in the dark woods / Annelise Ryan.
Description: New York: Berkley Prime Crime, [2023] |
Series: A Monster Hunter mystery; 2
Identifiers: LCCN 2023022889 (print) | LCCN 2023022890 (ebook) |
ISBN 9780593441602 (hardcover) | ISBN 9780593441619 (ebook)
Subjects: LCSH: Cryptozoology—Fiction. | Murder—Investigation—Fiction. |
LCGFT: Detective and mystery fiction. | Novels.
Classification: LCC PS3568.Y2614 D46 2023 (print) |
LCC PS3568.Y2614 (ebook) | DDC 813/.54—dc23/eng/20230526
LC record available at https://lccn.loc.gov/2023022889
LC ebook record available at https://lccn.loc.gov/2023022890

Berkley Prime Crime hardcover edition / December 2023
Berkley Prime Crime trade paperback edition / December 2024

Printed in the United States of America
1st Printing

For my auntie Mame

DEATH
in the
DARK WOODS

PROLOGUE

⌐

The loud snap of a twig alerted Bodie Erickson, and he stood slowly, staring into the fog and trees in front of him. Sharp movement caught his eye and in the undulating mist he could just make out the shape of a buck standing between two trees on a ridge about thirty yards ahead. He centered the animal in the crosshairs of his compound bow.

A distant sound, a guttural ululation made the hairs on Bodie's neck rise as it echoed through the air. The buck's head rose, eyes wild, nostrils flaring as it exhaled anxious puffs of warm breath into the chilly morning air. Filmy tendrils of fog slithered and flowed silently between the trees, making gooseflesh race along Bodie's arms. Sensing more movement off to his left, he briefly looked away from the buck but saw nothing other than shifting fog. He shook his head and sighted in on the buck again, but something, either that preternatural sound or Bodie's movement, had it flashing the white of its tail as it disappeared into the woods.

Cursing, Bodie climbed down from his tree stand and swore (not for the first time) he was done hunting deer in the Chequamegon Forest. If not for the bad luck he had here he'd have no luck at all. Screw it. Wisconsin was full of places to hunt. Time to move on.

When he reached ground level, he leaned his bow against the side of a nearby trunk, pulled off his fingerless gloves and tucked them into one armpit. Then he blew on his hands to warm them, his breath creating tiny clouds in the brisk October air and leaving beads of moisture in his beard. Irritated, he stomped his feet, as much to get the circulation going as to vent his frustration. He'd been in that damned tree stand since aught-dark-thirty and all for nothing.

He put his gloves back on and began taking his mobile stand down from the tree. He'd removed the main portion and set it on the ground so he could fold and strap it together into something more manageable to carry when he heard a loud crack behind him. He turned slowly, wondering if the buck had circled around or if another one might be nearby. As his eyes searched the surrounding trees, he reached back for his bow, cursing to himself when he realized it was too far away and the bulk of his stand was a tripping hazard on the ground behind him. Muttering another curse, he turned and sidestepped the tree stand to get to his bow. As he reached for it, he heard the snap of a foot crushing undergrowth behind him.

Bodie turned and stared into the fog as it swirled and flowed around the trees. It seemed denser now than it had minutes ago, and he shivered. He wasn't sure if the chill was due to the cold or to the crazy thoughts running through his head because he'd heard stories about how the Chequamegon Forest was haunted by spirits and monsters, everything from screaming banshees and the requisite number of Bigfoot sightings to killer bears, wolves, and wildcats. Bodie knew the latter threats were all too real and he carried bear spray with him as a backup. As for the more imaginative rumors, he'd never put much stock in such nonsense. Until now. Something about the woods felt eerie, off, wrong somehow.

He heard more snaps emanating from the surrounding brush and it sounded like they were coming from several directions at once. The sounds suggested a big animal, at least as big as the buck he'd seen earlier, and he grabbed a bolt and readied his crossbow, unsure where to aim. He squinted, trying to see something . . . anything out there in the undulating whiteness and thick growth of trees. As wind soughed through the branches overhead, he realized luck was with him because he was downwind of where he thought the sounds had come from. He stood with his crossbow at the ready, scanning, searching, struggling to make sense of the shadows he saw in that eerie curtain of shifting fog. Thick tendrils of mist curled around the trees like ghostly fingers reaching for something.

Give it up, Bodie. Go home.

He was about to heed his inner voice and release the tension on his bow when he heard another loud *crack*. Then another. And another. Footsteps. Coming toward him.

Bodie's pulse quickened, and he stared into the fog toward the ridge, desperate to spot the animal. It occurred to him it might be a bear rather than a deer, in which case his bolt wouldn't be much help unless he scored an extremely lucky shot, and even then, pure adrenaline might drive the beast onward long enough for it to do him some serious damage if it didn't kill him outright. He wished he was up in his tree stand rather than at ground level. He'd not only have a better view of what was ahead, he'd be safer. Yes, bears could climb trees, but at least the extra height would provide him with a small advantage and a little extra time to ready his bear spray.

The smell hit him then, a rank, pungent, musky odor, and in a parting of the fog he saw a flash of dark brown fur moving between the trees.

There! Only about thirty yards away!

The way the animal moved struck Bodie as wrong, but before he had time to figure out why, it stopped and rose to a frightening height, sending Bodie into panic mode.

He let his bolt fly and heard it land with a solid *thunk* that told him he'd hit flesh. There was a crash, followed by the echoes of a bloodcurdling, unearthly scream in the thick morning air, making Bodie think those stories about banshees might be true after all.

He heard something coming toward him then, but not from the direction where he'd shot. This time it was coming from off to his left, from a dense growth of tall bushes, the branches of which swayed, cracked, and then exploded.

Bodie had enough time to register that it wasn't a deer, bear, or wolf, though he wasn't sure what the hell it was. He saw a blur of big, brown teeth, shaggy fur, and bloodshot eyes, and then the creature was upon him, biting, clawing, ripping, and shrieking.

Bodie howled with pain as he dropped his bow—useless now—and fumbled for his can of bear spray. He found it, flipped off the plastic guard, and depressed the lever, unleashing a stream of noxious liquid as the creature bit hard into his scalp. The spray hit

Bodie as well as his attacker, and rather than scaring the animal away, it angered it. Bodie's eyes were on fire and watering profusely, his tears mixing with blood and all but blinding him. The animal kept up its ruthless attack, coming at him from all angles, tearing at his clothes, his skin. Bodie tried to push it away with his free hand, but something was wrong.

Oh my God! Where the hell is my hand?

The animal went for his face.

Bodie let go of the bear spray and fumbled at his belt, pulled his knife from its sheath and then dropped it as the creature bit down hard on his arm. He was completely blind now and his right arm wouldn't work anymore. The animal was at his back waging a frenzied, relentless attack and, weakened from blood loss, Bodie fell to his knees and then onto his back in a last-ditch act of desperation. It didn't work. The creature had incredible strength, and it flipped Bodie's body over like he was a rag doll.

Bodie's mind took a strange detour then, his thoughts oddly calm and detached as he puzzled over the fact that he hadn't seen his bolt anywhere in the creature's body. Had he missed it, or had the animal pulled it out? Then he remembered how this creature had come from a different direction than where he'd shot.

Good God, are there more than one of them?

Blind and weak from his flailing attempts to stop the attack, Bodie was helpless to defend himself as the creature began tearing at the flesh of his neck. Mercifully, there was no more pain by then, just a waning instinct to survive and an awareness of the stench—a raw, not-quite-rancid, animalistic smell.

Bodie's last bit of awareness was the sound of the animal's bloodcurdling ululation echoing through the chilly morning air.

CHAPTER 1

I looked up as the bell above the door to my store, Odds and Ends, jingled to announce a new arrival. A blond, blue-eyed fellow in a police uniform entered and I immediately broke into a big smile at the sight of him.

"Jon! Hello!" I hurried over to greet him, my dog, Newt, close on my heels.

"Hello, Morgan," he said. A mini tornado of red, brown, and yellow leaves swirled in behind him, carried on a gust of brisk fall air before the door closed. He did a quick surveil of my store, taking in the customers browsing the aisles. It was mid-October and Mother Nature was flaunting her colors, a vibrant, vivid display known to draw tons of leaf peepers to the area. Lots of visitors meant lots of shoppers for the store. If only all shoppers equated to buyers.

"This is a surprise," I said.

It was. Mostly. Jon Flanders was the Chief of Police for Washington Island, which is located off the tip of the Door County peninsula here in Wisconsin. While I'm quite fond of Jon and have seen him several times over the past few weeks, his unexpected arrival unsettled me a little. I mean, it wasn't as if he decided to drop in because he was in the neighborhood. Getting to my store in Sister Bay required him to take a half-hour-long ferry ride and then do a bit of driving. Plus, he was in his uniform, suggesting he might be here on official business.

Newt was clearly glad to see him. He walked up and pushed his massive head into Jon's hand while wagging his tail hard enough to threaten inventory on some nearby shelves.

"Looks like business is booming." Jon said with an approving nod, stroking Newt's head.

"It is. What brings you by today?"

He turned his attention back to me and, for a moment, his eyes warmed, his expression softening. Then he got all serious and businesslike. "I want you to meet a DNR warden by the name of Charlie Aberdeen who should be here in a few minutes."

"Okay," I said slowly, trying to parse this out. "Can I ask why you want me to meet a DNR warden?"

He winked at me, and I saw a wicked gleam in his eyes. "You'll see," he said vaguely. "I rather enjoy keeping you in suspense for now, though I will let you know Charlie is driving down here from Bayfield and wants to hire you. If you decide to take the job, I'm hoping you'll do it pro bono. Money is an issue."

"Hire me? You mean as a cryptozoologist?"

Jon nodded.

While I own Odds and Ends—a combination mystery book-store and oddities vendor—I also do work on the side searching for cryptids, creatures thought to exist despite there being no proof. Jon and I met a couple of months ago when he hired me to look for a Loch Ness–type monster in Lake Michigan after a couple of mysterious deaths had occurred.

His pro bono request wasn't a big deal. I don't search for cryptids to make money; I do it because I love it and to continue the work my parents did in the field. Jon knew this, though he hadn't known it when he first hired me. I find a willingness to pay can sometimes be a good indicator of sincerity and motive. I'm a cynic at heart, and I approach my cryptid searches from a position of science and reality, not speculation and rumor. There are hucksters out there claiming to be cryptozoologists, and I'm always eager to distinguish myself from them.

"I only charge people to determine their level of commitment and seriousness," I reminded Jon. "A recommendation from you serves the same purpose, assuming I decide to take the case."

"Oh, you'll take it," he said with a knowing grin, managing to both annoy and intrigue me. "Assuming Charlie's willing to trust you."

That gave me pause. "What do you mean?"

Jon's mouth twitched. "Charlie has already dealt with a fellow claiming to be a cryptozoologist and things didn't go well. Apparently, the fellow sounded all excited at first, but after they discussed plans for him to come to the area and help out, the money game began."

"He wanted cash up front," I said, nodding. I'd heard of similar scams before.

"Yep. The DNR and the local law enforcement agencies want nothing to do with this, so Charlie offered to pay this guy a small fee. It wasn't going to be nearly enough. First, he wanted round trip airfare from Connecticut, a rental car, accommodations once he got to Bayfield, and an agreement to pay an hourly fee. Then he asked for a bunch of expensive equipment, a local guide, and a large upfront deposit."

This MO sounded familiar. "Do you happen to know this guy's name?"

"The last name is Baumann. I think his first name was . . ." His face scrunched up in thought and he tapped the side of his head a few times. "Herman? No, that wasn't it, but it was something like that."

"Hans," I said.

Jon snapped his fingers, getting Newt's attention. "Yes, that's it! Do you know him?"

"I'm afraid I do, mostly by reputation. I only met him once, about five years ago, on a trip with my parents, but I've followed him and his antics online for years. He's a shyster. If there's a way to bilk gullible folks out of their money, he'll find it."

"Good thing Charlie ditched him then," Jon said. He focused more fully on Newt, who had been whining for attention ever since the first head scratch. Jon reached down—he didn't have to go far since Newt stands more than two feet at the shoulder—and sandwiched Newt's head between both hands, giving him a good, hard rub. "How ya doing, Newt, old boy?"

Newt, who is not just big but also nearly blind, wagged his tail so hard he brushed a display of shrunken heads—fake ones, the only real one I had was in a glass case elsewhere in the store—off a nearby shelf. I quickly picked them up and replaced them after telling Newt to sit so his swishing tail disturbed only dust rather than the merchandise.

I had just returned the scattered heads to their rightful spots when the bell over the door tinkled, and a woman walked in. She was pretty with a pale, flawless complexion, shiny black hair with bangs, and huge blue eyes rimmed with thick, dark lashes. I pegged her as in her late twenties, maybe early thirties. She was dressed in boots, blue jeans, a khaki shirt, and a vest with an embroidered patch from the Department of Natural Resources on the right shoulder. A name tag on her shirt read C. Aberdeen.

Charlie was a woman? I did a fast mental adjustment in my head, feeling strangely disoriented.

Jon waved at her, and she smiled as soon as she saw him, making a dimple in her right cheek deepen. She started toward him but then her gaze shifted inexorably to Henry, and she stopped, staring in astonishment. Henry is a mummified corpse that typically sits on a chair along the edge of the book section of the store near the entrance. He's our unofficial mascot and greeter, though he tends toward the taciturn. Currently, he was suspended on a wheeled pole to make it look like he was standing, something we do with him every year in preparation for Halloween.

C. Aberdeen pointed and said, "Is that—"

"Real?" Jon finished for her. "It is. Meet Henry."

She moved closer to get a better look—Henry was wearing a large, floppy hat set at a jaunty angle to hide some of his face since he was missing his nose. Seeing how curious she was, I decided to enlighten her and offered up an abbreviated version of Henry's history.

"Rumor has it that Henry was a forty-niner who went west to look for gold and eventually headed up to Alaska. Unfortunately, he fell into a crevasse in the ice up there, died, and became mummified. He's had some travels since and ended up here when my father bought him."

Warden Aberdeen looked at me with a surprisingly whimsical smile, and then did a quick surveil of my place. "I wondered what a store called Odds and Ends might be about," she said, zeroing in on three eerie-looking African masks I had hanging on one wall. "I don't think I ever would have guessed."

"The store was my parents' idea. They were both fascinated by anything weird, unusual, or strange in the world, and they collected oddities during their travels. My mother was also an avid mystery reader, so she decided to dedicate part of the store to books. Those would be the 'ends' in Odds and Ends since someone always dies in a mystery."

"Ah, I get it," she said. "Very clever. Such a unique place." Her gaze settled on Jon, and she smiled warmly. "You look just like your picture. Nice to meet you in real life."

Jon returned her smile and extended a hand for her to shake. "You look younger in real life than you do in your pictures," he said. Their hands clasped and they did a token shake while Warden Aberdeen beamed at Jon. The amount of time the two spent eyeing one another made me a tad uncomfortable. Finally, Warden Aberdeen shifted her gaze to Newt, who was obediently sitting at my side. "May I?" she asked, pointing toward him.

"Of course." I was pleased and impressed she showed no fear of Newt. He's a sweetheart, but he can look and seem intimidating at times. Plus, I find dogs are a good barometer for people and their personalities.

Warden Aberdeen—Charlie, I reminded myself, though my prior association of a man with the name was proving hard to shake—walked over to Newt, bent down, and stroked his giant head. Newt closed his eyes in momentary ecstasy and then gave her a big, wet kiss up one side of her face. I thought she might rear back from Newt's slobbery display of gratitude, but instead she let out the most delightful, heartfelt laugh before returning the gesture by kissing Newt's muzzle.

She straightened and cocked her head to one side. "I apologize for my manners. I imagine you must be Morgan Carter. I'm Charlotte Aberdeen, but everyone calls me Charlie."

She extended a hand, which I shook. "Pleasure to meet you. And this slobbery fellow is Newt," I said, nodding toward my dog, who was gazing up at Charlie with blatant adoration. "Let's go upstairs to my apartment so we can talk."

I looked toward the counter where one of my employees, Devon Thibodeaux, was checking out customers. He appeared busy, so I looked for my other employee, Rita Bosworth, who's always easy to spot thanks to her rhinestone-studded eyeglass chain and a tall, lanky frame topped off with a messy bun of snow-white hair. I caught Rita's eye—she was always tuned in to me, it seemed—and pointed toward the ceiling. She nodded and I turned back to Jon and Charlie.

"Follow me." I led them through the store displays to a locked door and, once I opened it, upstairs to my apartment, the place I'd called home my entire life even though I hadn't spent much time in it.

"Oh, wow!" Charlie said as we emerged on the upper floor. She did a slow spin, taking in the large open area that made up my living room, dining area, and kitchen. Bright, cheery daylight streamed in through the tall windows on the front wall, bathing everything with a warm, inviting glow. The décor was eclectic and colorful, filled with items my parents had bought during their travels around the world. There was no theme to the furnishings, no attempt at a color scheme, or any real organization to any of it, yet it all seemed to work, the colors blending or complimenting each other, the unrelated items fitting together in a welcoming and cozy way.

"Yeah, that was my reaction, too, the first time I saw it," Jon said. He looked over at me and smiled.

Feeling a little embarrassed, I said, "Charlie, have a seat in the living room. Can I get you something to drink? I have lemonade, or I can fix you a cup of coffee or tea if you like. I also have a few beers in the fridge, if you'd prefer."

"I'd love a cup of coffee," Charlie said, wandering into the living room and running her fingers appreciatively over the arm of my Adirondack chair. "Black is fine."

"Jon?"

"Coffee sounds good to me, too."

I saw the two of them exchange warm smiles and turned away to focus on my coffee machine. "Three coffees, coming up," I said, hoping I sounded more chipper than I felt.

CHAPTER 2

I set a pot of coffee to brewing while talking over my shoulder to Charlie, telling her where the various pieces in the house had come from. I'd covered the dining room and most of the living room pieces and was explaining how the Adirondack chair she'd just been admiring had been a gift from someone I'd met during a recent case I'd done with Jon.

"Exquisite craftmanship," Charlie observed, giving the chair arm an appreciative stroke.

I started to reply but was overcome with emotion that made the words stick in my throat. That chair had sentimental meaning for me. To cover, I busied myself setting cookies out on a plate, along with cream and sugar for the coffee.

Charlie, oblivious to my emotional strangling, filled the void. "Yes, Jon mentioned the two of you recently worked together on a case. He said you're a cryptozoologist? What a fascinating field of work."

"Yes, I am, and it is," I managed, grateful for the change of subject. "I'm always on the hunt for the latest cryptid."

"I take it Bigfoot qualifies?" Charlie said without missing a beat.

I looked at her, intrigued. "It does." I held up a finger. "Hold that thought."

The coffee was done brewing, and I poured three mugs and added them to the tray with the other items, carrying it all into the living room and setting it on my glass-topped coffee table. Jon and Charlie each took a mug, Jon adding sugar to his—the man had a sweet tooth—and I took the remaining mug after adding a dollop of cream. Since Charlie had settled into the Adirondack chair and Jon had chosen the leather armchair next to it, I sat across from them on the Bali daybed that served as my sofa, the cushions and pillows of which were covered with hand-dyed Indonesian fabrics in purple, orange, and red colors that will always remind me of my mother.

I was ready to give Charlie my undivided attention. "Okay, tell me why you're here."

Charlie had just bitten into a cookie, so it was her turn to hold up a finger. She chewed and swallowed, licking at a few errant crumbs on her lips before taking a sip of coffee.

"I'm here because there's something strange going on in the Chequamegon National Forest," she said finally. "We've had some Bigfoot sightings in the area, a couple of which have been rather . . . disturbing."

I shrugged. "There are always Bigfoot sightings in heavily forested areas. Hundreds of them every year all over the country. Heck, all over the world. It's nothing new."

Charlie shot a worried look toward Jon, and he gave her an encouraging go-ahead nod. Charlie squared her shoulders and swallowed hard, as if to brace herself before she spoke. "It's true, we certainly have our share of Bigfoot sightings up north, but this was more than just a sighting. One of them may have torn a man apart."

She dumped the words out there and they sobered the atmosphere faster than an AA meeting. I narrowed my eyes at her. "Can you be more specific?"

Charlie grimaced. "I can, but it's not pretty."

"Just tell me."

"All right. Ten days ago, the body of a bow hunter was found with his face, scalp, and one hand torn away, his clothes half ripped off, and deep gashes and bites all over his body. One of his arms was nearly severed."

I shrugged. "That's tragic, but it could have been from a sick or cornered animal, like a bear, a coyote, or a wolf. Maybe even a cougar. They're making a comeback in the region."

"Yes, that's what I thought at first blush," Charlie said. "But I know the attack wasn't from any of those animals you mentioned because there was a witness. And now we've had a second victim turn up with similar injuries."

Okay, that upped the ante. I shot a glance at Jon, who smiled smugly. He knew this case would intrigue me. "Tell me more," I said to Charlie, taking a cookie and settling deeper into my seat.

"Well, to start with, we do get Bigfoot sightings in the area. As you said, it's the perfect setting for them, between all the forested land and the uninhabited islands in the Apostles. Generally, we wardens take these reports with a grain of salt and laugh over them later when we meet up for a beer. The city and county cops typically get the calls first and pass them on to us because they don't want to deal with them. They slap a 'crazy' label on anyone making such a call. But this incident from ten days ago was clearly different."

"You mean the first victim you mentioned?"

She nodded. "He was hunting in the Cheq and . . ."

"The what?" I interrupted.

"Sorry," Charlie said. "Habit. Cheq is a nickname for the Chequamegon portion of the Chequamegon-Nicolet National Forest." I nodded and rotated my hand in a continue gesture. "Anyway, this fellow had taken down his tree stand, probably planning to pack it in. The witness was also bowhunting and he said he heard something like a shriek and a scream combined. He thought it might have been a hunter who was injured so he tromped through the woods toward the sound. Seconds later, he came across a man standing at the base of a tree, bow in hand. The witness was about to holler to the guy, to ask if he was okay, but in the next instant, this huge apeman burst out of the trees and began attacking the hunter. The witness said he was shocked at how violent and frenzied the attack was."

"Did he try to intervene?" I asked.

Charlie grimaced and shook her head. "He said he thought about trying to shoot the creature with a bolt but feared he might hit the other hunter instead. He also said the other hunter employed bear spray, but rather than deterring the creature, it incensed it. The witness feared the creature might see or smell him and come after him next, so he decided to retreat and go for help.

But just as suddenly as the attack began, it ended. He said the creature retreated into the woods and simply disappeared."

"'Creature'? Is that the word the witness used?" I asked.

Charlie nodded.

"And how did he describe this creature?

"He said it was a large apeman."

"And he saw this from how far away?"

Charlie extended her hand and waggled it from side to side. "Forty, maybe fifty yards, give or take." I stared at her, and she added, "In a heavily wooded forest. With thick fog." She let out a sigh, shoulders sagging. "To be honest, the guy was so traumatized by what he saw I don't know how much of his story can be trusted. He said he went up to the victim and checked to see if he could provide any first aid, but it was obvious the guy was beyond help."

"And he said an 'apeman' attacked this hunter? He used that exact term?"

Charlie nodded.

"Did anyone test the blood alcohol of the witness?"

Charlie squirmed a little in her seat. "We didn't. It didn't occur to anyone at the time." I started to ask another question, but she cut me off. "I know, I know. It seems like he must have seen something else, like a bear or a wolf. But the guy didn't strike me as someone who would exaggerate or imagine something, even if it was foggy."

"This happened when, again?" I asked.

"Ten days ago, at the start of the month. There were articles about it in the local paper. It was big news in our neck of the woods."

"You said there was a second victim?"

Charlie nodded, frowning. "This one apparently happened two

days ago based on the ME's preliminary assessment of the time of death. There was no witness, and we only found the body yesterday. The victim was fishing along the banks of a lake in the Cheq and his body was found a few feet from the water with injuries similar to the ones they found on the first guy, though not as extensive. His throat, face, and scalp were ripped and torn in places, and the cause of death was exsanguination from a neck wound that severed the carotid artery. He likely bled out in a matter of minutes."

"Who found the body?"

"Another fisherman. The ME estimated the victim had been dead for twenty to thirty hours when he was found, though I haven't seen the final autopsy report yet."

"Was there evidence of scavenging on the body?"

"Yeah, but only a little and the cooler weather kept the bugs to a minimum." She paused, finishing off her cookie.

"Tell her the rest," Jon prompted.

Charlie took a slug of her coffee before continuing, as if it were a shot of whisky she hoped might brace her. "There was a smell," Charlie said, wrinkling her nose. "The first victim had this strong, rank odor clinging to him. The best way I can describe it is as a mix of ammonia, fecal matter, and bad body odor. The witness to the first victim said the smell came from the creature. No such smell was noted on the second victim, but his body was out in the elements longer, so it could have dissipated."

I logged this detail away. "Anything else?"

"Tell her about the bones," Jon said.

Charlie looked over at him and smiled in a way I found curious and a little disconcerting. Clearly the two of them had been talking about this at length, and I couldn't help but wonder if there was something going on between them. I hoped not, though technically it wasn't any of my business. Except. . . .

Jon and I had recently declared an interest in one another, and that kind of made it my business, didn't it? Granted, we'd agreed to go slow because of our recent histories, his with a wife and child who were tragically killed in a horrible accident three years ago, and mine with a fiancé who turned out to be a homicidal sociopath. When it came to heavy emotional baggage—both known and hidden—Jon and I had enough between us to sink the Titanic without the help of an iceberg.

"Right, the bones," Charlie said, giving Jon a Princess Di–worthy look from her downcast eyes. "Thanks for the reminder." She cocked her head to one side and looked over at me. "It's not unusual for me to come across an animal carcass in the Cheq. Sometimes it's little more than scattered bones, but I've also found relatively intact bodies on occasion, typically animals like squirrels, raccoons, rabbits . . . prey that raptors have killed but can't carry off because they're too heavy. I also find the occasional deer that's been taken down by animal predation and abandoned for some reason, though the scavengers tend to make quick work of those. And of course, there's the usual collection of roadkill because the roads in the Cheq range from paved sections to barely discernible, rutted dirt paths. The cause of those deaths is typically obvious, and with other carcasses I can frequently tell what happened. For instance, I might see puncture wounds made by talons, or tears in the flesh made by ripping teeth or the claws on a bobcat or wolf. Bear wounds tend to be large and gaping. After a while I can just look at a body if it's not torn completely apart or fully decomposed and tell how the animal died. It's one of my superpowers," she concluded with a grim smile.

Oddly enough, this declaration warmed me to her.

She cleared her throat and finished off her coffee before continuing. "But lately I've been finding animal carcasses that have been skinned, disjointed, pulled apart, and then gnawed on."

"Okay," I said with a shrug. "Lots of animals do that."

"Do they then put the bones in a neat and orderly pile?"

I didn't answer her because she continued on before I could. But we both knew the answer was no.

"The ME who did the autopsy on Bodie Erickson, the first hunter who was killed, had a forensic odontologist examine some of the bite marks on the body and he said some of them were indicative of grinding molars."

I arched my eyebrows. "Molars? You're sure?"

Charlie nodded. I saw her smile in Jon's direction again and took a sip of my coffee to hide my annoyance. I was in no position to be jealous of Jon's relationship with another woman. I hate emotions sometimes. Give me science instead. Or math. Something straightforward, clinical, and dry that doesn't make me feel like my guts are being turned inside out. It's been two years since my ex-fiancé murdered my parents, and I'm still healing. New emotions, if they're too intense, tend to rip the scabs off the old ones, leaving me in pain. It's easier for me to simply bury them. Newt is the only emotional outlet I can tolerate these days.

"Then there's the footprint," Charlie said.

"Footprint?" I echoed, nearly choking on my coffee.

"One large, five-toed, humanoid footprint found at the scene of the second victim," she said with a definitive nod. "The reports of

Bigfoot sightings in the area over the years have occasionally in-cluded footprints. This one at the lake was much more defined than any others I've seen."

I experienced a thrill of excitement at this news, an emotion more in line with what I felt capable of handling. Charlie had me hooked and the look on Jon's face told me he knew it. I scooted forward to the edge of the daybed and set my mug on the coffee table, ceramic meeting glass tabletop with a clatter. Clapping my open palms on my knees, I looked at Newt and smiled.

"I suppose we better pack our bags, buddy," I said. "It looks like we're taking a road trip."

CHAPTER 3

⌒

After exchanging phone numbers and email addresses, I assured Charlie she wouldn't have to pay for my services if she promised not to advertise the fact I was doing the job pro bono. She did, however, tell me she had arranged through local "connections" to obtain a one-bedroom suite for me in downtown Bayfield near the ferry landing.

"I hope that's okay," Charlie said. "I know it seems presumptive of me, but Jon said he was sure you'd want to help me out." I shot Jon a sly look. "Plus, the leaves have peaked and last weekend was the Apple Festival, so things are still booked solid right now. I know the owners of a motel in downtown Bayfield, and they owe me a favor. They agreed to let you stay in a suite that's part of a detached home affiliated with the motel. They're remodeling after a small fire last month elsewhere in the house, and while there's still finishing work to be done, the basics are there. They just got occupancy clearance and the location is good, right across the street from Lake Superior. It's private, and you can bring Newt."

I thanked her, took down the details, and then Jon and I walked her out to her car. Once she pulled away, we returned to my apartment.

"I'm curious," I said when we were back upstairs. We settled on the stools at my kitchen island and picked at the remains of the cookies. "How is it Charlie knew she could get to me through you?"

Jon blushed—a trait of his I'd grown used to and generally found charming—color surging up his neck and onto his face like a red tide, turning his ears a hot pink. It offered quite the contrast to his pale blond hair and deep blue eyes.

"I might have mentioned you in an online forum," he said sheepishly, flinching a little, as if he expected me to hit him or something.

"What kind of forum?" I asked with a sinking feeling.

I didn't hide the fact that I was a cryptozoologist available for hire, but I didn't advertise it either. Cryptozoology attracts its share of nutjobs simply by its nature. Add in all the con men like Baumann who are looking to make a buck off naïve, vulnerable people, and you have the perfect recipe for a conspiracy hullabaloo. My parents were the reason I was drawn to the field. They had traveled far and often while I was growing up, dragging me along with them, hoping to find proof any of these intriguing, mysterious creatures existed. Any oddities they happened to come across along the way were just extras to help fill out the store shelves.

I wasn't as obsessed with the work as my parents were. I tended to treat my cryptid hunting as more of a hobby than a job despite my qualifications—I had degrees in biology and zoology—and I worked hard to distinguish myself from the likes of Hans Baumann. Plus, while I did have the store to tend to, my parents had left me quite well off, enough so that I didn't have to work at all if I didn't want to.

"The forum is a closed site, not public," Jon assured me, apparently sensing my unease. "It's a casual place where law enforcement officers can get together and chat informally, share their experiences, ideas, thoughts, problems . . . that kind of thing. Sometimes we even solve crimes by sharing things. Other times, someone might toss out a problem they're having and ask for help. It's a national forum with law enforcement folks from all over the country, so there's a good variety of backgrounds, knowledge, and experience."

"Is Charlie someone you've chatted with regularly on this site?" I hoped my question sounded casual but felt the weight of it as soon as I uttered the words.

"No," he said, as he swallowed a piece of broken cookie. "In fact, up until a week ago, I'd never chatted with her at all. I don't even know if she's posted anything there before." He paused and frowned. "Sadly, these online forums can be like any other segment of society. There are social strata and hierarchies. The wardens and rangers of the world tend to rank lower on the totem pole in law enforcement and, because of past abuses by other members, many of them prefer to keep a low profile. I think Charlie might be one of those. If she wasn't before, she will be now."

"Why?"

"Because she was soundly ridiculed and made fun of for her inquiries, even though she tried to camouflage what she was looking for. She made out like she was merely searching for similar deaths that might indicate a killer's signature, but she didn't hide her own biases well enough, and they quickly sniffed out her true meaning. Bunches of posts started popping up suggesting she get in touch with the real world instead of Agent Mulder, quit watching reruns of _The X-Files_, and check herself into rehab."

I shook my head with disgust. "The internet can be a cruel place. Did you get ridiculed, too, when you responded to her?"

His prior blush had receded, but it returned in full force within a millisecond. His face was like a flashing neon sign. "No, but I replied to her privately. I didn't want to give the trolls more fodder and I thought you might be able to help her."

I nodded, my anxieties lessened with his explanations. "I can try," I told him. "It will mean spending time up there talking to the locals and looking into these sightings and deaths." I paused, thinking. "It sounds like I might encounter resistance. I don't suppose you'd be able to come along?"

Jon tilted his head and smiled. "I'd love to, to be honest, and I'm happy to know you'd want me along, but I can't abandon my work here on such short notice. I should be free over the weekend, though, and in the meantime, I'll be a mere phone call away. You can use me as a sounding board, or even as a research assistant, though I doubt I can compete with the likes of Devon."

Most folks would have a tough time competing with Devon Thibodeaux when it came to research. As an IT graduate from New Orleans who quickly discovered the majority of jobs he could get required about as much brain power as the zombies that so fascinated him, he'd come to Door County on vacation several years ago and had wandered into the store, intrigued by the oddities in

Odds and Ends. He'd been exposed to, and had a fascination with, dark arts and voodoo during his formative years in New Orleans, and when he saw my parents were looking for full-time help, he'd decided to apply for the job on a whim. He'd been with the store ever since, and because he was such a whiz at digging up information online, I paid him extra to do research on the side for me when I needed it.

"Devon can handle the research," I said. "But will Charlie be able to get me autopsy reports and the like, since she isn't a police officer?"

"As a conservation warden, Charlie is as much of an LEO as I am."

"LEO?"

"Sorry, law enforcement officer," Jon explained. "From what she's told me I gather she already has access to the necessary reports and files. It sounds like she works closely with other law enforcement officers in the area and the person in charge of both death investigations is one of her cohorts in a nearby town. Deaths in the Chequamegon Forest fall under the purview of the conservation wardens, though as often happens in thinly populated areas, other local LEOs help out whenever needed. Charlie or her cohort should be able to get you whatever you need, but if they can't, let me know and I'll do what I can to help from my end."

I gave him a wan smile. "I still wish you could come along. It would be nice to have you there to help with the procedural stuff."

His expression faltered and he looked away. I sensed a sudden coolness in him, and it momentarily puzzled me until I replayed what I'd just said.

"Jon, I wasn't implying the only reason I want you to come is to help me cut through red tape. I'd love to have you at my side simply for your company and to provide me with a sounding board I can trust."

He gave me a smile that was clearly forced.

I reached out and touched his arm. "I hope you know I'd enjoy your company anywhere, anytime." He sighed and blinked rapidly, as if bracing for the "but" he knew was coming. "But you know I'm not ready yet for heavy entanglements."

"Who said anything about heavy?"

"You know what I mean."

"I do. I get it," he said, pulling his arm free. "Frankly, with everything that happened to you in New Jersey, it's a wonder you'd ever trust anyone again."

"And with everything that happened to you in Colorado, I'm amazed you'd ever open up your heart again."

We looked at one another for a long time, his face a mix of empathy and sadness, mine most likely the same. I felt an urge to hug him but resisted it. Every time I felt drawn to him, memories of the last time I'd had the same feeling with someone else made me step back and put barriers up. I had no idea how to get past such an instinctive reaction, and what's more, I wasn't sure I could. Or should.

"I've had a little more time to recover than you've had," Jon said, finally looking away. His head dropped and his next words were barely above a whisper. "But I won't lie to you. There are moments when the reality of it strikes from out of nowhere, hitting me like a gut punch. Particularly with Bjorn. That's not to say I mourn my wife any less. But the love you feel for your kid is different, more intense, more important somehow." He squeezed his eyes closed and swallowed hard before continuing.

"You're given this amazing gift of a tiny life to nurture and protect. It's a huge responsibility, but also a magnificent opportunity. Losing it in such a sudden, arbitrary way breaks you." He paused, the muscles in his throat and jaw struggling to get words out past the strangling emotions. "It was my job to protect my little boy and I failed," he said finally, his voice breaking on the last two words.

Tears spilled from his eyes, dropping into his lap. It wasn't until I blinked myself that I realized I was crying, too. I slipped off my stool and gave in to the urge, hugging him, resting my cheek against his chest, feeling the irregular, gasping breaths he took as he tried to get his emotions under control. Eventually, he wrapped an arm around my waist and held me tight.

Here I was thinking I was the damaged one, forgetting how his loss had been just as bad, maybe worse. Losing a child had to be devastating. We'd both suffered horrible events that had forever altered our lives, tainting everything we said, did, or thought with grief and all its accompanying emotions: anger, sorrow, sadness, guilt, depression, and a hollow emptiness that could never be filled. Time and distance softened the pain bits at a time, but it didn't take a genius or a shrink to know Jon and I both had work to do before we'd be ready to pursue a serious romantic relationship. Slow and steady was my mantra.

When I finally, reluctantly released my hold on him, he did the same and I moved away to give him a moment of privacy. I instantly missed his warmth and the sense of security I'd felt when he held me close; I'd liked the feeling. But then I'd also liked it when my ex-fiancé, David Johnson, had done it, too, enough so that I'd agreed to marry him after knowing him for only six months. I'd not only been duped by a clever and murderous con man who was still out there some- where, my naivete and recklessness had led to my parents' deaths.

"I should probably pack and get ready to leave in the morning," I said, swiping at the remnants of tears on my cheeks. "But I wouldn't mind some company for dinner if you can stay."

Jon slid off his stool with a wan, apologetic smile. "I would love to, but I need to get back to the island. I'm on call tonight because the guy who was going to do it is out sick and one of my other em- ployees is on vacation until Friday."

"Of course," I said, mentally cursing the geographic complica- tions in our relationship. As if we didn't have enough other things to make it difficult. "I get it. You need to be able to respond quickly if there are any calls."

"To be honest, there aren't likely to be any. Life on the island tends to be non-eventful, but we just never know, especially during busy tourist times. You can bet the second I gamble on things being slow and decide to stay on the mainland, five urgent calls will come in."

My store and Washington Island—where Jon lived and worked as the chief of police—weren't far away as the crow flies, but they might as well have been on two different planets when it came to quick transports. The ferry connecting the two had limited scheduled runs during the day and none at night. Jon had patrol boats he could commandeer in a pinch, but the stretch of water between the peninsula and the island was known as *Porte des Morts*, or Death's Door, because the waters there were so treacherous. Hundreds of shipwrecks filled the small stretch of water already—so many that they were stacked on top of each other in places—and the rocky shoals combined with the unpredictably treacherous weather made any kind of speedy transport over water, particularly at night, a fool's errand.

"I'd offer to come to your place and cook but I want to get an early start in the morning," I said. "I do owe you a dinner, though."

He waved this away with a little *pfft*. "No scorecards, okay? I love to cook and I'm happy to do it. Just not tonight." He glanced at his watch. "I should get going so I can catch the four o'clock ferry." He glanced at his phone and added, "Besides, if the notifications on my phone are any indication, your store is pretty busy right now."

"You still have my security camera feed on your phone?"

He nodded, looking a little guilty. "I put it on there when I installed the cameras for you, but if it bothers you, I'll take it off."

I thought about it for a second and decided I kind of liked having him watch out for me. "No, it's okay."

Newt and I walked him downstairs where I saw the store was bustling, just as Jon had said. It was a Wednesday, typically one of our busiest days for two reasons. One, it's the middle of most people's vacation weeks as many of the rental places run from Saturday to Saturday and tourists often tire of sightseeing by midweek, and they're ready to shop, kick back, and relax. And two, new releases for books come out on Tuesdays, so Wednesdays mean there will be a selection of new inventory to browse.

I saw Rita watching the two of us out of one corner of her eye and decided to take advantage of the store's busyness to avoid any awkward goodbyes with Jon. I gave his hand a squeeze and said, "I need to help Rita and Devon. I'll be in touch."

Jon held on to my hand when I went to pull it away, and he gave me a squeeze of his own. "Give me a holler once you get the lay of the land up there. If my employee is feeling better and back to work, I'll come check on your progress in person this weekend."

It surprised me how much the possibility of him joining me lifted my spirits. "That would be great," I said, hearing the earnestness in my voice and hoping he did, too. "I can always use the support."

He chuckled. "It's hard for me to imagine you needing anyone or anything for support." He reached down and patted Newt's big head. "Well, except for this guy."

Newt looked up at him with tongue-lolling affection and, once Jon departed, my dog looked as disappointed as I felt. Newt let out a sad little whimper at one point and I bent down close to his head, rubbing my hands vigorously through the fur around his neck.

"I know, Big Guy," I whispered in his ear. "I like him, too. But for now, it's just you and me. Okay?"

As I straightened, Newt gave my hand a big, wet, sloppy lick, his way of letting me know he was there for me. The gesture provided me with as much relief and joy as any human support could and, as I made my way to the checkout counter, I idly pondered if this was a good thing.

Was there room in my heart for two men, one of them human, the other a canine?

CHAPTER 4

Living on a peninsula made driving anywhere challenging at times as it forced me to traverse the length of it just to reach the main part of the state. The entire trip to Bayfield was going to take more than six hours. I briefly considered chartering a plane and flying instead, but in the end I decided to stick with my original plan. I've always enjoyed driving, and time in the car would give me a chance to sort through my thoughts, both those related to the case at hand and some that weren't.

Business in the store on Wednesday night died down after eight and I was able to leave Devon and Rita to go upstairs to pack. I wanted to get an early start, so I loaded everything I could into the car the night before. The first things in were my suitcase, a large bag of Newt's food, a box of his favorite treats, and five rolls of poop bags. Did I mention he's a big dog? The final items I loaded were a handful of gadgets I'd inherited from my parents' stash of toys, things they used to aid them in their cryptid hunts. I'd lost one of these—a remote-controlled underwater camera—on my first case with Jon but had since replaced it and had even ordered one for the Washington Island police department as a gift because Jon fell in love with the thing. I had other items in my arsenal I thought might come in handy, including a drone, night vision binoculars with an infrared light, and a high-resolution, handheld, infrared thermal imaging camera. Thinking I might want to do some nighttime prowling or stakeouts, I also packed a flashlight, a headlamp, my superwarm down sleeping bag, and a hooded, down parka. Temperatures at night were likely to be hovering just above freezing. To ensure our safety in the woods during hunting season, I also tossed in a blaze orange hat and vest for me and a blaze orange harness with reflector strips for Newt.

When the store closed, Devon left straight away. He had a hot and heavy new relationship going with a local EMT he'd met several weeks ago. But Rita, who was widowed and had no one to go home to, lingered. I'd already told both of them I would be gone for an indefinite amount of time, where I was going, and why, and they'd assured me they had the store hours covered. I also told them I might need to call on them for long-distance help. Devon's online capabilities made him an invaluable tool, but Rita was useful, too. She and her husband had owned a rare books store that Rita had been forced to sell after her husband's death, but all those decades spent reading and handling moldering old books had left Rita smart, well read, and something of an amateur historian.

As I processed the day's receipts, which turned out to be exceptionally good—many of our browsers *had* also been buyers—Rita hovered in the doorway of my office, which was tucked beneath the stairs leading up to my apartment. I braced for what I knew was coming.

"Are you sure you want to go traipsing up north to look into this mess? Seems to me you might take a lesson from how things went with the last investigation like this you got mixed up in."

"It all turned out okay in the end."

"You almost died."

"You have such a flair for the dramatic," I said, rolling my eyes at her. She scowled at me, and I softened. "I appreciate you looking out for me, Rita. I promise I'll be careful. And I'll have Newt with me. It will be okay."

"It better be," she grumbled, her scowl deepening. "Because if you think I'm going to take care of this store if you end up dead, you've got another think coming. Knowing my luck, your ghost will be stuck here with all the other creepy stuff, and I'm not doing any séances or weird ceremonies to free your sorry-assed spirit."

I bit back a smile. "That's okay. Devon will do it," I teased, refusing to get sucked into her dark thoughts. "You know how he loves zombies. Maybe he'll reanimate me, and then I can keep Henry company."

Rita appeared horrified by the idea.

"Come on, Rita. Relax. It will be fine. Jon said he might even come up for the weekend to join me." I saw Rita's expression ease a smidge. "You can help by assuring me you'll manage things here while I'm gone. Knowing the store is in your very capable hands will give me the peace of mind I need to stay focused."

"Of course," she said, with mild reproach. "You know you can rely on me."

"I do, and it matters a lot. Thank you."

Mollified, she started to leave but then turned back, head slightly cocked. "One more thing?"

"Sure."

"Remember the discussion we had about estate planning after your parents died?"

I did, and the reminder unsettled me.

"I can see this question troubles you," Rita said, eyeing me more closely. "You're not as confident about this trip as you're trying to let on."

"You're being rather . . . inquisitorial tonight," I said with a sly grin.

Rita and I engaged in an informal war of vocabularies from time to time, tossing out words that were big or obscure—sometimes both—during our conversations, constantly trying to outdo or stump one another. Rita almost always outshined me—I've had to look up the meaning of several words she has used on me—but I thought I might have had her this time. More importantly, I was hoping it would divert her attention away from the topic at hand.

"That's a good one," Rita conceded with a nod and a smile. "And yes, my insights into your mind are quite keen. Which is how I know you're only . . . equivocating to distract me."

Busted.

We stared at one another until Rita wrinkled her nose and shook her head. "Yeah, mine was lame compared to yours. You win this one, but your efforts to distract and divert me have failed. You can do better. And I haven't forgotten my original question."

No surprise there.

Rita might appear doddering with her white hair, glasses, and old-fashioned dresses but the mind behind that wild hair was as keen as any I've ever known. "No, I haven't done a will yet, or any of the other stuff, but I'll get to it eventually," I said impatiently.

Rita gave me a castigating look and folded her arms over her chest.

"Maybe now isn't the best time to bring it up," I said. "You're spooking me."

"Good!" Rita punctuated this comment with an emphatic *I Dream of Jeannie* nod. "You should be spooked, young lady. You've spent half your life gallivanting around the globe searching for ungodly creatures and dealing with all sorts of weird, unseemly folk. It worries me."

"I'm only going upstate this time," I pointed out. "And I don't think I've ever gallivanted in my life. What does it mean, anyway?"

Rita saw right through this second attempt at a diversion, and she was having none of it. Her lips disappeared into a thin line and one foot started tapping with irritation.

Truth was, her words plucked at my heart strings, so after a moment's hesitation, I got up from behind my desk and walked over to her. Her eyes grew wide as I reached out and pulled her to me, her body as straight and rigid as my ironing board.

"I love you, too," I said, wrapping my arms around her.

It took her a bit, but eventually her body relaxed, her arms squirmed loose from where they were trapped between us, and she hugged me back.

When I finally released her, she turned away quickly, and I heard her sniffle. "You drive carefully tomorrow," she said over her shoulder and before I could manage a response, she was gone.

I went back to my chair and dropped into it, suddenly exhausted. Emotions did this to me all the time and it was one of the reasons I steadfastly tried to avoid them, at least in their more intense iterations. After my parents died, my emotions were like bubbles, thin skinned and ready to burst at the slightest hint of pressure. And when they did burst, as they seemed inevitably inclined to do, I would lose control, unable to think straight or talk right or function at the most mundane of tasks. My grief had flayed me bare, leaving me raw and exposed, with an unbearable pain I feared would never end. I'd hated those feelings and with time I'd learned to avoid the triggers. Sadly, doing so tended to set me off from the people around me.

Though I'd known Rita and Devon before my parents died, my relationship with both of them changed dramatically afterward. Before, I was so preoccupied with myself, my life, and with David Johnson and our imagined future together that Rita and Devon were little more than peripheral characters orbiting on the outside spheres of my life. Afterward, they became my center, my all, the only support system I really had.

My father had been an only child and while my mother had siblings and her parents were both alive as of a decade ago, she had written them out of her life when she married my father. I only knew about them because I found a letter from my maternal grandmother to my mother when I was snooping around in my parents' office one day. I'd asked my mother about them once and all she said was they didn't care about her or me, only my father's money, and they weren't worth a second thought. I'd half expected them— some of them anyway—to show up for the funerals, but they didn't. I don't know if they opted not to come or simply didn't know what had happened.

In the wake of my parents' deaths, Rita took on a parental role, and I'd happily let her, desperate for at least the illusion of a loving family. Back when my grief was still new and raw, when it had rendered me vulnerable and afraid and all I wanted to do was curl up under my covers and block out the monsters in the room, I'd needed that from her. Nowadays I didn't need it so much as tolerate it, a sign of progress on my part.

Devon on the other hand, who I'd long suspected might be at the very high-functioning end of the spectrum, treated me like a boss. He didn't like high emotion any more than I did unless it involved romance and a girl, but occasionally he would say or do something to let me know he cared. I did the same with him and for us, it was a perfect relationship.

I adored them both but knew they could be gone from my life at any moment, through death or simply through life and a change of plans. They were impermanent, temporary, and under no obli- gation to keep me in their lives. Knowing this had left me afraid to care too much about them, fearful I might open my heart too far and have to feel that grief, or some semblance of it, all over again.

I had the same problem with Jon. Learning to love again, learning to trust again came hard for me, though I'd made some progress. Newt had helped immensely. When he'd shown up behind my store a year ago, battered and bloodied and clearly in need of help, it was the first lowering of my defenses since the murders of my parents. I'd cared for him and loved him without limitation or hesitation, and in return he gave me back ten times the love I gave him. He asked nothing of me and gave everything in return. My walls began to lower, and I began to heal.

Unfortunately, I still had a long way to go.

CHAPTER 5

Despite wanting to get an early start the next day, I found sleep hard to come by. My brain refused to shut down and I kept replaying memories of past Bigfoot hunts I'd been on, a bit of bittersweet nostalgia because my parents had been on them, too. God, how I missed them. I longed to be able to discuss this trip with them, to have them help me plan things out and identify what I needed to look for. I didn't have them physically, but I had the next best thing: their records.

My parents had maintained a home office full of books, papers, diaries, recordings, articles, magazines . . . anything and everything to do with cryptids of any type. The Bigfoot, or Yeti, or Sasquatch—pick your name—made up a sizable chunk of the information they'd accumulated over the years because it was one of the better known, more frequently seen, and popular cryptids.

Sightings occurred all over the world with regular, even alarming frequency. Hundreds of scientific and not-so-scientific articles, journals, and books had been written on the topic, and my parents had a slew of them.

And so, after tossing and turning for more than an hour, I got out of bed and went into my parents' home office. It was a room I didn't venture into often, the memories it held still proving quite painful. But I'd spent endless hours in there while growing up, sorting through all the stuff my parents had, listening to their lively debates on various topics and reveling in their excitement as they planned trips to exotic places to investigate reports of recent sightings. They had instilled their love of the hunt in me and, since it was what was keeping me from being able to sleep, I figured I might as well indulge it.

At the center of the room was a large partner's desk made of rare cocobolo wood from Mexico. While I had childhood memories of how and where other pieces in our apartment had been found, purchased, and delivered from all over the world, the desk had been there as far back as I could remember. My parents used to sit on opposite sides of it, facing one another, the surface covered with drink glasses, soda cans, snack residue, pencils, papers, magazines, books of all kinds and, in later years, their respective laptops. They would discuss and debate the logic (or lack thereof) behind hypotheses, sighting reports, and scientific debates regarding whatever cryptid they were focused on for the day, one of them often playing devil's advocate. The resulting discussions were typically lively, loud, emphatic, sometimes funny, and occasionally adversarial. But in the end, they would get up from their respective seats and walk arm in arm from the room, discussing dinner plans or other innocuous subjects as if the loud, harsh words that had echoed inside those office walls had never been uttered.

Currently, the top of the desk was cleared of all clutter, the only things on its surface a handful of glass rings scarring the finish. In sharp contrast, the rest of the room looked like borderline hoarder chaos, with overflowing bookcases, filled file cabinets, and stacks of papers, magazines, and books all along the walls. Despite the appearance of disarray, things were relatively organized if one knew where to look. And I knew exactly where to look to find what I needed. I gathered up the articles and books I felt would be most relevant and carried them out to the living room, away from the ghosts of my parents and their desk.

When it comes to the creature known as Bigfoot—actually with all cryptids—there are three camps of thought: the skeptics, the believers, and the folks who simply see it all as a way to make a buck. This latter group's primary interest is in selling Bigfoot-related items, things like T-shirts, footprint casts, and guidebooks on where to find a Bigfoot and what to do if you're successful.

I float in between the first two groups, preferring to linger in the land of "plausible existability," a phrase my mother coined years ago. But while I'm open to the existence of such a creature and would be beyond delighted to encounter one, I'd have to see irrefutable scientific proof of their existence before becoming a staunch believer.

To be honest, of all the cryptids my parents and I had ever searched for, a giant apeman was the one I considered the least likely to exist. My reasoning for this was because it was the most popular of all the cryptids out there and, according to the lore and sightings recorded throughout history, it had been seen on every continent in the world except Antarctica. It was known by dozens of names, all of which translated to a version of wild or wilderness man: Bigfoot, Sasquatch, Yeti, Bagwajiwininiwag, Yeren, Sokqueatl, and others. While the names and details of these creatures differed slightly from place to place, they had been talked and written about for more than six hundred years. Given this ubiquity, it made little sense that no one had ever found verifiable evidence of one—no scat, bones, hair, or dead bodies.

Despite this, descriptions of the creatures remain consistent in many regards. Most describe the animals as at least eight feet tall, powerfully built, upright-walking, and covered with hair, though depending on where in the world the sighting occurs, the hair may be chocolate brown in color or snow white. Sightings from centuries past may well have been literal wild men, humans with an aversion to contact from other humans, chose to live off the land, and gave little attention to personal hygiene. Other sightings were easily attributable to bears, other wild animals, or hoaxers. But a few remained more credible, less easily dismissible, and those were the ones that interested me the most.

Some sightings were more sensational and well known than others, such as the famous 16-millimeter film of what is supposed to be a Bigfoot captured by Roger Patterson and Bob Gimlin in Northern California in 1967. To this day, no one can agree on whether the film is legitimate or just an elaborately executed hoax.

There are those who claim to have collected "scientific" evidence, though most of it is pseudoscience in my opinion. In the year 2000 in the Pacific Northwest—a hotbed of Bigfoot sightings and an area some consider the birthplace of such sightings in North America—a Washington State University physical anthropologist, a professor of anatomy from Idaho State University, and a journalist carefully examined a plaster cast made by what they claimed was a Sasquatch. It became known as the Skookum cast because it was obtained in an area known as Skookum Meadow in the Gifford Pinchot National Forest. After a heavy rain, they used apples and melons as bait overnight, setting them out in the middle of a big mud puddle not far from Mount Saint Helens. Supposedly a creature took the bait, laying while it ate and leaving behind impressions of its body in the mud. Casts were taken of these impressions—a hairy hip and leg for example, as well as other identifiable body parts—and after careful examination they were declared to be proof of a Sasquatch.

The skeptics descended and the debates began, including those who said the impressions had been left by an elk kneeling in the mud to eat the fruit. The original team's conclusion claimed the impressions weren't made by any known animal but rather from an unknown primate. This conclusion was bolstered when hair samples found in the casts were removed and analyzed. They were all identified as belonging to known local fauna—deer, elk, coyote, bear—except for one with unique primate characteristics. Not proof per se, but a nugget of hope that helped perpetuate the rumors, stories, and supposed sightings.

One fact remained, however, and for me it was the biggest argument against the existence of such a creature. No one had ever found the bones or dead body of a wild, giant apeman. A lack of this type of physical evidence was easier to explain for water-bound cryptids like the Loch Ness Monster because the deepest regions of our oceans and lakes remain largely unexplored. But relatively few places above ground remained unexplored, uninvaded, or un-developed by man. Bottom line: Bigfoot had nowhere to hide.

Still, human imagination knows no bounds and far-out the-ories have been put forth to explain why no one has ever found proof of the existence of Bigfoot. These ideas included one positing alternate, crisscrossing dimensions in certain areas that allowed the creatures to temporarily set foot in our dimension long enough to leave behind a print or be seen by someone before getting sucked back into their own dimension. Proponents of this theory believed the creatures could only cross over for short periods of time before complex laws of physics I didn't begin to understand (and sus-pected may have been made up) dictated they must return to their own dimension, which was where they all ultimately died. This far-fetched theory conveniently explained sightings and footprints while also offering a nifty escape clause to explain away the lack of any real proof.

Don't get me wrong; I'm open to the existence of cryptids. But Bigfoot was low on my list because of the scientific approach I take to my work.

After studying some maps, I realized the Chequamegon portion of the Chequamegon-Nicolet National Forest was an ideal setting for Bigfoot sightings: heavily wooded areas with nearby freshwater sources and scant human populations. I decided my first order of business, once I saw the full collection of evidence Charlie pos-sessed, would be to visit the sites where the two men had died. Then I'd talk to people who claimed to have recently seen the creature and examine the areas where those sightings had oc-curred. Interviewing the witness to the first victim's attack would

also be key. If there was a Bigfoot on the rampage in the Chequamegon National Forest, I didn't want to believe it could, or rather
would, inflict the kind of injuries these two victims reportedly had.
I supposed a rogue homicidal creature was possible, just like there
are rogue homicidal humans, but my mental image of the creatures, if they did exist, had always run more along the lines of a
wild, skittish, but otherwise curious and friendly animal.

Before going back to bed for the night, I mentally planned out
the initial phase of my trip. While waiting on the ME's report for
the second victim, I'd try to keep my own biases and excitement in
check. No easy task. I knew the odds of finding irrefutable proof of
a Bigfoot, or better yet, one of the creatures themselves, were extremely long.

So why was I so excited?

CHAPTER 6

Newt and I managed to get on the road by a little after five the next morning. It was a weekday, and I wanted to beat the worst of the rush hour traffic in Green Bay. Once we were outside the city, the autumn colors, warm sun, and bright blue sky made for a serene and peaceful backdrop.

Newt rode in the back seat—the front seat was too small for him on a ride this long—and he spent most of the time looking out his partially lowered window, though he did take a couple of short dog naps. He was utterly fascinated when I drove alongside railroad tracks for a stretch where a train moved slowly along, hauling cars filled with colorful containers—green, red, gray, yellow, blue—stacked two high. I doubted Newt could see the colors, or even make out any details of the cars given his poor eyesight, but the movement, sound, and smells held him transfixed for a while.

I drove through small towns and past roadside stands selling squash, pumpkins, maple syrup, and a varied assortment of apples. Newt's nose went crazy when I drove by a horse farm that also had a couple of donkeys. The scenery was classic Wisconsin autumn: rivers and small lakes everywhere, fields full of dairy cows and tall corn, trees of all types sporting magnificent fall colors, Fleet Farm stores and Kwik Trips in every town, plaid flannel shirts in abundance, and farm equipment and implement dealers every fifty miles or so. The start of my drive was over flat land interrupted by the occasional glacial drumlin, but it got hillier and rockier the closer I got to Lake Superior and my final destination.

I arrived in Bayfield a little past noon and the bright sun and cloudless sky overhead had warmed things up to an unseasonably balmy sixty-four degrees, a pleasant surprise in an area where the average daily temps for October tended to range in the low to mid-fifties and significant snowfalls weren't uncommon. Here, the majority of the trees remained green much like those back home. The Great Lakes have some kind of delaying effect on the color change and trees close to the water tend to turn a week or so later than the ones located more inland.

The suite Charlie had arranged for me was one of three units in a detached house, and as she had promised, my unit afforded me a small view of the lakefront and a location within easy walking distance of shops, art galleries, cafés, the ferry, and other amenities. It also had its own outside entrance, allowing me to come and go whenever I wanted without worrying about disturbing other renters. When sleep eludes me, I sometimes prowl around at night.

The best asset for me, of course, was that it allowed dogs, albeit for an extra fee. The joke was on them, though; I would have been willing to pay any amount to have Newt with me. After checking in at the motel office, I went across the street to my suite and unpacked most of the car. I sent off quick texts to Jon, Devon, and Rita to let them all know I'd arrived safe and sound, and then I called Charlie to let her know I was in town.

"How was your drive?" she asked.

"Lovely. This is my favorite time of year. There's something about the brisk autumn air and the smell of the leaves . . . I love it."

"I hear you. I'm a spring girl myself, but fall is a close second."

Enough with the polite chitchat. I was eager to get down to business now that we had the niceties out of the way. "Do you want me to meet you at the police station here in town? Or do you have an office nearby?"

"I do have an office, one I share with another warden, but if you don't mind, I'd prefer to come to your suite. I'll bring my files with me."

Charlie's desire to meet here triggered a prickle of wariness in me. What was she hiding? And who was she hiding it from? I didn't know much about her and should have had Devon do a deep dive on her rather than simply taking Jon's acceptance of her as a sign she was okay. Live and learn. I'd correct my mistake later.

"You can come here," I told her. "But I can't offer much in the way of hospitality. I don't have any provisions yet, just what I brought with me in a small cooler."

"Not a problem. There's a great little sandwich shop near you and they make a yummy BLT on sourdough. How does that sound?"

"Delightful," I said. "How soon will you get here? Should I run and get the sandwiches now?"

"I'll get them. My treat. It's the least I can do."

"I don't want you to go to too much trouble. Is it on your way?"

She laughed. "In Bayfield, pretty much everything is on the way. Think of it as my way of saying thank you for coming here."

"All right. Thank you."

"I'll be there in half an hour or so."

Half an hour gave me enough time to take Newt outside for a quick walk in the park area along the lakefront across the street. He had his nose to the ground the entire time, sniffing so hard he snorted at times, making me laugh. He so loved exploring all the new territory with its accompanying smells that he whined when I said we had to go back.

Charlie arrived five minutes after we returned to the suite wearing a bulletproof vest and a utility belt that included a taser, a baton, some sort of multipurpose hand tool, two sets of handcuffs, a flashlight, a mobile radio, extra ammo, and a holstered gun in addition to her work uniform. She looked ready for battle.

"I take it you're on duty?" I said.

She smiled. "What was your first clue?"

I relaxed, thinking maybe this was why she'd wanted to come here. She didn't want her coworkers to know what she was . . . or wasn't doing. We settled in at the table in the kitchen area and she slid a small cardboard container toward me.

"Here's your sandwich," she said. "And I got you an iced tea, too. Peach. It's delicious. Hope that's okay."

"Sounds perfect."

The sandwich was wonderful with thick, lightly peppered bacon, crusty sourdough bread, and thick slices of ripe, juicy tomato. The tea was lightly sweetened and bursting with flavor.

As we ate and drank, I slipped Newt a piece of bacon while

Charlie gave me a quick rundown on the shops, eateries, and other attractions nearby, including directions to an area she described as "an unofficial off-leash dog park" that the locals used at one end of town. When we were done eating, she removed a small stack of folders from a shoulder bag she'd carried in with her.

"I'm not the primary on either of these cases, though I was part of the investigative team for both deaths and do have access to all the files," she explained. "Bruce White is the primary on both. He's a warden out of the Washburn office and we work together all the time. This is what we have so far on the two victims." She slid the folders toward me but kept her hand atop them. "I should warn you; these aren't for the weak of heart. In addition to background information on each of the victims, there are scene shots, autopsy photos, and a couple of rather explicit reports. Are you sure you want to see it all?"

"I'll be fine," I told her, though even as I said this, my stomach churned ominously.

Charlie removed her hand from the folders, and I slid them the rest of the way toward me, spreading them out. There were three folders total, two with the victims' names on them. The third one was labeled MISC. REPORTS, and I considered looking at it first since it piqued my curiosity, but I held off and started with a victim folder instead.

The name on the label was Bodie Erickson and the first thing I saw when I opened it was a picture of the gruesome and bloody scene where his death had occurred. I reared back instinctively and swallowed hard. "Oh, my," I said. "You weren't kidding."

"Are you okay?" Charlie asked, looking concerned.

I took in a bracing breath, released it slowly, and nodded. "I am.

I just didn't expect that to be the first thing I saw. Bit of a shock, but I'm okay."

"Sorry," Charlie said, grimacing. "I threw things together in a hurry and didn't even think about how it might present."

I dragged my eyes from the photo—this proved to be surprisingly difficult; it had a strange, rubbernecking effect on me—and narrowed my eyes at her, in need of a breather before I continued. "I'm getting a sense you're being somewhat furtive about my involvement in this. Am I imagining it?"

Charlie raked her teeth over one corner of her lower lip. "The cases have both been attributed to bear attacks and they're considered closed, though the second one won't be officially closed until the ME releases his final report."

"What's the holdup? It's been, what, a couple of days now since the body was found?"

Charlie nodded, giving me a half-hearted shrug. "We got the final report on Bodie Erickson's case the next day, so I don't know why this one is taking so long. As to your first question, yes, there are folks in these parts who would rather keep these deaths under wraps."

"Why?"

"It's not good PR for the tourist trade, and that's the lifeblood of this area. Don't get me wrong, rumors of a Bigfoot sighting might attract some people. In fact, there's a large wooden cutout of a Bigfoot that circulates around town, and it's become something of a game with both locals and visitors to try to find it. But rumors of a viciously homicidal Bigfoot might have the opposite effect."

She had a point, but I got the distinct feeling there was something she was still holding back from me. "Can I expect any help from the Bayfield city police?"

"Probably not." She looked away and chewed at her lip.

"How about the county sheriff's office?"

She winced, still not looking at me. "Yeah . . . again, probably not. Technically the cases fall under our jurisdiction because hunting accidents and the Cheq Forest are our domain. The other agencies chip in and help out when needed, which to be honest is fairly often. Sometimes that gives them a sense of ownership they don't really have."

"Okay," I said, thinking. "Can I at least count on support from the DNR then?"

She forced a smile. "You have *my* full support." She made a valiant effort to sound chipper.

I leaned back in my chair and sighed. "You could have told me this before I came all the way up here."

"But then you might not have come."

This was an incorrect assumption on her part. The lure of the hunt was something I would have found hard to resist, but I let her believe she was right. It wouldn't hurt to have her a bit beholden to me.

She leaned forward and jabbed a finger atop one of the folders. "I've seen bear attacks and the resultant injuries the victims have, and I'm certain these men were not attacked by bears," she said vehemently. "I'd bet my life on it."

Now we were getting to the nitty-gritty. I wanted to keep her talking, so I cocked my head to one side and stared at her, letting the silence stretch between us and do the heavy lifting. It took longer than it might have with some people, but eventually she caved.

"It's not just the injuries. There weren't any bear tracks near either victim, or any bear scat close by. I'm sure because I looked and I'm something of a scat expert." She scoffed. "Another one of my superpowers," she said, chuckling and shaking her head. "The things we take pride in, eh?"

I smiled back but remained silent. It worked a little quicker this time.

"And there are those weird bone stacks I mentioned. There's a picture of one in there somewhere. Bears don't do that. Something else is out there, and people have seen it. Plus, the witness to Erickson's attack swears it wasn't a bear."

"Stress, fog, the horror of what he saw . . . it can add up to an unreliable witness," I said.

She shook her head, clearly frustrated, and I felt certain she'd heard this same argument from others before. She folded her arms over her chest and jutted her chin toward me. "Then explain the footprint," she said with thinly veiled belligerence.

"Footprint?" I said in my best skeptic's tone. It was the least reliable evidence so far, in my opinion. Too easy to fake.

Charlie reached across the table, grabbed the folder for the second victim, and began shuffling through its contents. After a moment, she removed a large, color photo and pushed it across the table at me.

The picture showed rust-colored, sandy-looking dirt speckled with red, yellow, and brown leaves dropped from nearby trees. The ground was dry and marbled with visible cracks, but there was no mistaking the imprint at the center of the photo. It was a large footprint, oddly human in its appearance though its size—measurable not only by comparison to the leaves near it but the two rulers on the ground beside and above it—was much bigger than the average human print. It measured nearly twenty inches long and eight inches wide, and there was a fuzziness to the edges suggestive of movement.

"We discovered it in the area where the second victim was found," Charlie said.

"Okay," I said, already noting a problem with the footprint but opting to keep it to myself for now. "I want to visit and examine the sites where these deaths occurred. Will you be able to take me to them?"

"I can. I have the day off tomorrow and we should visit these sites first thing. The weather has been dry for some time, so the footprint should still be there, but the forecast for tomorrow night is calling for a thunderstorm and the rain might wash it away."

"First thing tomorrow it is," I said.

"If you're ready to jump into things today, I can try to arrange an interview with the man who found the second victim."

"That would be great. What about the witness to Erickson's attack? Any chance of talking to him today?"

Charlie shook her head. "He refuses. That poor guy was pretty messed up by the experience. It was all we could do to get him to talk to us at the time of the incident. I think he's got a bad case of PTSD. I suppose I can ask him again if you want but no promises. You can stay for a few days, yes?"

"Sure. However long it takes." I cocked my head to one side, studying Charlie. Something about this whole scenario bothered me. "Why are you so determined to investigate these deaths?

Wouldn't it be easier to just accept the explanations already offered and leave it be?"

She gnawed on her lip again, her gaze briefly darting around the room before finally settling on Newt. Then she said, "I've seen it."

Her voice was so low and hushed I began to wonder if I'd imagined it. I turned an ear toward her and leaned forward. "Say again?"

Her back went rigid. "I've seen something in those woods," she said. "It wasn't any animal I've ever seen before, or since. I can't say for sure what it was, but it wasn't human." She paused and looked at me then, pinning me with her gaze as she said, "You have to believe me, Morgan. There's definitely something out there."

CHAPTER 7

A hundred questions leapt to my mind, but I leaned back in my chair and simply said, "Tell me."

She sagged a little, appearing wary but also relieved, as if she'd needed to unburden herself for some time. Her gaze fixed on something out a nearby window as she began to speak.

"It was . . . I was thirteen, so . . ." her eyes closed briefly as she did the math . . . "sixteen years ago." She tensed again and looked at me, posturing as if expecting a blow.

I gave her my best reassuring smile. "I'm intrigued," I said, not a lie. "Tell me about it . . . when, where, what you saw, any significant details like sounds it made or smells you noticed."

This seemed to ease her anxiety a little and she nodded almost imperceptibly. She reached for her iced tea, took a swig, and set the cup back on the table resolutely.

"Let me start by telling you I'm the only child of a well-meaning but hapless mother and a drunken, abusive father who desperately wanted a boy. He named me Charlotte so he could call me Charlie, and he spent my entire childhood doing his damnedest to turn me into the son he never had. He blamed my mother for not giving him a boy and took it out on her regularly. Whenever I failed to live up to his expectations, which was often, he'd toughen me up by slapping me around."

She paused, flinching as if she'd just felt one of those slaps. Her face contorted into something between a smile and a grimace. "Not all of my father's efforts were for naught. I can work on car engines, I have a talent for wood carving, and I know how to fix most things that break down around the house. I'm also an excellent shot because my father started me on a rifle almost as soon as I was able to hold one. We shot at trees, bottles, and cans, and I got to be quite good. It made me happy to know I could please him with something, but it was never enough, and I was so blinded with relief at having something I was good at, I didn't realize where it would inevitably lead.

"When I turned twelve, my father started talking about taking me hunting with him. I tried to tell him I had no desire to shoot or kill any animals, but he didn't want to hear it. If I voiced an objection, he'd just slap me upside the head and yell at me to shut up and do as I was told. For a year we bantered back and forth. He was determined to take me along on a hunting trip and I was equally as determined not to go. My mother didn't have the backbone to stand up to him and I knew it was inevitable when he bought me hunting gear for Christmas when I was twelve and made me take the hunting safety course the following spring. After a year of fighting with him and getting smacked around, I caved."

Charlie paused, took another sip of her tea, and stared out the window. Her physical self may have been in the room with me, but the rest of her was mired in memories from her past. Any hint of a smile was gone and when she spoke again, her expression was somber.

"Leading up to our first outing, I told myself it wouldn't be so bad because I honestly believed my father did more drinking than shooting when he went hunting. He typically came home half in the bag and without a kill." She took in a deep, shuddering breath and looked at me. "Then again, the man clearly had a mean streak, so maybe he simply enjoyed watching things suffer and die. Who knows?" She shook her head as if to shake away the thought.

"Anyway, I thought the trips were just a way for him to escape my mother's constant nagging about his drinking and if he got drunk enough it might make the trip more tolerable. Maybe I could miss on purpose, and he wouldn't notice what a lousy shot I was all of a sudden."

As I listened to Charlie's story, my heart broke for the child she'd once been and the child still cowering somewhere inside her. Her relationship with her father, with both of her parents, was something I struggled to relate to. I'd been so close to both of mine, and we all got along for the most part, even managing to avoid the tension and acrimony that typically accompanied the teenage years. Not that we didn't argue. We did, but we tended more toward intellectual debate than actual arguments.

It probably helped that we lived a life of privilege, never lacking for anything and possessing the ability to have or do things others couldn't afford. My childhood was magical and idyllic, and my parents reminded me often of what a privilege our lifestyle was. They instilled in me the importance of kindness, humility, and the need to share with those less fortunate.

It wasn't until I reached adulthood and started dating seriously that things got tense in our household, primarily between me and my father. Pressure built around his need to investigate every tiny detail of any man I dated, and it cost me several relationships. Sadly, our inability to see eye to eye on the matter crescendoed toward a life-altering and earth-shattering conclusion: the murder of my parents by a man I was about to marry.

Morbid images from that awful time threatened to pull me out of the moment, but Charlie's eerie, monotone voice jerked me back to the present.

"My father didn't make things easy for me," she said, her expression as dead as her tone. "He was determined to have me kill something and he upped the pressure by telling me he'd lost his job and there would be no more money coming in, something I later learned was a lie. He said I had to bag a deer because we needed the meat to get through the winter. If I failed, we'd starve to death, and it would be all my fault. I cried and told him I didn't want to kill anything, he had to do it, but he said he couldn't because his hands shook too much." She let out a humorless laugh. "That part was true enough, at least until he'd refueled his tank with enough alcohol to stop the tremors."

I tried to imagine what it must have been like for Charlie as a young girl. What a scary way to live.

"Dad drove us into the Cheq and parked in a pullout near a small lake. As we hiked into the woods, he instructed me on how to find and bag a deer. He talked about the importance of staying downwind, how to identify deer scat and tracks, and what to look and listen for. As we worked our way deeper into the woods, my father worked his way through the better part of a twelve pack in the cooler, topping off each can with slugs from the flasks he carried. When we got to a spot he thought was good, he showed me how to put up the tree stand. Then we both climbed up there and sat, about fifteen feet up, me on his lap." She let out a deep, shuddering breath and closed her eyes before continuing.

"I'm not sure how long we sat in that damned tree stand but it was late November, and I remember feeling cold and tired but not daring to complain. The cold didn't seem to bother my father at all, probably because of all the alcohol he was drinking. He was close to finishing off the two flasks stashed in his pockets. After what seemed like an eternity, we heard something crashing through the trees and we both looked toward the sound. That's when we saw it."

She paused, and it was all I could do not to reach across the table, grab her by the shoulders, and shake her. "Saw what?" I prompted. "What did you see?"

"It was big . . . and hairy . . . and dark, with eyes that looked . . ." She faltered on this one, her mouth twisting as she struggled to come up with the right word. The one she finally settled on wasn't one I expected.

"The eyes looked surprised," she said, appearing rather bewildered herself.

"Did it see you?"

She nodded.

"How far away was it?"

"I'm not sure. I'd guess about thirty yards. It stood on two feet like a man, but it wasn't human."

"How could you be sure?"

She considered my question for a moment. "The proportions were wrong," she said finally. "It was humanoid but not human." She shook her head. "Sorry, I can't describe it any better."

"That's okay. What did it do?"

"It raised its nose to the air and sniffed, though how it could have smelled anything over its own stench is beyond me." She wrinkled her nose with the memory. "It was really rank, a pungent mix of stale urine and something like rotting meat and vegetation."

"Did it make any sounds?"

"Not at first, but my father grabbed the rifle from me and tried to aim it. I was straddling his knee and his efforts nearly knocked me out of the tree stand. I yelped and grabbed at him to keep from falling and he tried to shake me off. That's when the creature let out this strange, horrible sound, something between a howl and the noise warring Indians made in old cowboy movies." She paused and I saw a shiver shake her. "I've not heard anything like it before or since. It made my hair stand on end."

Her story was having the same effect on me. "Did your father shoot at it?"

"No." She sat bolt upright for a second, her eyes glassy and unfocused. Then she collapsed back in her chair. "He had a hold on the rifle and when he tried to shake me loose, the barrel swung toward me. I was afraid he might accidentally shoot me because I knew he was drunk and he was panicking." This came out in a rapid surge, a flood of words rife with tension and emotion. But then she paused, and her next words were uttered with all the emotion of someone reciting a grocery list.

"I shoved the rifle away as hard as I could and he lost his balance, fell out of the tree stand, broke his neck, and died."

I sat momentarily stunned and then echoed the last part to make sure I'd heard her right. "He died?"

She looked at me through dead, cold eyes. "Yep, though not right away. He went down headfirst and landed on his back. I'll never forget the way he stared up at me from the ground, his mouth opening and closing like a beached fish."

Gooseflesh raced up my arms. The calm, casual way she said this was chilling. I realized what a plague of nightmarish memories this woman's childhood must have been and was once again reminded of how little I knew about her.

Charlie, either unaware or indifferent to my discomfort, went on. "Eventually his mouth stopped moving and his eyes glazed over. That's when I knew he was dead. Later I found out he'd broken his neck and paralyzed everything below his shoulders. He couldn't talk because he couldn't breathe, but it took a full minute or two for his brain to shut down from the lack of oxygen."

"What a horrific experience," I said. "I'm so sorry that happened to you."

She raked a hand through her bangs, leaving a section of them standing straight up. Her eyes had a too-bright shine to them, making her look like a madwoman. For all I knew, she *was* a madwoman. Her childhood traumas had to have done some damage to her psyche—how could they not have—and I wondered if I'd made a terrible mistake in coming here.

Hoping to ground her in something less grim than memories of her father, I asked, "What about the animal?"

She smiled and suddenly her eyes looked normal again. "Right. By the time I stopped watching my father and looked back to where it had been, it was gone."

Talk about anticlimactic. I tried to hide my disappointment and skepticism, but I had some serious concerns about her story and pondered the best way to broach them. The last thing I wanted to do was add pressure to what I suspected was an already fragile spirit.

"Do you think the trauma of what you saw, of what happened to your father could have colored your memories of the event in any way?"

"There was no trauma," Charlie said matter-of-factly. "My father's death came as a huge relief to me."

My discomfort over this declaration must have shown because she quickly amended her statement.

"Oh, don't get me wrong. He was my father and despite all his faults, I loved him on some instinctive level. All kids do, right? Even when they're subjected to horrible abuse? I've seen it in other families." She paused and sighed. "My father could be kind and caring at times, but I hated him for what he did to me and my mother. The violence and the drinking got so bad in the months before his death that he broke my mother's arm and whipped me with his belt so hard once he drew blood. I couldn't sit for days. We were terrified of him and his temper, and I feared he'd lose what little self-control he had one day and kill us. And so, the over-whelming emotion I felt as I looked down at his dead body was one of simple relief." Her tone was unapologetic. "I wasn't traumatized, and my mind remained perfectly clear throughout the whole incident."

"Did you tell the authorities what happened?"

"Eventually. I hiked back to our car, but I got lost and wandered in the woods for a bit trying to find my way. Once I got to the car, I realized I didn't know how to drive it, so I followed the dirt road out to a more main one. I think it was hours before a couple of other hunters came along in their truck and stopped to help me. They had a CB radio, and they were able to get a warden to come out and meet me so I could take them back to my father's body."

She paused, took a drink, and sighed. "There was a sheriff assigned to watch over me, and I did try to tell him what I saw, but he shut me down, obviously skeptical. So, I let it go. There were already enough questions about what had happened."

No doubt. "Have you seen this creature since?"

"I haven't, but not from a lack of trying," she said with a derisive chuckle. "To be honest, it's one of the reasons I went into this profession. Calls about Bigfoot sightings aren't popular among law enforcement officers and anytime one comes in, I volunteer to take it. People know I'm interested in the topic, though they don't know why. Other than the sheriff years ago, you're the first person I've ever told about what I saw."

I supposed I should have felt honored, but I couldn't help wondering if I was being played. Skepticism tends to be my default in these matters. My doubts must have shown.

"I know how it sounds, Morgan," she said. "Believe me, there are days when I doubt myself. I've walked through those woods in the Cheq hundreds of times, beginning in the spot where my father died and circling out from there. Over the past decade I've searched all the islands in the area from one shore to another. And in all that time, I've found nothing."

She paused and looked at me as if she expected me to raise an objection or make a point that would undermine her story. When I didn't, she continued.

"I know it sounds crazy, but I know what I saw and even though I've never seen it again, I think I might have heard it twice. It wasn't the same exact sound I heard on the day I saw it, but it was similar and unlike anything else I've heard in those woods. Please believe me. There's something out there."

Her earnest tone and pleading expression were hard to ignore.

"I believe you," I said finally, and in return she gave me a big smile. I felt a twinge of guilt because I knew she didn't realize I only believed her catchall statement about *something* being out there.

Just what it was, however, remained to be seen.

CHAPTER 8

On the heels of Charlie's horrific story, my nerves were a bit on edge, and I jumped when there came a loud pounding on the door to my suite. Newt leapt to his feet and let forth with one of his deep, menacing barks. I gave Charlie a puzzled look. "Who on earth could that be?"

"Jon, perhaps?" she said hopefully, heading for the door. "Is he coming up?"

"He's hoping to, but not until the weekend."

"Oh." Charlie's disappointment rang clear with that single word. She paused at the door with her hand on the knob and looked back at me with a questioning arch of her eyebrows.

"Yeah, go ahead," I said, my curiosity piqued.

Charlie swung the door open to reveal a tall, pudgy, uniformed police officer out on the porch. He had a deeply receding hairline and a sagging face with jowls, making him look like a hound dog.

"Hello, Charlie," he said.

"Buck," Charlie said, her tone cold. "Why are you here?"

Buck stuck his head inside and peered around the corner toward the table where I sat. I gave him a finger wave but said nothing. Newt let out a mild but warning *whoof.* If anything got him more worked up, there'd be a whole lot of racket going on.

"Can I come in, Charlie?"

Charlie let out a weighty sigh, cocked her hip to the side and, with one hand still on the door, planted her free hand on the frame, barring Buck's entry. "It's not my place to say."

Silence followed, wherein neither person at the door seemed willing to ask my permission. I let the silence stand and waited, curious to see who would cave first. My money was on Buck.

Not taking his eyes off Charlie, Buck finally said, "Ms. Carter, would it be all right if I came in to chat with you?"

It took me a second or two to interpret what he said because his voice was low and deep, and he barely moved his lips when he spoke, talking like he had a mouthful of marbles. I didn't like the idea of a visit from the police so soon after my arrival, but the fact that he knew my name intrigued me.

Charlie turned and looked over at me, eyebrows raised in question, her body still effectively blocking the entrance. I gauged Buck to be in his fifties and not in the best of health, yet despite his receding hairline, over-the-belt paunch, and the prominent nose capillaries I could see from twenty feet away, he could have tossed Charlie aside easily enough if he wanted to. He stood well over six feet tall and filled the doorframe.

"Let him in," I said. Charlie stepped aside and waved Buck through.

He didn't hesitate, coming in fast and surprisingly light on his feet for his size. One meaty hand was thrust at me. "Ms. Carter, I'm Deputy Buck Weaver with the Bayfield County Sheriff's Department. Pleasure to meet you."

Was it? I went ahead and shook the proffered hand, expecting a bone-cruncher but pleasantly surprised to get a firm but reasonable shake instead.

I gestured toward one of the chairs around the table. "How is it you know who I am?" I asked as he settled in. Charlie shut the door and came over to join us.

"Not much goes on in these parts I don't know about." Buck mumbled this with a smile, but it didn't exactly warm the cockles of my heart. There was an underlying tinge of intimidation in his words.

"He's most likely been talking to Kyle, my ex-fiancé, who also happens to be his son," Charlie said. She gave Buck a withering look. "I told Kyle not to tell you anything."

"Rest assured, little lady," Buck said with a hint of condescension. "Kyle didn't say a word. I happened to run into Maureen this morning over at the coffee shop, and she was quite happy you'd arranged to have someone stay here in the suite. She mentioned the name of the person who'd be staying, and I did a little research. No biggie."

I had to focus hard on his words because of his marble-mouthed mumble.

"Maureen is the proprietor of this place," Charlie explained, though I'd already surmised as much on my own. Small towns.

They're the bane of privacy. Charlie probably interpreted my look of confusion as wonderment about how Buck came by his knowledge as opposed to my difficulty in understanding the words rolling out of his mouth.

"Is it true you go hunting about for Sasquatches and the like?" Buck asked, leaning back in his seat with his hands folded over his belly. He chuckled, clearly amused by the idea. "Seems like a tough way to make a living, yet I understand there are two of you here in town looking for Mr. Bigfoot."

I had no idea what he meant when he said there were two of us, though I had a strong suspicion. "I'm here alone. I don't work with anyone else."

"Is that right?" He scoffed. "Takes all kinds, I suppose. Don't you have a husband to keep you at home?"

"I don't see how that's any of your business."

"I'll take your answer and the ringless finger as a no." He cocked his head to the side. "You're one of those spoiled rich kids, aren't you?" I bristled at the comment and tried to keep my reaction from showing, but Buck's smug expression told me I'd failed. He was good at finding the right buttons to push. "Oh, yeah, I know all about the Carters in Door County," he went on. "I also know both of your parents are dead and you are the primary suspect in their murders."

Charlie shot me a look. Clearly this tidbit was one Jon had neglected to share with her.

"I *was* the primary suspect," I clarified. "I'm not any longer."

"Riiight," Buck said, his voice rife with sarcasm. "And now you get to spend the family millions trotting around wherever you want looking for big, bad monsters." His eyes grew huge and round, and he held his hands up and waggled his fingers as he spoke. I half expected him to lunge at me with a loud, "Boo!"

Newt sensed my growing state of agitation and nudged one of the hands in my lap. I let my palm rest on his head and the act instantly calmed me. Clearly, the primary objective behind Buck's impromptu visit was to intimidate and rattle me, to make me feel uncomfortable enough to pack it in and go home. It was equally clear to me that Buck didn't know who he was messing with.

"Deputy Weaver," I said in my sweetest voice, "I understand my presence here in town displeases you for reasons I don't quite fathom. I also understand you came here to deliver a message to me, one intended to send me back where I came from. Clearly, you're a man of stature in these parts, one who's used to getting his way and having others do what you tell them to." I swear Buck actually puffed out his chest a little. "We call those kind of folks bullies where I come from."

Buck instantly deflated in his seat and scowled at me. "Now listen here, young lady," he said.

I lunged forward, leaning across the small table. "No, you listen, Deputy. Your kind of intimidation not only doesn't work on me, it motivates me to find out why it is you don't want me here."

Buck shot eye daggers at me and shifted in his seat, making his chair squeak beneath his weight. We engaged in a stare-off and Buck blinked first.

"Okay, let's not get too worked up here," he said with a smile I could only describe as unctuous, making me wish for a second that Rita was here so I could toss the word at her. "I'll save you the trouble and tell you why we don't want or need you here. These deaths you've come to investigate, they're closed cases. They were bear attacks, nothing more. Sad, yes, but nothing exotic and certainly not the work of Mr. Bigfoot. And spreading a bunch of unfounded rumors is likely to scare off the tourists."

His tone was condescending, as if he were trying to explain something to a toddler. It irritated me. "It's close to the end of the tourist season, anyway, isn't it?" I said with a shrug of indifference.

He shook his head. "We get visitors year-round and there's more to it. Our citizens have been rightly upset over these grisly deaths and they're doing everything they can to put it all behind them. The last thing we need is a couple of charlatans, however well intentioned, riding into town on their high horses and stirring up the pot again."

This guy had a knack for mixing his metaphors. "I take it you aren't a believer," I said.

He laughed. "Hell, no. Are you?"

"I'm open to the possibility, but I'm also fully grounded in science. I'd need proof to be convinced."

"What kind of proof? Fake footprints you can sell to gullible, unsuspecting tourists?"

"That's not fair, Buck," Charlie said. "You know perfectly well there are shops around here selling Bigfoot-themed items. Heck, you can buy a T-shirt around the corner with *I partied with Bigfoot in Bayfield* printed across the front of it."

"That's different," Buck said, clearly displeased with Charlie's interruption. "Those things aren't associated with gruesome deaths."

"They are now," I said. "And I'm not here to sell stuff or convince anyone of anything. I'm here because—"

"Because Charlie here asked you to come and look into it, right?" Buck shot Charlie a castigating look. "To feed her childhood conviction about how some imaginary Bigfoot monster out there killed her daddy."

I didn't answer, caught off guard by his reply. Not the meanness of it—I expected that from Buck by now—but rather the revelation it contained. I glanced over at Charlie and saw her flush red.

"Oh, yeah, I know all about Charlie and her little addiction to the idea of Bigfoot," Buck said, calling my attention back to him. "Who do you think helped investigate her father's death?" I must have looked puzzled because he elaborated. "When I got called out to the scene when her father died, I was put in charge of keeping Charlie here company while the wardens dealt with the body. She tried to convince me she saw Mr. Bigfoot in the woods and that's why her father fell out of the tree stand."

I looked over at Charlie again. "This is the person you tried to tell?"

Charlie cringed and nodded. "He's the only person I said anything to. And as soon as I realized he didn't believe me, I dropped the whole thing."

"Except you never really did, did you?" Buck said. "You've been chasing the same hallucination your entire life."

"It was *not* a hallucination!" Charlie insisted, her eyes welling with tears.

Buck sighed and shook his head woefully. "I warned Kyle about you, told him you need to be seeing a shrink. Told him you might have pushed your daddy out of that tree stand."

"He fell," Charlie said through gritted teeth.

"Yeah, right," Buck sneered. "Good thing Kyle finally decided to dump you."

"I dumped him," Charlie snapped back.

"Yeah, right," Buck said again, this time punctuating the comment with a deep chuckle. Then he stood, shoving his chair back in the process, and leaned across the table toward me. "You seem like a nice young lady, Ms. Carter. I'd hate it if Mr. Bigfoot attacked you or anything else bad happened to you. And I really don't think you're going to find much of a warm welcome in these parts, so why don't you do us all a favor and head on home?"

With that, he straightened, adjusted his utility belt, and gave Charlie a nod. "I'll show myself out." Seconds later he was gone, leaving two stunned women in his wake.

"Good grief, Charlie," I said. "Is he always like that?"

Charlie nodded, smiling grimly and still looking flustered from her own verbal scuffle with Buck. "Pretty much. He's got an attitude problem and it has kept him from getting promotions over the years. There are rumors—unproven, mind you—of excessive force issues in his past."

This didn't surprise me. "And you were engaged to his son?"

Her smile fleshed out into something more relaxed and genuine. "I was, but Kyle is nothing like his father. He's kind, thoughtful, generous. . . ."

"Is Kyle in law enforcement, too?"

"No, he's a lawyer. He does corporate stuff and finance."

I detected a wistful tone in her voice when she spoke of Kyle, making me suspect she still had significant feelings for him. "Why did you break off the engagement?"

"It just didn't feel right," she said, making a face like she'd just sucked on a lemon. I wondered if the idea of Buck Weaver as an in-law had played a role. "Kyle keeps saying he wants to move down south to Georgia or Florida, somewhere warmer, and I can't imagine leaving here. I love this region of the country and I love my job. I know I could probably get a similar job elsewhere, but I'm just not keen on starting over. The islands, the lake, the woods in the Cheq, it's all home to me as much as the house I live in. How can I leave it?"

I had a suspicion the experience with her father and her subsequent obsession with Bigfoot might have something to do with her attachment to the area. She wasn't leaving until she validated her childhood sighting.

"I'm glad Kyle didn't take the breakup too hard," I said.

Charlie smiled. "Yeah, that's why I think it was the right decision. He took it a little too well. Then again, our relationship has always been one of those on-again, off-again things." She let out a wistful sigh. "Kyle's a good guy. I don't know how or why, given who he grew up with, but in this case, like father, *not* like son."

I slapped my thighs and gave her a smile. "Okay then. What do you say we get back to the stuff in these folders?"

"Buck didn't scare you off?"

"Hell, no. If anything, he made me even more determined to get to the bottom of this mystery. I've got a feeling Buck is hiding something relevant to all of this, and I'm going to find out what it is."

Charlie gave me a worried look. "Be careful. Buck has connections around here. If he wants to, he can make life miserable for you."

"Let him. I have no tolerance for bullies and I'm not about to let some pompous, misogynistic, testosterone-overloaded, mumble mouth push me around or tell me what to do."

Charlie's eyes grew wide at my rant; then she laughed. "Morgan Carter, you and I are going to make a great team!"

CHAPTER 9

⟵

The remainder of the information in the folders—even the grimmest parts—seemed mundane after hearing Charlie's story and enduring Buck's visit. I skimmed the reports and narrative summaries for Bodie Erickson, the first victim, and found the information oddly clinical in its detail given the gruesome nature of the scene, perhaps an effort by those involved to distance themselves from the horror. There was one exception: the statement from the poor fellow who had witnessed the attack, a thirty-two-year-old man by the name of Bob Keller, who was a candidate for PTSD if ever I saw one. His only description of the "creature" attacking Erickson was "large, hairy, and insanely aggressive, ripping and tearing at the man in a frenzy of bloodlust." His description didn't sound anything like a bear or a typical bear attack, and the wounds on the victim didn't resemble any I'd ever seen on other victims of such attacks.

One possibly relevant finding was a pool of blood located about thirty yards from where Erickson had died and a trail of smaller drops between this second pool and Erickson's body. The investigators tried to explain away this puzzling blood evidence by surmising the animal Erickson had shot had been gravely wounded yet had still managed to attack Erickson despite the eyewitness's account of a second animal that had come from another direction.

The whole thing made little sense to me. I couldn't imagine an animal attacking Erickson after being wounded with a bolt arrow and then heading back to the spot where it had been shot to sit and bleed out. Everyone agreed the amount in the second pool of blood was indicative of a mortal wound, so why hadn't they found a carcass anywhere? I supposed scavengers could have dragged it off, but judging from the size of the attacking creature as described by the eyewitness, I didn't think so. None of it made sense. I had too many questions and, without the ability to observe the original scene, not enough answers.

I moved on to the folder for the second victim, a forty-two-year-old fisherman named Pete Conrad, and immediately noticed a difference in his wounds. Erickson's injuries suggested a frenzied ripping and tearing, whereas Conrad's wounds appeared cleaner and more precise. Pete Conrad's throat had been gashed deep enough to sever the carotid artery, a long, slightly ragged line across his neck that had caused him to rapidly bleed out. Erickson's neck, on the other hand, looked as if it had been gnawed on in places and, despite a gaping wound, the large vessels had miraculously remained intact. The majority of Erickson's bleeding had come from his scalp, his face—or what was left of his face—his nearly severed arm, and his severed hand. This difference might explain why there appeared to have been more of a struggle in the first case than there was in the second. Pete Conrad had bled out and died quickly. Erickson, sadly, had not.

The sites where their bodies were found differed, too, not only in the general milieu—one deep in heavily forested woods, the other along the somewhat open shoreline of a lake—but also in ease of accessibility. Erickson died in a spot not easily reachable and requiring a significant hike through the woods. Conrad, on the other hand, had died by a lake that was isolated but still accessible by vehicle.

I studied a map in Bodie Erickson's file that showed where in the forest his body had been found and where his vehicle had been parked. There was a lake not too far from the site of his death, but it was still a hike.

One other difference I noted in the written reports was how no one attending to Pete Conrad had mentioned a distinctive odor whereas several people had noticed it with Erickson. Charlie had mentioned it, too, in reference to her childhood experience, so clearly it had stuck with her. Not surprising since smell is one of the most evocative senses. Not knowing what significance, if any, the smell issue had, I logged it away for future reference.

Since there were no witnesses to Conrad's death, the summation from the law enforcement officer in charge—the conservation warden out of the Washburn office named Bruce White that Charlie had mentioned earlier—contained conjecture. Conrad had been found four feet from the water's edge and there was a tackle box upside down not far from his body, its contents strewn over the ground. Another picture showed the footprint I'd seen earlier but from a different, wider angle. The report said it was located a distance from the body, but in the only area where the ground was soft enough and clear enough to leave a discernible print.

How convenient.

One final bit of evidence got me excited. A thick, coarse hair had been found on Bodie Erickson's body stuck in the blood of his wounds and it had been collected and sent off for DNA analysis. Two similar hairs had been found and collected from Pete Conrad's body.

I looked at Charlie, who was standing nearby watching me and chewing on the side of her thumb. "Tell me about these hairs," I said. I saw a gleam in her eyes and the reason for her excitement became readily apparent with her explanation.

"They were all sent off for DNA analysis, which will likely take weeks, maybe months. There's a backlog and they weren't prioritized since both cases were preliminarily determined to be accidental deaths. The gross examination of the hairs found on Pete Conrad determined they were likely from a bear. They could be the result of incidental contamination, likely picked up from the ground or nearby plant growth during his struggle."

"Didn't you say you didn't find any evidence of bear prints or scat in the surrounding area?"

Charlie nodded. "I did but that doesn't mean they weren't there. There's such heavy undergrowth in both areas, and with as dry as it's been this summer, the ground isn't very conducive to making prints. We got lucky with the big one left in the dirt road."

Did we?

She made a dismissive wave gesture and the gleam in her eyes brightened. "More important is the preliminary report on the hair found on Erickson since it says it appears to be simian in nature," she said excitedly.

I frowned at her. "Really?"

Charlie nodded, looking positively gleeful.

I shuffled the papers about. "Why didn't I see that in here?"

Her smile disappeared like a drawing on water. "What do you mean? It's in there."

I sifted through the pages more carefully and Charlie moved closer, watching me. "I don't see it," I said.

"The ME's findings on Pete Conrad aren't in there because it was a phone report," she said, eyeing the contents spread out on the tabletop. "But everything else should be here. I printed out the entire file and that preliminary hair report was part of it. I saw it two days ago." She pushed the pages around herself and opened all the folders to examine their contents. Then she straightened and ran a hand up through her bangs. "Maybe it's still in the printer," she said, looking doubtful and confused. "But I swear it was there. I saw it with my own eyes."

"I believe you," I said. "You went out to both sites, right?" She nodded. "Did you find any evidence at the second site of a large creature moving through the woods? Things like broken limbs? Crushed plants? Disturbed ground?"

"We found broken limbs and branches everywhere but none of it was conclusive. It's been an unusually dry summer here and the vegetation has suffered as a result, making it hard to tell what caused the branches to break. It could have been deer, or other fishermen, or whatever else your imagination can drum up. It looked as if Mr. Conrad had followed an established trail through some shrubbery to gain access to the separate part of the lake where we found him, but whether or not an animal followed the same trail was impossible to determine."

"Was there any blood along the trail or near the footprint? Or any hair snagged on a branch anywhere?"

"Not that we found."

My imagination drummed up all kinds of possibilities, but I mentally pushed them all aside, focusing instead on Charlie's use of the pronoun *we*. "Were there a lot of people at both of these sites?"

She nodded. "Sure. The LEOs in this area all tend to chip in and help out where and when needed and both of these deaths were all-hands-on-board situations. Even if they weren't, most folks would have showed anyway. We don't get this level of excitement around here often, so all of us adrenaline junkies tend to gravitate toward the juicy cases like these."

"Did you arrive at both scenes early in the investigations?"

She wagged her head from side to side. "Kind of. Within the first couple of hours anyway. I was on duty for the Erickson case, so I was part of the first team on scene, but I got called in for Conrad's."

"I'm curious about the smell you mentioned with your childhood experience, something that also came up with the Erickson case. Yet I don't see any mention of a smell with Pete Conrad. Did you notice anything when you were there?"

"I didn't, but Erickson's death was witnessed, and we were on scene within an hour or so of the attack. Conrad, on the other hand, was dead for a day or more before he was found according to the medical examiner, so if there had been any odor, it might have dissipated by the time anyone got to the site."

A reasonable explanation. Plus, it seemed the struggle between whatever had killed these men and the men themselves was much more prolonged in the Erickson case, making the transfer of odors more likely.

There was something else about Pete Conrad's death bothering me, a nagging niggle in my brain, but I couldn't isolate the specific thought at the time. Since I was done reviewing the information on the two men, I went for the third folder. Inside it were four photos: two labeled as footprints, though they were both smudged partials I thought required a great deal of imagination to find any resemblance to a Bigfoot print; a picture of a supposed Bigfoot sighting, a grainy shot from a long distance of something lurking in a heavy grove of trees that could have been anything from a bush to a shadow; and a final picture of a large, neatly stacked pile of animal bones. Behind the pictures were more typed-up reports.

"What's this?" I asked, tapping the last photo.

"It's one of those bone piles I told you about. They're always neatly stacked like that and picked relatively clean. The bones are from small animals—squirrels, mice, rabbits, even a bird in one case. I've found them throughout the Cheq, and once I found one on an uninhabited island in the Apostle chain."

"Interesting," I said. There were no animals I knew of indigenous to the area that would stack bones in such an orderly, organized manner. Would a Bigfoot do something like that?

"They are intriguing," Charlie agreed. "They look like something, or someone, used the spot in question as a dining place. At first, I thought maybe campers had cooked something over a campfire and stacked the bones, but I've never found any evidence of a fire at any of the sites. Just the bones, neatly stacked, occasionally with bits of dried tissue still clinging to them. Whatever ate the animals those bones belonged to, ate them raw."

While the idea was disturbing, this didn't necessarily rule out humans. It took all kinds, and I'd met raw meat enthusiasts before. "Do you think the bones could have been collected by someone who wanders the woods looking for carcasses and then builds these little piles as a form of art expression or a type of spiritual ceremony once he's collected enough of them? Sort of a bone cairn?"

"I suppose," Charlie said, though I could tell she didn't believe this for a second. It did sound far-fetched.

"Maybe for a type of Native American ritual?" I posed, unwilling to let the idea go just yet even if it did make me seem a bit desperate.

Charlie tilted her head to one side and stared over my head at the wall behind me. "Well, the Anishinaabe did have a tradition with bear kills," she said. "Bears commanded considerable respect among the tribes and whenever they killed one, specific rituals were routinely followed. Beaded costumes got laid out beside the carcass and part of the tongue would be removed and hung for days. The carcass was then carefully disjointed instead of being chopped up as this was considered a way to show respect for the animal. They'd hold a big feast everyone would partake in, and afterward the bones were collected and piled together, never scattered about or left for the dogs because that was considered a sign of disrespect."

"I'm familiar with some of those rituals," I told Charlie. "I studied religions and mysticism in college and spent time on the customs and beliefs of the local Native American tribes. But you said these bones were from a mixture of animals, mostly small ones. I'm not aware of any Native American rituals related to those."

"Neither am I," Charlie said. "That's why these piles got my attention. Whenever I've found one of them, I've gone back days or weeks later to see if the pile grew, but it never did. Sometimes I found them collapsed and scattered; other times they appeared untouched. I finally got smart and took the picture you're holding to have a baseline to use for monitoring this particular pile. I found it four days ago but haven't been back since."

"Where did you find it?"

"In a small clearing about a quarter mile from the Erickson site."

There was no denying that this bit of information excited me. Any of the carnivorous or omnivorous animals normally found in the area—not counting humans—wouldn't have the sophistication, or table manners, if you will, to create such a neat pile of largely unbroken and mostly clean bones. Wolves, wildcats, badgers, even bears merely crunched, ripped, and tore at an animal carcass. A Bigfoot, however, particularly if it had prehensile fingers, might very well dine with more sophistication, much as we humans do.

Could a human be the answer to it all? Might there be a crazed person out there living off the land in the Chequamegon National Forest, an unkempt, smelly, hairy, and potentially violent human responsible for both the sightings and the deaths? I had to admit it was possible though it seemed improbable, particularly given the harshness of the winters in the area. Without an abode or other form of shelter, survival would be next to impossible. And surely if there was a place for a human to live, it would have been discovered by someone exploring the forest. Granted it was a huge area filled with isolated spots, but between wardens, rangers, hikers, campers, fishermen, hunters, and exploring sightseers, the likelihood of such a thing going unnoticed was too small to seriously consider.

Unless...

"Charlie, do you know of any caves in the Cheq?"

She shook her head. "There are shoreline caves on nearly all of the Apostle Islands, but I've never come across any caves in the Cheq. Of course, I haven't explored every square inch of the forest either." She tilted her head and looked off to the side for a moment, her brow furrowed. "However," she said, holding up a finger, "to the southeast of us is the Gogebic Iron Range, also known as the Penokee Range, a busy iron-mining district in the late 1800s and early 1900s. One or two of the mines remained active as late as the 1960s but most were abandoned earlier in the century. None of them are in use anymore, but there's still a network of underground tunnels running all through the area. I'm not sure how easy it would be to access them today because the mine entrances are closed, but who's to say what a determined person ... or animal might be able to do?"

I felt a surge of excitement at the idea and logged the information away for future use before moving on to the remaining pages in the third folder. Three were typed narratives: police reports for complaints of a large apelike creature spotted in or around people's homes within the city of Bayfield within the past two months. The last four pages were less official looking anecdotal summaries typed up on plain paper, also dated within the past two months.

"Those are my unofficial reports," Charlie said, pointing to one of the latter pages. "As I mentioned before, people in these parts know I'm interested in Bigfoot, so they sometimes come to me with their sightings when they don't want to file an official report because they're afraid it will make them look crazy."

It certainly could, I thought. I wasn't above such prejudices myself because I knew there were cases my parents and I had investigated in the past where the people *were* certifiably crazy. I returned the pages to the folder and leaned back in my chair, thinking. Charlie must have interpreted my thoughtfulness as doubt or hesitancy because she walked over and put her hands on the table, leaning toward me, her expression serious and pleading.

"Look, I know lots of people think this Bigfoot stuff is nonsense," she said. "And I'll be the first person to admit there's no conclusive proof these two deaths have anything to do with one. But I also know there's something out there, Morgan. I know because I've seen it, clear as day. It was *not* my imagination."

She pinned me to my chair with both the intensity of her gaze and the strength of her conviction. While I didn't doubt she had seen something in those woods when she was a kid, the accompanying trauma of the event still made me question the reliability of her memories. Still, the other evidence she'd presented was compelling enough to create a tingle along my spine, a sensation I knew meant the hunt was afoot.

More than anything, I wanted to bag a Bigfoot.

CHAPTER 10

~

Since the witness to Bodie Erickson's bloody demise didn't want to talk, Charlie gave me the phone number for Mitch Hollander, the man who had found Pete Conrad's body out at Pine Lake. I dialed the number and put the phone on speaker mode so Charlie could listen in. A woman answered and when I asked for Mitch Hollander, she hesitated and then asked who was calling.

"My name is Morgan. I'm looking into the death of a man whose body was found in the Chequamegon National Forest a few days ago. I understand Mitch was the person who found the body and I'd like to ask him a couple of questions."

"Are you a cop?"

I sighed, impatient with this third degree but resigned to having to deal with it. "No, I'm more of a private investigator. The relatives of the man who died have questions about what happened and I'm trying to help them out."

"Mitch said they thought it was a bear attack."

"I'm not at liberty to discuss any details with anyone other than Mitch Hollander. Can I please speak with him? Or are you going to continue obstructing justice in this matter and make me turn it over to the police?"

Silence. Charlie arched her eyebrows, looking at me with new-found respect, but as the seconds ticked by, I worried I'd misjudged the woman on the phone. Was she one of those stubborn, anti-government, conspiracy-theory types who would refuse me regardless of what I threatened, cops and potential jail time be damned? I didn't have the power to do anything to her despite my vague threats, but I was banking on her not knowing that and having enough fear of governmental and police authority to cave.

Finally, I heard her holler, "Mitch! Phone is for you," followed by the clatter of the handset being dropped onto a solid surface. After a half minute of waiting, we heard approaching footsteps, and then the handset being picked up.

"This is Mitch."

"Hi, Mr. Hollander," I said, hoping the more formal use of his name might lend me an air of authority, something I needed since I had none. "My name is Morgan Carter and I'm looking into the death of Pete Conrad, the man whose body you found out at Pine Lake a few days ago. I'd like to ask you some questions if you have a moment."

"Um, sure, though I don't know what there is for you to look into. They said he was attacked by a bear."

"Yes, well, that was the original thought, but new evidence has arisen suggesting a different scenario."

"Oh, okay. Wow."

"I understand you live in Madison. How is it you happened to be here on the day in question?"

"I discovered Bayfield and Lake Superior a couple of years ago when I went up there on a fishing trip with some buddies of mine. I fell in love with the area, and I've been trying to get back ever since. I finally got five days in a row off and decided to go on my own since I couldn't get anyone to come with me on such short notice."

"And had you fished at Pine Lake before?"

"No. I'd only been out on Lake Superior, but I didn't realize I'd picked such a busy week. When I got up there, I discovered all the fishing charters were booked. I couldn't find a house or motel room to rent and ended up camping in the back of my pickup. Since I couldn't get out on the big lake, I decided to look inland for places to fish."

"Pine Lake isn't exactly a large spot or even a popular one from what I understand. How is it you ended up there?"

"Well, it's funny how fate plays out sometimes, you know? Because I was forced to sleep in my truck, I stopped at a local store in Washburn to pick up some things and then went to a nearby restaurant to grab a bite. They were advertising all-day breakfast, which sounded good to me even though it was closer to lunchtime. I asked the waitress if she knew of any good fishing spots in the area and she said she didn't, but then this fellow who was getting something to go came over to my table and said he knew of a spot. Said he'd overheard some fellas heading back home to Chicago a few days earlier claim they were pulling huge pike and bass out of a place called Pine Lake. I had no idea where that was, of course, but this fella had a map of the Chequamegon National Forest"—he totally butchered the pronunciation, coming out with Cheek-qua-me-gin—"in his car and he showed me where it was and how to get there. Right nice fella, he was."

"And you went out there straight away once you were done eating?"

"Sure did. I was disappointed to see there was another car there because I was hoping I'd have the place to myself, though I didn't see anyone, of course. There was a pier at the bottom of the road where I parked but it was crooked as hell and unusable, and all the shoreline right there was marshy. That fella in the restaurant had shown me part of the lake that was kind of separate from the main, so I started walking around looking for it and then I found the body."

"It must have been quite a shock for you."

"You can say that again."

"I'm curious, did you see any footprints in the area?"

"No, but I wasn't really looking for any. I just hightailed it back to my truck and drove back into town to get help. Once I told them what I'd found, they wouldn't let me go back out there."

"It's probably just as well you didn't have to see the body more than once."

"Yeah, I sometimes have nightmares about it. His throat was gaping open and the flies . . ." His voice trailed off and I imagined him grimacing on the other end of the line.

"Mr. Hollander, did you notice any unusual smells when you found the body?"

"Smells? I mean, there was that sickly kind of smell of early decay."

"Of course. Anything else?"

"Not really, no."

"Okay. I think those are the only questions I have for you for now, but I might want to talk to you again."

"Um, sure. I guess."

"I hope it hasn't put you off of coming back to the area sometime in the future," I said, feeling the need to put in a plug for the tourist industry.

"Heck, no, though I think I might stick to fishing in Lake Superior from now on."

I started to thank him and say goodbye but then thought of one more question. "Mr. Hollander, do you happen to know the name of the man in the restaurant who recommended Pine Lake to you?"

"Sorry, no—wait, his first name was Jim. I remember the waitress called out to him when his takeout order was ready."

"That's great, Mr. Hollander. Listen, thanks for taking the time to talk to me. I appreciate it. And I hope your future fishing trips are less eventful."

"It was an exciting one, all right," he said. "I hope the fellow's family is doing okay. If you talk to them, will you let them know I'm praying for them?"

"I will. Thanks, and you take care."

I ended the call and gave Charlie a quizzical look. "How come he didn't notice the giant Bigfoot footprint?"

"Because the victim's car was parked practically on top of it. We even dusted the hood of the car to see if there was a handprint on it." I arched my eyebrows in question. "There wasn't," she said. "It's a narrow strip of dirt road there and Mr. Hollander would have had to park behind Conrad's car. If the pier he mentioned had been in better shape, Hollander might have seen the footprint on his way to use it because it's located directly in front of where we found the footprint. But as you'll see when we go out there, the thing is obviously unusable. We've closed off access to the lake, so the print should still be there if no one hiked down past our barriers. Will it be okay if I come by to get you at eight tomorrow morning?"

"That will be fine."

"Great. I should get back to work but I'll see you tomorrow at eight a.m. sharp." With that, Charlie left my suite, closing the door hard behind her.

Left to my own devices, I decided to walk around the downtown area with Newt and check out the local businesses and shops. Every place I went into had owners and employees who were more than willing to expound at length on the recent deaths, though everyone bought into the current party line and attributed the deaths to a rogue black bear. A fair number of people had stories to tell me about previous encounters with black bears, both in the wild and in town on those occasions when the animals had ventured inside the city limits to raid garbage cans, garages, or even homes. While many of these encounters might have been heart-stopping in the moment, I quickly learned these sightings were common but actual attacks were relatively rare.

Whenever I brought up the topic of Bigfoot, the locals would laugh and play along with me, acting as if it was a big, inside joke all the townsfolk shared. Given what Charlie had told me about the cutout image making the rounds about town, it apparently was an inside joke.

"Oh, right! Big Harry," one lady at a bookstore said, presumably taking the name from the 1987 movie *Harry and the Hendersons*. "Harry's a kind soul. Wouldn't hurt a fly. Don't blame poor him for what that bear did."

Despite this bit of group-speak advertising, I sensed the recent deaths, even if they had been attributed to bear attacks, had folks edgy. I overheard more than one whispered conversation on the topic as I browsed, and I sensed the cheerier responses I got on the topic were simply folks wanting to whistle past the graveyard.

I found a shop around the corner from my suite that sold the shirts Charlie had mentioned. They had a giant silhouette of a Bigfoot at the center and the words *I partied with Bigfoot in Bayfield, Wisconsin*, printed on the front. I bought one, just for grins. Then I took Newt, who had patiently waited for me on the sidewalk outside of each store I visited, for another walk along the lakefront, where I let him chase geese.

While there, I saw a trio of guys working on one of the piers and decided to approach them and see what their take on the subject might be. "I'm visiting the area and I've heard there's a Bigfoot around here," I said. "Any idea where I can go to see one?"

Two of the guys looked at one another like they thought I was crazy. The third guy looked at me serious as a heart attack and said, "Don't mess around with them. They're dangerous."

The other two guys burst out laughing, making the third guy frown.

"Go ahead and laugh," third guy said to his two compadres. "But I'm betting neither one of you want to be out in the Cheq at night anymore, do you?"

The smiles faded from the two men's faces. One of them made a flippant gesture and muttered, "Get serious, dude. Those were bear attacks." Then all three of them went back to work, effectively dismissing me.

Yep, there was a definite undercurrent running through the city, one folks didn't want to talk seriously about. Between that and Buck Weaver's charming welcome, it became obvious to me my job wasn't going to be an easy one. I wasn't too worried, however. I've never been one to shy away from obstacles, even those in the shape of a big, hairy apeman.

CHAPTER 11

⌒

I returned to my suite and spent the late afternoon and early evening hours once again going through the folders Charlie had left behind. This time, I took down notes on things I wanted to follow up on and studied the pictures and reports more closely. When I thought I'd gleaned as much as possible from them, I placed a call to Devon.

"How are things at the store?" I asked when he answered.

"Oddly slow for a Thursday. How are things in Bigfoot country?"

"Interesting," I admitted. "Hopefully I'll have a better feel for it all tomorrow. The DNR warden is going to take me to the sites where the two men were killed and we're also going to visit some local folks who claim to have seen a Bigfoot recently."

"Sounds sketchy," Devon said.

"Yeah, it might well be, though I do think there's something odd going on here. Along those lines, I have a bit of digging around I'd like you to do."

"Happy to!"

"Great. The first thing I need is a deep dive on this conservation warden, Charlie Aberdeen. She seems levelheaded enough on the surface, but an incident in her past raises concerns for me." I summarized the childhood story Charlie had told me but left out the characterizations she had shared with me of her father.

"I don't know if you'll be able to find any news reports about it given it happened sixteen years ago," I said. "But give it a shot and see if anything turns up. Also, do the usual poking around on social media and other online sites to see what you can suss out about our Ms. Aberdeen in more current times."

"Will do."

"Also, see what you can dig up on a Bayfield County sheriff by the name of Buck Weaver. I'm not sure if Buck is his real name or a nickname. He's been with the department for at least sixteen years and has never been promoted. Rumor has it it's because there have been problematic events in his employment history. If that's true, I'd like to know what they were."

"Got it. Anything else?"

I gave Devon the key names involved with the case, those of both victims, the witness to Erickson's death, and the man who found Pete Conrad's body. Devon would get the basics, some of which I already had in the folders Charlie had given me, but he would also dig a little deeper to see what hidden gems he could find. Those were often the more telling details, and it was the kind of digging Devon not only excelled at but enjoyed.

"That's it for now, though I'm sure I'll have more for you after tomorrow."

After ending my call with Devon, I placed one to Jon, or Flatfoot Flanders as I often thought of him these days, thanks to Rita. She'd slapped the moniker on him not long after I'd first met him, and I was having difficulty shaking it off. I feared slipping one of these days and saying it to his face.

He answered my call with, "How's it going up there?"

"Hello to you, too," I teased.

"Oh, sorry," he said, not sounding sorry at all. "I didn't think you were into the social niceties. I had you pegged as more of a get-down-to-business kind of gal."

"Yeah, okay," I conceded, smiling. He had me dead to rights. "As to your question, I'm not sure how it's going. There are intriguing things to investigate here, but there are also things about Charlie giving me pause. How well do you know her?"

"Not well, to be honest. I only met her online about a week ago, though I saw her posts on the law enforcement site before then. And I only met her in person yesterday when you did. I've chatted with her in private rooms online over the past few days and what I've seen so far hasn't raised any red flags. Otherwise, I never would have given her your name. What's bothering you?"

Did I really believe Charlie might have intentionally killed her father by pushing him out of a tree stand? Buck had implied the possibility. And if she had, what difference did it make to what we were doing now? Might she be a bit out of kilter mentally because of what happened all those years ago? Probably, but then so was I. My own mental state since the murder of my parents had been dicey at times. Shouldn't I give Charlie the same benefit of the doubt I wished I'd had when my parents were killed?

"I don't know," I told Jon. "Something about this case feels different. *She* feels different. And I was hoping you might be able to dig a little deeper into her background."

This was met with silence, but I could hear Jon breathing and knew the call hadn't dropped. Was he simply sorting through the possibilities in his mind, or was he hesitant because he was uncomfortable with my request?

"I don't know, Morgan," he said finally, giving me my answer. "I don't like the idea of looking into someone's background unless I have a reason to. She hasn't committed any crimes you know of, has she?"

That was the million-dollar question, wasn't it? But I wasn't willing to push it. Jon was clearly uncomfortable looking into her past and I had Devon looking into it anyway.

"No worries," I said, letting Jon off the hook. "It's not a big deal, and I don't want you doing anything if it makes you uncomfortable. Forget I asked."

There was another extended silence and then Jon said, "You already have Devon working on it, don't you?"

"I plead the Fifth."

He chuckled. "If it helps, I plan to come up there for the weekend. I can drive up tomorrow after work. It will be around eleven before I can get there, but we could start fresh on Saturday morning, and I wouldn't have to leave until late afternoon on Sunday."

"I'd love to have you with me on this," I told him. "But it's a busy time up here and I don't think you'll be able to find a room.

Charlie had to pull strings to get me this suite and even then a bit of lucky timing was involved." I paused to give him time to offer up a solution but when he didn't jump in with anything, I leapt out of the proverbial frying pan. "My suite does have a nice-sized sofa, though, so if you're okay with sleeping on it, you're welcome to stay with me."

I sucked in my lower lip and held my breath as I awaited his answer. Our relationship thus far was a mildly romantic one marked by a couple of dinners together and a few kisses, but nothing more. Jon knew I needed to take things slow. Glacially so, according to Rita.

"That would be fine, if you're sure?" he said. "I don't want to make you uncomfortable."

I let out the breath I'd been holding, closing my eyes with relief. "I'm sure," I said, and I was. Even though things between us were moving slower than maple sap in springtime, I was comfortable in Jon's company and trusted him. Plus, I liked having him around. The world always looked brighter, the colors more vibrant, when I was in his presence.

"I'll feed you when you get here," I said, "but odds are it will be reheated takeout. I have a kitchen in my suite, but I haven't stocked it and I'm honestly not much interested in cooking. Plus, it sounds like Charlie has a big day planned for me tomorrow."

"I'm fine with that. Figure on me getting there late. I'll text you when I'm on the road. Also, if it makes you feel any better, Charlie would have had a fairly extensive background check run prior to being hired for her current job."

"Good point," I said. I'd let him make his own judgments once he got here and had a chance to spend more face-to-face time with her. "Goodnight, and I'll see you tomorrow."

After ending my call with Jon, Newt was looking at me with tongue-lolling anticipation, desperate for a walkabout. I found the night vision binoculars I'd brought along, and I tossed them, a flashlight, and a bottle of water into my backpack, along with a collapsible bowl for Newt. Then I grabbed my wallet and stuffed it in the back pocket of my pants. Finally, I grabbed a towel from the bathroom and shoved it in my backpack, too. Newt loved to swim and if I found a spot for him to splash around in Lake Superior, I wanted to be able to dry him off afterward. I would have considered going for a swim myself—the two of us do early-morning swims in Green Bay as soon as the water reaches a tolerable temperature in the spring and until it gets too cold in the fall—but Lake Superior rarely gets above sixty-five degrees this time of year and that's a bit too frigid for my tastes without a wet suit.

I walked Newt across the street to the lakefront park we'd visited earlier and let him off leash. He made his way down a wall of large boulders to the water's edge and then took himself for a quick swim while I watched from a nearby bench. The park was nearly empty, and I guessed this was because it was just after six in the evening and most folks were probably eating dinner. After ten minutes of watching Newt swim, paddle, splash, and chase random ducks and geese, I called him out, dried him off the best I could—his fur tended to hold water for hours—and leashed him back up.

We went back to my building, got in the car, and headed for the dog park Charlie had told me about earlier. Bayfield is situated along the shores of Lake Superior on land where glaciers and old lake borders have left behind deep gullies and rocky bluffs. The unofficial dog park was an abandoned soccer field located atop one of the steep hills near the outskirts of town, and it was bigger than I expected, easily the size of two football fields side by side. The open grassy area was surrounded by woods on three sides—one of those sides containing the dirt road I drove up to get there—but the fourth side had a steep, grassy drop-off. I decided to walk the perimeter beginning with the wooded sides, knowing it would provide an olfactory treat for Newt.

The sun skidded down below the horizon as we walked, and while the setting wasn't particularly menacing given the vast open field, we were utterly alone in the growing darkness. I found myself feeling edgy as the shadows lengthened and the surrounding woods revealed dark voids. Newt dodged in and out of the tree line, nose to the ground, happily sniffing this new world, while I took the flashlight from my backpack and used it to illuminate the path ahead. We made it around to the side with the steep, grassy hill without incident. I walked over to the edge and saw the grass ended about twenty feet below where it gave way to a heavily wooded ravine with even steeper sides that I guessed were thirty or forty feet high.

I tried to shine my flashlight into the bottom of this gorge, but the shadows swallowed the light. I turned the flashlight off, gave myself a minute to let my eyes adjust, and then removed the night vision binoculars from my backpack. After powering them up and turning on the attached infrared light, I scanned what I could see of the ravine, which seemed to go on forever. Newt acted like he wanted to go down there to explore, but I told him to stay, and he dutifully sat and stared into the abyss instead.

The sides of the ravine were not only steep, they also were

littered with trees, shrubbery, deadwood, and roots that would make any climb up or down a hazardous trip. At the bottom, I saw what appeared to be a dried-up creek bed currently being navigated by a scurrying racoon. A movement higher up and to the left revealed an owl in a tree, its head pivoting as it searched for something to eat. Beside me, Newt let out a whine, followed by a low growl.

I looked down at him, thinking he was simply being impatient, but when I saw the ridge of fur raised along his spine I knew it was more.

"What is it, buddy? Did you see something?"

I turned around and scanned the vast, open field behind us with the binoculars, but when nothing showed up along the edge of the woods or in the field, I turned back to focus on the ravine.

I slowly scanned along the dry creek bed at the bottom using the binoculars and then froze when I saw something large move off to the right. At first, I thought it must be a person, because it appeared to be standing on two feet. But something about the shape of it, and seconds later, the way it moved, made me rethink my assumption. The thick brush and trees obscured my view as it darted in between shrubs and trunks, my jerky movements with the binoculars sometimes making me lose track of it. But I could tell it was large, dark, and covered with fur from head to toe.

Newt barked as the creature disappeared around a curve and I stood there stunned, staring through the binoculars at the spot where I'd last seen it. After a moment, I scanned what I could see of the ravine's length and saw nothing, though the goose bumps on my arms and legs lingered for a long, long while.

CHAPTER 12

I wasn't sure what I'd seen, but it hadn't been a bear based on its shape and the way it moved. My heart raced, galloping inside my chest as much from excitement as fear. Questions flooded my brain. Had I just seen a Bigfoot? Could I now join the ranks of those who claimed such? Were the townsfolk right? Was a Bigfoot hanging around the area after all? Was it homicidal? Had it killed those two men? And where had it gone? Should I go down into the ravine to try to track it?

A worried whine from Newt convinced me now wasn't the best time. Besides, navigating the steep sides of the hill and the obstacle-studded ravine in the dark, even with my flashlight or my night vision binoculars, would have been a fool's errand.

"Let's get out of here," I said to Newt.

Despite being the brave boy he is, he needed no convincing. I turned the flashlight back on and we did a quick walk to the car with me doing frequent over-the-shoulder checks while Newt sniffed the ground with vigorous interest. I cursed my stupidity when I remembered my binoculars had the ability to take pictures and record video. Had I been quicker on my feet, I could have captured evidence of what I saw in the ravine, evidence that might have proven valuable later after more in-depth study.

On the short drive back into town, I half expected to see the animal appear in the beam of my headlights. I kept my cell phone close by, thinking I would try to snap a quick picture, but the drive was uneventful other than the loud gurgling of my stomach, a reminder that I hadn't eaten dinner. I pulled up outside of the bistro Charlie had recommended because it was conveniently located only two blocks from my suite. I parked at the curb and saw it had an enclosed porch area for those souls brave enough to face the fall chill and a sign indicating dogs were allowed there. It was a perk I thought I might take advantage of on a future date, but right then I felt the need for warmth and human company. Besides, Newt was still damp from his earlier swim, and I feared the smell of wet dog might be offensive to other diners on the porch, if there were any. I told Newt to stay in the car and went inside, making my way to a bar just past the cashier's station by the entrance. The place was bustling, so I was pleasantly surprised to find an empty stool at the end of the bar. I slid onto it and ordered a glass of Chardonnay to sip on while I perused the menu.

"The lemon garlic fettucine is superb," said the man seated beside me. "Particularly if you're a vegetarian, though I typically add the roasted chicken option. The pizzas are quite good, too."

I glanced over at him—handsome, dark hair, blue eyes, probably in his forties, nursing a beer—and smiled. "Thanks. I was just about to settle on a pizza and your recommendation seals the deal."

"Happy to help." He cocked his head to one side and gave me a quick head-to-toe perusal. "Are you visiting or new in town?"

"What gives me away?"

He shrugged. "Haven't seen you in here before. I grew up in this town, so I know you're not a long-term resident. That leaves me with either visitor or newcomer to the city. Given the time of year and the influx of tourists, I'd guess visitor."

"Good guess. But I'm here on business."

"Really?" he scoffed, obviously amused.

"Yes, really." The waitress came then to take my order and I gave it to her, asking her to package it up to go. I hoped the interruption would dissuade my seatmate from more conversation, but no such luck.

"I'm sorry, but I have to ask," he said once the waitress was done. "What kind of business brings you to our lovely little city? It's not like Bayfield is a big commercial hub. Aside from fishing, the only business happening in these parts is centered around the tourist trade."

"Spoken like a rep from the chamber of commerce," I said teasingly.

"That's because I am one," he countered. "My brother, Trip, and I own a couple of wilderness supply stores . . . camping gear, tents, sleeping bags, lanterns, meals in a bag, that kind of thing. We have a store here in Bayfield and one in Washburn."

"Sounds like a good business for the area. You said you've lived in Bayfield all your life?"

"Between here and Washburn." He extended a hand. "Name's Lloyd Mann."

I shook his hand, which was damp with sweat from his beer bottle. "Morgan," I said, purposely leaving off my last name.

Lloyd leaned back and gave the fellow on his right an elbow nudge. "This handsome fellow over here is my brother, Trip. Hey, Trip, say hi to Morgan."

Trip bore a strong enough resemblance to his brother, I would have guessed they were related had I not been told. He glanced my way, nodded politely, raised his right arm, which was enclosed in a cast, and then went back to watching the TV at the end of the bar.

Having been summarily dismissed, I took a long drink of my wine and looked hopefully toward the kitchen area, letting my body language tell Lloyd I wasn't interested in more conversation. But he was either oblivious or indifferent.

"I really am curious," he said. "What sort of business brings you to Bayfield?"

Resigned, I sighed and said, "I'm a cryptozoologist." I hoped this might shut him down, but I'd underestimated Lloyd.

His brows dipped down ever so briefly before his eyes widened and he smiled. "You hunt for fabled monsters and the like?" Apparently this was a rhetorical question because Lloyd didn't give me time to answer. "What sort of creature are you hunting for here in Bayfield?" His posture turned rigid, and he drew back from me almost imperceptibly, as if bracing himself for the answer.

I bit the bullet. "I'm looking for Bigfoot."

Lloyd stared at me for several seconds before he burst out laughing. "Oh, my goodness. You hear that, Trip?" he said, giving his brother an elbow in the ribs. Other patrons in the place turned to look at us. "This lady is hunting for Bigfoot. Takes all kinds I guess, doesn't it, Trip?"

Trip looked at me again and smiled apologetically. Then he looked at his brother and said, "Yes, it does, you jackass. Now leave the lady be and quit bothering her."

"I'm not bothering her," Lloyd whined, looking at his brother like he'd lost his mind before turning back to me. "Am I bothering you, Morgan?"

Before I could figure out how to answer this loaded question, Lloyd's eyes shifted to something behind and above me. "Buck!" he bellowed. "You're late. I thought you'd be here by seven."

"I'm here now."

There it was, that deep, marble-mouthed grumble I'd heard earlier in the day. Buck Weaver was the last person I wanted to run into, and I wished I could shrink down and pull into a shell so he wouldn't see me. Lloyd promptly dashed those hopes.

"Hey, Buck, this pretty little lady in your seat is named Morgan. And guess what?" he snorted. "She's here looking for a Bigfoot."

The little lady in your seat. I should have known when I found an empty stool in such a crowded place it was too good to be true.

Behind me, Buck said, "Yeah, I heard. I made it clear that her so-called investigation isn't welcome around here."

"Oh, for heaven's shake, Buck," Lloyd said with a big smile. He reached over and clapped a hand down on top of mine. His eyes had a too-bright, brittle look to them. That, and the use of "shake" instead of "sake" told me he was well into his cups. "Ease up, big fella," Lloyd went on. "She's looking for a freaking Bigfoot. It's not like she's doing anything, you know, la-git-a-mitt." He pronounced the word slowly, concentrating on each syllable, and then punctuated the comment by withdrawing his hand and taking a long slug of his beer.

Resigned, I spun around on my barstool and looked up at Buck. "Good to see you again," I said with forced cheerfulness.

"Is it?" Buck tilted his head to one side and narrowed his eyes at me, a sneer of a smile on his face.

I slid off my seat. "I didn't realize you owned a barstool here. Sorry if I trespassed. My order should be ready soon and then I'll be out of your way."

"You need to be *on* your way," Buck grumbled. "Out of town."

I laughed. I'd had about enough of Buck Weaver and his compensatory bluster. "What is this, the wild, wild West?" I said.

Lloyd snorted a laugh, and it didn't go over well with Buck, who didn't much like being the butt of anyone's joke. His face looked like the kind of storm known to spawn F5 tornadoes. Fortunately, the waitress chose that moment to arrive with my order and I eased past Buck and went to the register to pay. When I was done, I looked at the trio of men seated at the bar and gave them a big smile.

"Ta-ta, fellas," I said in my best cheery tone, giving them a little finger wave. "Maybe I'll see you around town again in the coming days." It was my not-so-subtle way of letting Buck know he wasn't scaring me off, though a little voice inside my head warned me it might not be a smart idea to antagonize the man. What was it Charlie had said? Something along the lines of how Buck had connections and ways to make my life miserable.

I've faced down tougher things than you, Buck Weaver, I thought, as I left the bistro with my shoulders squared, feeling eyes boring into my back. *So, have at it.*

Though I didn't know it at the time, it was one of those be-careful-what-you-ask-for moments.

CHAPTER 13

I had trouble getting to sleep and then slept later than planned, so when Charlie knocked on my door the next morning I was still in my pajamas. She, I noticed, was in her uniform, gun at her side, though sans vest and lacking the other accoutrements she'd had the day before.

"Sorry, I'm running behind," I told her after inviting her in.

"No problem. I brought you a latte and a biscotto from a coffee shop I frequent. Hope that's okay."

It was better than okay. We sat at the small table and Charlie filled me in on the day's schedule over our morning repast. My biscotto—a little softer than biscotti I'd had in the past—was a delightful mix of shortbread, cherries, and pistachios.

"I know you want to see the sites where the two men were killed, so those are definitely on the agenda for today," Charlie said. "But first I'd like to take you out to see a man who claimed he saw a Bigfoot creature two weeks ago. He strikes me as credible, and he lives just outside of Washburn on the edge of the Cheq, so it's on the way. Getting to the spot where he saw the creature will require a bit of a hike though, as will getting to the site of Erickson's death, so you might want to dress accordingly."

"Got it." I debated telling her about my experience last night with the ravine but decided against it. Why I made the decision, I couldn't say. It just felt right at the time. I dressed, grabbed my coat and the backpack I'd prepared with water and snacks for Newt, and in less than fifteen minutes we were on our way.

It was a brisk but beautiful fall day, with white puffy clouds drifting across an azure sky. Newt was buckled into the back seat of Charlie's SUV with the window down and his head hanging out, eagerly sniffing the air. The temperature hovered in the low forties, but the forecast promised a warm-up to the high fifties by midafternoon. With the heat on in Charlie's vehicle, we were comfortable enough, and Newt wasn't fazed at all at having forty-degree, fifty-mile-an-hour wind blasting him in the face and making his ears flap crazily as we headed out of town on Highway 13.

"The man we're going to see is Nathan Hotchkiss," Charlie explained as she drove. "The area where he lives is sparsely populated, with just a handful of houses sitting on dozens of acres of mostly wooded land between Washburn proper and the edge of the Cheq. Nathan owns one of those houses and about fifty acres around it butting up to the Cheq. Other than dirt lanes, old logging roads, and ATV trails, it's mostly wilderness out there."

"Did Nathan say how it was he happened to be out in the middle of this wilderness?" I asked.

"He was walking with his dogs. He lets them run loose on the property. There's a small pond on his land and as they neared it, the dogs alerted and began to growl. Nathan looked up, saw what appeared to be a large apelike creature across the pond, and then he grabbed his phone to try to snap a photo. By the time he got the camera ready, the creature had retreated into the woods. That was the blurry picture you saw in the folder I brought you. Unfortunately, it was the only shot Nathan was able to get. He said the creature, and I quote, 'dissolved into the trees.'"

"This happened in broad daylight?"

Charlie nodded but also gave me an indecisive waggle of her hand. "It was midafternoon, but it happened back in August when the trees were all leafed up, so it would have been very shaded. I know from personal experience how shadows can create interesting optical illusions." Her voice sounded eerie as she said this, and I wondered if she was flashing back to her childhood experience.

"What does Nathan do for a living?" The question was a routine one, geared toward developing a personality profile, something I do for all "witnesses" who report a cryptid sighting.

Charlie wrinkled her face like she'd just sucked on a lemon. "Yeah, I should probably prepare you for Nathan. He's not the easiest person to get along with, or to talk to. He can be a bit abrasive." From the way she said this I gathered it was an understatement. "As for what he does, he's retired. He was a hedge fund manager who apparently did quite well for himself. He grew up in the area, moved to New York for college and career, and then decided to come back here to his roots when he retired at the age of fifty-three. That was three years ago. He bought a chunk of land

and put up a house, though rumor has it he has plans to replace the existing place with something bigger."

"Got it," I said.

"Also, as I mentioned, Nathan's two dogs have the run of the property and they'll likely be outside to greet us when we arrive. They're big but friendly. Does Newt get on well with other dogs?"

"He does, but we'll take things slow and easy to make sure everyone gets along. If there's any doubt, I'll leave Newt in the car. He won't like it, but he'll do okay."

Charlie turned off the main highway after we drove through Washburn and onto roads with sparse development and heavily wooded acreage. "I think someone might be following us," she said at one point.

"What?" I wondered if I'd heard her right and thought surely I hadn't. "Why?"

"A Land Rover Defender followed us out of Bayfield and stayed behind us all the way into Washburn. Having it behind us on the main highway is no big deal, but it has followed us turn for turn since we left the highway, keeping a safe distance behind us. I only noticed it because I have vehicle envy. I'd love to own one of those Defenders someday but can't afford it yet."

I glanced in my side mirror and saw a silver vehicle behind us. When I looked out the back window, I could tell it was, indeed, a Land Rover. Charlie slowed to turn into a gravel driveway, and the Land Rover continued on down the road.

"Maybe it was nothing," Charlie said as she pulled up in front of a large A-frame home.

The two dogs Charlie had warned me about were outside and they came bounding up to the car to greet us. They were friendly, if somewhat exuberant, mutts—a mix of collie, lab, and maybe some German shepherd—and after greeting us with tail-wagging jumps, they swiftly shifted their attention to Newt. There was a minute or two of butt-sniffing hellos and, once everyone was content, we made our way to the front door. I was surprised no one had come out to greet us and had a powerful sense of being watched. We knocked and waited a long minute before anyone came, making me wonder if the delay was intentional. When the door finally opened, it was done fast and with a bit of a flourish, perfectly framing the person who stood on the other side.

The gentleman in question—and I use the term loosely—was a grizzled fellow of medium height with beady, brown eyes and a hawklike nose. Something about him reminded me of a man I'd met on my first case with Jon Flanders, a hygienically challenged fellow with a hoarding problem who hadn't left me with a particularly good first impression. That had changed once I really got to know him, however, and I reminded myself of this fact as I found myself instantly disliking what was quickly revealed to be the bellicose and paranoid personality of Nathan Hotchkiss.

"I don't understand why the hell you're bringing another one of these hucksters out here," Hotchkiss bellowed at Charlie after introductions had been made. "Bunch of damned shysters trying to rob people of their money." He shifted his gaze in my direction, craning his neck forward and bringing our faces into uncomfortable proximity. "Do I look like an idiot? Do I seem addlebrained to you?" he asked accusingly. He jabbed a finger in my direction, though he thankfully refrained from poking me with it.

"Do you think I suffer from senility or dementia?" he went on. "Or maybe you think I use drugs because I lived in New York City all those years and held a high-pressure job. He must use drugs then, right? Wrong. Others in my profession did, but not me." He tilted his head to one side and gave me a questioning look.

Wow. Charlie's warnings hadn't been nearly stringent enough.

"I don't want your money," I told him. "I'm just here to investigate some recent sightings and I understand you had one."

Newt, sensing the rising tension, left the other dogs and shoved his huge body between me and Hotchkiss, forcing the man to step back. I was grateful for the space. Hotchkiss's breath was like a foul blast furnace. Newt didn't growl, but his message was clear.

Hotchkiss blinked rapidly several times, staring at Newt as if the dog had manifested out of thin air. Then he folded his arms over his chest and gave me a grudgingly acquiescent look punctuated with a resonant sigh.

I reached down and patted Newt reassuringly on the head while flashing my best customer-service smile at Hotchkiss. "I'm confused by what you just said, Mr. Hotchkiss. Has someone else been talking to you about what you saw? About this creature in the woods?"

Hotchkiss narrowed his eyes down to tiny gunner slits and gave me a rueful smile. "Don't act like you don't know about the other monster hunter fellow who's been poking around. You charlatans are all in cahoots together."

"Mr. Hotchkiss, I assure you I work alone and I'm not in cahoots with anyone. I'm a professional cryptozoologist with college degrees in zoology and biology. I approach each potential sighting of a cryptid with a jaundiced eye. I'm a realist and I believe in science. I'm not swayed by rumors or monies from interest groups."

He still looked skeptical, though I sensed a slight softening. My next comment was a calculated one, based on the information Charlie had given me about him beforehand. "I understand your skepticism," I said with a gentle but knowing smile. "While I have no need to swindle anyone out of their money, I'm keenly aware of how many people out there would like to swindle me out of mine." This triggered a noticeable change in his expression, and I knew I had him.

"Lots of hands out once folks know you have money," he said, nodding slowly.

"Yes, there are." A suspicion was building in my mind. "I take it someone else came to talk to you about your sighting. Someone who tried to convince you to sponsor his investigation into said sighting perhaps?"

Hotchkiss looked mildly surprised as he nodded.

"I think I might know the man you're referring to," I told him. "Was his name Hans Baumann?"

"That's him, all right," Hotchkiss said, eyes narrowed. "You're saying you don't work with him?"

"That's what I'm saying, yes. As I mentioned before, I'm a professional cryptozoologist and I've spent years investigating sightings of all kinds of creatures. In the course of doing so, I've run into Mr. Baumann before and have good reason to believe his intentions aren't always the most . . ." I hesitated, searching for the proper descriptive but not wanting to be too scurrilous. "His intentions aren't always the purest," I said finally. "He's interested in finding money whereas I'm interested in finding a cryptid if there's one out there to be found. I promise you, I don't want or need your money and won't ask for any."

Hotchkiss's brow furrowed. "*If* there's one out there? Are you saying you think I made it up? You think I'm just trying to make a quick buck or earn notoriety?"

Yikes, that didn't take long to turn. Nathan Hotchkiss was certainly a prickly little pear.

"No, that's not what I think at all," I said, trying to remain calm and pleasant. "Though I don't really know you, so I'm basing that assumption on how you haven't sought out attention from the press, you are clearly reluctant to chat with me today, and you were willing to share the photo you took with the DNR warden here. Those are the actions of someone looking for the truth, not the actions of an attention-seeking nutter."

This seemed to amuse him. He grinned wryly, sighed, and said, "Fair enough, lady. What did you say your name was again?"

"Morgan Carter."

Hotchkiss looked down at Newt, frowning for a second or two before his face relaxed into a smile. "And this guy's name?" he stroked the top of Newt's head, which my dog was all too happy to allow.

"That's Newt," I said. "We're a team."

Hotchkiss nodded his approval. "Okay, then, where do we start? Want to take a hike out to where I saw the creature?"

"I would very much like to, yes," I said. "And perhaps along the way you could tell me exactly what happened on the day in question."

"No problem." Hotchkiss walked over to a hutch along one wall of a room we could see into and opened a drawer. He removed a handgun, checked the chamber, dropped out the ammo clip, gave it a cursory once-over, and then slapped it back into place. After tucking it into the waist of his pants, he then walked over to a door, opened it, reached inside, and came out bearing a rifle. He slung this over his shoulder, looked at us expectantly, and said, "Ready?"

I made sure to retrieve Newt's leash from the car before we set out. The last thing I wanted was for my dog to be running loose with this Hotchkiss guy armed and ready.

Some days this monster-hunting thing isn't all the fun it's cracked up to be.

CHAPTER 14

We followed Nathan Hotchkiss through the wooded wilderness surrounding his home, heading toward the edge of the Chequamegon Forest. We hiked along trails covered with dead leaves, twigs, and the occasional half-buried tree root to trip us up. Despite the serious reason for our journey, I relaxed once we were underway, enjoying the way the warm sun on my head contrasted pleasantly with the brisk autumn air on my face. I drank in the sounds of birdsong, of the wind whispering all around us, and of the dried leaves crunching beneath our feet. The play of dappled sunlight shining down through the trees and creating mosaic patterns on the sandy, russet-colored dirt was my idea of an art show. It was a little slice of heaven and, as I inhaled the musty, crisp smells of autumn, I remembered why it was my favorite time of the year.

We weren't far from the house when Charlie leaned in close to me and said, "Do you think this Baumann guy came out here anyway after trying to get me to pay his way?"

"I do. That's his MO. Once he knew there were enough sightings to get a law enforcement officer to try to hire him, he saw the potential to make some money and hopped a plane out here on his own. Now he's most likely sniffing around, trying to figure out exactly what's going on. When was it you called him?"

"It was two days ago. Wait, no, three days ago now. Right after the second death and the day before I met you."

"I'll bet he's been out here since then, probably hopped a plane the minute he finished talking to you. Could be he heard about Erickson and the rumors about his attack and came out way back then. He might have already been here when you called him. He'll have contacted the local cops to get reports of recent sightings and talked to folks to get a feel for what the rumors are and who's involved in them. I'll bet he followed you from your office to find out where you work, where you live, and what you're up to with the investigation, and now he's busy laying the groundwork for his grifts."

"I get how he might have heard about the attack on Erickson already, but how did he know about Mr. Hotchkiss here?" Charlie asked, her voice just above a whisper.

"You filed a report about his sighting, didn't you?"

Her shoulders sagged. "Yeah."

"There's your answer. I'll bet if you talk to one of the other wardens in your office and ask if anyone came in or called recently asking about sightings, you'll find out Baumann was involved."

Charlie mumbled something I didn't hear clearly but I got a sense she was calling Hans Baumann a bad name.

Despite his curmudgeonly personality, Nathan Hotchkiss turned out to be something of a natural born storyteller. As we trampled through the trees along a path only Nathan could see, he began to talk, telling us about the day of his sighting, about how his dogs had been happily wandering about and sniffing out the trails of other woodland creatures when both had suddenly come to a standstill, nostrils flared and raised to the air, a ridge of fur down each of their backs.

"I figured it was either a coyote, wolf, or bear," Nathan said. "Maybe even a cougar. We've encountered them all out here at one time or another. I had my rifle at the ready, just in case. I didn't plan to shoot anything; I have no issue with the animals living out here. Live and let live is my motto. But I also know they're wild animals and they could attack me or my dogs. I figured if I didn't want to end up dead and a statistic on some damned DNR warden's report, I needed to be ready." He shot Charlie a look and added, "No offense meant."

"None taken," she said pleasantly.

"Anyway, if it hadn't been for the need to have my rifle at the ready, I might have gotten a better picture than I did, but I was holding the gun in both hands and by the time I was able to fish my phone out of my pocket and get the camera going, the dogs were running toward the beast and scared it off."

We came upon a large pond that—judging from the marks I could see—had shrunk down to nearly half its size during the hot, dry summer months, exposing musty, dank banks. There were trees encircling it and Nathan stopped about ten feet from shore, pointing toward the opposite bank, which I estimated was maybe a hundred yards away.

"It was right over there, standing beside those two birch trees. That's how I spotted it so easily. The critter was dark and, against the white bark of the trees, it stood out."

I stared across the water at the trees in question, imagining a Bigfoot standing in front of them, staring back at me. Behind the trees was an expanse of open field stretching back fifty yards or so, ending at a wall of trees even thicker than what we'd just walked through.

"That's the edge of the Chequamegon National Forest," Nathan said, seeing where my gaze was aimed.

I nodded and focused on the pond again. The upper, curved end of it to our left was maybe thirty yards away. To my right the pond extended down for what I guessed was the length of two, maybe three football fields. "Did your dogs stop at all on this side of the pond?" I asked Nathan.

"They tried to swim across it. It was hot and dry, and these two never pass up a body of water in the summertime, even when it's scummy and rank." He shot both dogs looks of tolerant disgust, which they returned with tongue-lolling smiles.

"Could you tell how tall the creature was based on any marks on those trees?"

Nathan stared off toward the other side of the pond, his forehead wrinkled in thought. "See the closest birch tree over there with the dogwood bush in front of it? The creature was about the height of that bush," he said. "I think." He winced and looked at me apologetically. "Like I said before, I was trying to get my phone out and focus the camera, so my eyes weren't always on it. By the time I looked up again, it was retreating. It had already run across that field and was about to disappear into the woods."

"Did you see it run?"

"Like I said, I was focused on getting my phone out and readying the camera," Nathan grumbled, his crustiness returning.

"Did you get a chance to see how it moved? Was it on two legs? Four?"

"It was on two when I saw it over there by the pond's edge," Nathan answered irritably. "I think it was still on two when it got to the trees beyond the field, but if you asked me to bet my savings on the fact, I wouldn't do it. It all happened fast and furious."

"Did your dogs ever make it to the other side?"

Nathan nodded, shaking his head woefully as he looked down at his mutts. "They swam across and scrambled up onto the bank over there but then they just stood there and barked. By then the creature was long gone."

I nodded and started walking around the closest end of the pond. It took fifteen minutes of hiking through scrub grass and snagging roots, and then circling around a small stretch of boggy marsh before I reached the birch trees on the other side. After telling Newt to sit and stay, I walked over to the tree with the dogwood bush in front of it and began walking an ever-widening arc around its trunk, traversing back and forth while dodging dried-up bushes and clumps of grass.

"Are you searching for prints?" Nathan asked after watching me for a bit. "Because if you are, you won't find any. I looked right after spotting the creature. Besides, it's been a couple of weeks now."

"You're assuming the day you saw this creature was the only time it came here. But this pond might serve as a regular watering hole and whatever creature you spotted might have come back. If it went down close to the water's edge where the bank is muddy, it could have left prints." I stopped, staring at the ground in front of me. "Like these," I said, pointing.

Charlie and Nathan both walked over to where I was and looked at a set of three depressions running close to the water's edge.

"Those are from a bear," Charlie said. "And a good-sized one."

Nathan scowled, shaking his head. "Yes, those *are* bear prints, but I'm telling you whatever it was I saw out here wasn't a bear." He was clearly agitated and growing testier by the minute.

Newt, who was still patiently sitting where I'd told him to stay, stood up and let forth with a low growl from deep in his throat. I waved him over to me and he came at a trot, trailing his leash through the plant growth. Just as he reached me, a breeze wafted over us, bringing with it a rank, animalistic odor. At first, I thought it must be Newt, but then his hackles rose, as did gooseflesh on the back of my neck.

All three of us—six if you count Newt and Nathan's dogs—turned and stared into the dense woods behind us, the nostrils of the humans flaring and working as hard as those of the canines. We all held perfectly still, no one speaking a word for a minute or more. The silence, which was absolute, felt unnatural. Or rather preternatural. The birdsong had ceased. The bullfrogs had quit bellowing, Even the wind had died away.

That was when we heard it, a sound both guttural and screeching, a sound filled with anger and fear, a sound that made my scalp tingle and my heart race. It was unlike anything I'd heard before and something I didn't think I'd ever want to hear again.

Nathan lowered his rifle from where it was slung over his

shoulder. The three of us scanned the trees, our eyes wide, our tension palpable. Newt pushed the top of his head against the palm of my hand.

"It's okay, buddy," I whispered, and he responded with a small whine.

"Maybe we should head back?" Charlie suggested, her voice a bit tremulous.

No one offered any argument, but no one moved right away either. I wondered if the others, like me, were reluctant to turn their backs on those trees. After a minute or so of staring at them, we trekked back the way we'd come, moving in unison as if an unspoken command had passed between us. We took turns casting glances over our shoulders—even Newt did so—and while I never saw anything, the sensation of being watched by someone or something was strong and inescapable.

CHAPTER 15

Little was said as we hiked back to Nathan's A-frame. Something was in the air out there and we'd all felt it. Maybe it was just nerves. Then again, maybe it was something more.

When we reached Nathan's house, he looked at me with disappointment and skepticism. "You think I'm nuts, don't you?" he said.

"I don't," I told him honestly. "I think you saw something out there but just what it was remains unclear."

Pfft. Nathan cast a disgusted look Charlie's way. "I told you this would be a big waste of time. Don't bother me again." He turned and strode into his house, slamming the door closed behind him.

I looked at Charlie and smiled. "That went well, wouldn't you say?"

She laughed. "Sorry. He's a crotchety fellow, but I thought his story bore further scrutiny. He doesn't seem the type to make up something like that."

"I agree, but unfortunately, we're no closer to the truth. Where to next?"

"Pine Lake, the site of the second death, that of Pete Conrad. I hope it's okay to visit these sites out of order. The Pine Lake site is closer and easier to get to than the site of Erickson's death."

"That's fine."

We said goodbye to Nathan's dogs, got in Charlie's SUV, and headed out. Charlie drove us over backcountry roads where forest surrounded us on both sides. Pavement gave way to gravel, and three times in a matter of a couple of miles we had to slow down for deer standing in the middle of the road. Newt's window was down enough for him to hang his head out and he sniffed the air with wild abandon, his tail wagging as he watched the deer make their graceful, bounding escapes. He looked like he wanted to gambol with them.

I lowered my window so I, too, could inhale the earthy wood scents. At one point, while watching Newt in the side mirror as he hung his head out his window, I noticed there was another vehicle behind us. I craned around to get a better look, but it was too far back and the dust we were kicking up obscured my view.

"I think it's the same car," Charlie said, seeing me look. "But it's hanging farther back this time so it's hard to see it clearly, especially with all this dust."

We eventually turned onto a narrow, rutted, uneven dirt road and Charlie flipped the car into four-wheel-drive, slowing us down to a bouncing crawl as we drove downhill. A few hundred feet later, we reached a small meadow sporting brown, dead grass and Charlie crossed it to yet another length of dry, dirt road. At the bottom of this second stretch, I saw the glittering surface of a lake in front of us surrounded by a mix of colorful trees and marsh plants in vibrant hues of red, orange, and green.

I got out and hooked Newt up to his leash. The ground beneath our feet was a mix of sand and dirt with an orange tinge to it and I feared Newt would be tracking plenty of it back to the suite later.

The view was breathtakingly beautiful, the lake before us a placid, isolated, smoothly serene body of water that sparkled in the late morning sunlight and reflected the fall colors of the bordering trees. Birdsong filled the air, and I recognized the melodic two notes of a black-capped chickadee, the down-slurred whistle of a cardinal, and the persistent *tap-tap-tap* of a woodpecker. A shadow overhead made me look up and I watched with awed reverence as a bald eagle swooped and swayed over the treetops surrounding the lake's perimeter. When looking at this location on the map last night I'd wondered why anyone would drive so far to fish in such a relatively small lake. Now I had my answer. It was a hidden treasure.

Directly ahead of where we'd parked, traversing the marshy shore plants and barely reaching the water, was the infamous wooden pier. It extended out twenty feet or so before making a dogleg turn to a section maybe half that length. Some boards were missing or had succumbed to neglect and the far end of the structure was tilted sideways at a steep, forty-five-degree angle. Our witness had been right; the thing was impossible to navigate.

"Here's the footprint," Charlie said, pointing to a spot in front of the car. "It's still visible."

I told Newt to stay and set my end of his leash on the ground. I didn't need him to go tromping all over the scene before I had a chance to look at it. Surprisingly, the print was still well preserved, an undisturbed, even depression in the sandy dirt. I squatted to study it more closely and snap a few photos with my phone. Then I scanned the surrounding area, noting how the sandy dirt road we'd driven on was bordered on both sides by bushes, trees, and steep banks. The footprint was located in about the only spot where it stood a chance of being made, seen, and not disturbed. What a coincidence.

"Conrad's body was found over there, on the other side of those trees," Charlie said, pointing off to our right. "There's a little side pool the lake feeds into, but because of the low water levels this summer, it's practically a separate pond all its own now."

I gestured with an extended arm. "Lead the way."

Charlie took off into the trees, marking out a path between bushes, roots, and overgrown ground cover. I grabbed Newt's leash and followed in Charlie's footsteps, emerging into another open area moments later.

The body of water in front of us was small, not much bigger than half a football field, and off to the far left of it I could see a narrow channel where the main lake trickled in. The bank in front of us was covered with dry, dead grasses and Charlie pointed to a spot about ten feet away and said, "That's where Conrad's body was, in the position you saw in the photograph, feet toward the water, head toward those trees. His pole was near his right hand and his tackle box was flipped over; the contents spilled out here." She waved her hand over a general area.

I recalled the photos from the file and could envision the scene as I stared at the spots Charlie was indicating. The ground where the body had been found was darker than the other areas and there was a small depression where Conrad's blood had saturated the ground enough to turn it muddy.

"Charlie, you came out here fairly soon after the body was found, right?"

"Within a couple of hours."

"How many others were out here at the time?"

"Two. Bruce White, the warden out of the Washburn office who's in charge of the case, and a county deputy."

"Not Buck?" She shook her head. "When you came through those trees from the road to here, was the brush broken or squashed down already?"

"There was evidence of a path of sorts through there, the same one we just followed. But I honestly don't know if it was there already from other fishermen, from Conrad, from the fellow who found Conrad, or from Bruce and the deputy. Maybe all of the above." She pointed off to our right where the shoreline rose up to a small ridge. "We did notice broken branches and flattened grass heading in that direction. And this dead grass we're standing on was squashed down considerably, crushed and flattened as if something heavy had tromped on it."

I studied the hillside she'd indicated. It was a steep rise covered with grass and other ground cover and the ridge above was heavily wooded. It wouldn't have been an easy traverse for any creature, much less a two-footed one.

The footprint had been pointed away from this area, seeming to imply the creature was heading toward the woods on the other side of the road. Had the animal originally come at Pete from somewhere around this pond? The growth directly across from us and to our left was thick enough to rule those approaches out, which left the steep hill to the right or the trees behind us.

I stared at the hill again, trying to imagine Pete Conrad standing where I was when he saw some huge apeman descending from the tree line toward him. The trail Charlie and I had just followed from the road wasn't well marked but it was passable enough. Why hadn't Pete Conrad tried to run? Had he been stunned into immobility? Had he perhaps tried to run but tripped? Had the creature somehow managed to sneak up on him?

"Was Pete Conrad wearing earbuds when you found him? Or did you find any on the ground near him?"

Charlie shook her head.

"Did he have any defensive injuries?"

Charlie squinted in thought, her brows drawing together and making a puzzled V above her nose. "I don't recall seeing any, but I also haven't seen the final autopsy report yet." Her eyes widened. "That seems a bit odd, doesn't it?"

"It does," I agreed. "You said Pete's vehicle was parked behind the footprint, pretty much in the same spot where we're now parked?"

She nodded. "Sometimes folks park in that small meadow above us because the road down here can get thick with mud that even a four-by-four can struggle to get out of. But it's been so dry this year it hasn't been an issue."

The fact of Pete Conrad's car being parked relatively close by made the apparent lack of any effort to escape on his part even more puzzling. Why hadn't he at least tried to get to it and lock himself inside? Or fight off whatever had attacked him? And why had he been attacked in the first place?

I looked out over the still pond as I mulled these questions and saw the surrounding trees and sky reflected in its smooth, glassy surface to near perfection. It was such a lovely, peaceful setting, making it hard to imagine the violence that had happened there. The why of it nagged at me. What had prompted the attack? Conrad wasn't being aggressive; he was fishing. Had fish been the lure? Had the animal that attacked him been so hungry and desperate for food it had killed for it?

"Did you find evidence Conrad caught any fish? Scales or fish blood of any sort?"

"No, from what we could determine, he'd been skunked so far, though he might have been a catch-and-release guy. We don't know for sure how long he was out here before he was killed because we couldn't track his activities from the day before. It could be he'd just started fishing. We did find a fresh-looking energy bar wrapper near where I parked, but we can't be sure it belonged to Conrad."

"What about his cell phone?"

"His wife said he carried one, but he didn't have it on him, and we didn't find it in his motel room. We're not sure what happened to it. It might be at the bottom of this pond. We tried to ping it, but there's no signal out here."

I took my own phone out of my pocket and examined the screen. Sure enough, I had zero bars.

A loud *snap* came from the trees above us and off to our right, making us both look. Charlie's hand moved toward her gun, and I found it interesting she went for it first, bypassing her taser and bear spray. I didn't see anything moving through the trees but noticed the birds had all quieted. Newt let out a low growl and a ridge of fur rose along his back as he, too, stared in the direction the sound had come from. I tightened my grip on his leash and placed my palm on top of his head, steadying him, keeping him at my side. The last thing I wanted was for him to charge off after a bear or wildcat.

Another *snap*, and the three of us—two humans, one dog—stood utterly still. The only things moving were Newt's flaring nostrils and three pairs of eyes as we scanned the surrounding woods. If I said I wasn't afraid, I'd be lying.

After a minute or so of heart-stopping silence, I looked over at Charlie. "I've seen enough. Let's go."

She gave me no argument and led the way back to the car. I didn't relax until she had driven up the hill and onto the main road.

That is, until I saw the same car we'd seen earlier, tailing us again.

CHAPTER 16

I was willing to bet the person behind the wheel of the car following us was Hans Baumann. This sneaky sort of shadowing was something he'd done in the past when my parents and I had investigated Bigfoot sightings elsewhere. And a vehicle like a Land Rover fit his profile. It was the perfect prop, designed to support the image and brand he wanted to project. I didn't think he owned it—driving here from Connecticut didn't seem his style—he would have rented something after flying here, all of it likely paid for by victims he'd managed to fleece over the years.

"Looks like we have a tail again," Charlie said.

"Yeah, I see. I think it might be Hans Baumann. I wonder why he's following us." It was meant as a rhetorical question; I was thinking aloud and wondering if Hans knew about my involvement here, and if so how, but Charlie answered anyway.

"I'm guessing it has something to do with you. Maybe he's hoping to gain notoriety by riding your coattails."

"Or maybe he's here hoping to find a way to discredit me. Though I'm not sure how he would know about my involvement. You haven't talked to him since the first phone call, have you?"

"Nope."

"And my name didn't come up at any time during that call?"

"No. I didn't even know about you then."

I thought for a moment, debating the pros and cons of a wild idea that had just popped into my head. "I don't suppose you could lose him?"

Charlie shot me a bemused look.

"I mean, surely you know the roads around here better than he does."

Charlie didn't answer me. She didn't have to. A grin spread over her face, and I saw the way her hands flexed on the steering wheel. I looked back to make sure Newt was clipped in and told him to lie down. Then I gave my own seat belt a reassuring tug a second before Charlie floored it.

The road ahead didn't offer much in the way of turnoffs for a distance, but then we came to an intersection and Charlie took a hard right onto a dirt and gravel road. We bounced and jostled along it for several hundred feet, and then Charlie took a left onto what was little more than an ATV or snowmobile trail. We fishtailed a little before she got the SUV back under control, and I wanted to look back and see how close Baumann might be, but I was afraid to tear my eyes away from the road. Charlie followed the trail for a few hundred yards more and then turned onto another gravel road. A couple of minutes and two turns later we emerged onto a paved road.

I looked back and saw we'd kicked up a hefty cloud of dust and dirt. It might make it easy for Baumann to track where we'd gone but might also make it hard for him to see us. Charlie stayed on the paved road for a couple of miles, bypassing one turn and taking the next one at a rate of speed bordering on reckless, though other than the earlier minor fishtail, she always had full control of the vehicle. She made one more turn, putting us back on a gravel road and slowed to a more reasonable pace. When I looked back, there was no sign of the Land Rover. A quick check of Newt showed him securely snugged down into the back seat, looking none the worse for wear.

"Impressive driving," I said to Charlie.

"I've done a lot of tactical pursuit training."

"Think we lost him?"

Charlie, grinning from ear to ear, shrugged. "Not sure but odds are he might guess where we're going anyway. He knows I think Bodie Erickson's death might have been at the hands of a Bigfoot because we discussed it during our phone call. And while he may not have known the exact spot where Erickson was found, he could have chatted with some locals or obtained copies of the reports to find out. The rumor mill around here is quite efficient."

I hadn't considered this. "Then why did you bother trying to lose him?"

Charlie turned and looked at me, her grin growing broader. "Because it was fun as hell."

Fair enough. I had to admit to feeling a certain sense of exhilaration myself.

Charlie pulled off our current road and onto another trail barely wide enough to accommodate the car. This time she slowed enough that I didn't feel like my kidneys were being rattled loose. When she stopped, I was relieved to put my feet on solid ground. There was no sign of the Land Rover.

"We've got a hike of a half mile or so," Charlie said, pointing toward the trees.

I unhooked Newt and let him out of the car but put him on his leash. Charlie set off on a purported trail—I'm not sure I would have recognized the narrow, meandering, leaf-covered path as such—and Newt and I followed. We walked in silence, the only sounds those of nature, Newt's constant sniffing, and the crunch of our feet on dead leaves. Fifteen minutes in, Charlie stopped at the foot of a large oak tree in a stand of smaller trees and shrubbery.

"This is where Erickson put up his tree stand," she said. "It looked like he'd just dismantled it because we saw fresh abrasions on the trunk and the stand was sitting at the bottom of the tree." She pointed off to the west. "The witness, Keller, had hiked further down the trail in that direction and was returning when he heard the commotion. He claims he saw the whole thing happen, but honestly, I'm doubtful."

"Why?"

"Look around us," Charlie said, waving an arm in an encompassing gesture. "The trees and bushes are so thick in here you can barely see ten yards in front of you, much less the fifty-yard line of sight Keller claimed. The terrain all around us is hilly, blocking how far you can see in any one direction unless you happen to be on top of one of these ridges. And there was a heavy mist, a common thing for this time of year because there's a lake not far from here."

"Why would Keller say he saw what happened if he didn't?"

Charlie held up her hands, palms skyward, in a classic gesture of bewilderment. "Who knows? My guess? He heard it happening. Heard Erickson's screams and started toward him but then caught a glimpse of what was going down and either backtracked and hid or climbed a tree. Then when the screams stopped, he approached, saw what had been done to Erickson, and the sight of it traumatized the hell out of him. In his mind he thinks the creature he saw attacking Erickson was a Bigfoot, but I watched his interview. The guy was so freaked out by the whole experience I'm not sure his accounting is reliable."

"Now you sound like me, a skeptic," I said. "And yet you, of all people, should believe Keller's story because you say you've seen the creature yourself." Newt was vigorously sniffing around the base of the tree, and I pulled him back away from it before he could lift a leg.

Charlie gave me a long side-eye stare and said, "I'll tell you why I'm skeptical of Keller's story. What was done to Erickson was horrible. Whatever attacked him literally tried to tear him apart. It was a vicious, violent, frenzied attack. You saw the pictures."

I nodded, staring at dark specks on the trunk of the oak tree, spots I suspected were dried blood spatter.

"The creature I saw when I was out here with my father never tried to attack us. If anything, it shied away from us. The sort of violence perpetrated on Erickson seems off to me."

"Fair enough," I said. She had a valid point. Bigfoot sightings and stories were prevalent in cultures all around the world, yet this sort of violence rarely accompanied the narratives. "Didn't you say there was a blood trail you found apart from Erickson's body?"

Charlie nodded, did a follow-me wave, and stepped off the path into the heavy undergrowth of bushes, trudging her way through tangled vines, over downed tree limbs, and up the side of a hillock. She stopped halfway to the top.

"Here we go," she said, pointing to a bush on her right. "We found traces of blood along this path, a couple of drops on the ground that I don't see any more, and some on leaves, like this." The branch she'd indicated was about waist high, with broad leaves on it, and it stuck out from the main body of the bush. One of the leaves, the one at the very end of the branch, was smeared with a rusty brown substance resembling dried blood. Judging from Newt's attention to it, it also smelled like blood.

Charlie continued up the hill and stopped at the top near a spot relatively clear of plant growth. "The pool of blood was here," she said. "It was a significant amount."

There was no visible evidence of any blood remaining, but I knew predators and insects would have eliminated much of it by now. Not all of it, apparently, because Newt's nose was glued to the spot. Unlike the other areas where blood had been, this one made a ridge of fur rise along Newt's back. When he finally lifted his nose from the ground and sniffed the air, he let out a low, rumbling growl.

Charlie pointed down the opposite side of the hillock, deeper into the woods. "We tracked a trail of blood droplets from here off in that direction for maybe twenty feet or so and then nothing."

I looked back toward the big oak Erickson had used for his tree stand and was able to see it easily from where we stood. Of course, the fog might have complicated things, but perhaps not enough to keep Erickson from shooting at something. Particularly if the something had been atop this ridge. That kind of morning mist tends to favor low-lying land.

"Maybe Erickson shot at a bear, hit it, and rather than killing it, he only incensed it. Then it came at him and mauled him to death," I surmised. "Keller might have seen glimpses of the bear but in his shock with the horror of what was happening, he morphed it in his mind into a Bigfoot because he'd heard of another sighting or had it in mind for some other reason."

Charlie reached up and scratched her head. "Maybe," she said. "But none of the blood samples we collected from on and around Erickson's body were anything but human. The samples we collected between his body and here were also human. This pool of blood, however, was from an animal, though we don't know what kind yet. If it was a bear and it had been injured enough to bleed such a large amount here, how had it managed to not leave any of its blood on or around Erickson's body, or between it and here?"

Charlie's questions were good ones, and I had no ready answers. "I don't know," I admitted. My stomach chose that moment to growl so loudly it made Newt start. I laughed, glanced at my watch, and saw it was just shy of noon. "You hungry?"

"Clearly you are," Charlie said with a chuckle. "I know a place in Washburn where we can grab a bite. I can get us there in twenty minutes, fifteen if you let me drive like before."

CHAPTER 17

It took more than thirty minutes to get to the eatery Charlie had in mind. We still had to hike back to the car, but Charlie drove the route in sixteen minutes rather than twenty, apparently still revved up from our earlier antics. She pulled into the parking lot of a small café located on the main road through town.

"This place not only makes great sandwiches, there's an outdoor patio with gas heaters so we can keep Newt with us," she said. "They also happen to make the best coffee in town. None of those fancy drinks, though, simply good, plain coffee. I don't know about you, but I could use a warm-up. It's nippy today and I've got a chill."

After resurrecting memories of what she'd seen at Erickson's death site, I doubted her chill was solely attributable to the temperature, but there was a definite bite in the air and coffee sounded good. We left Newt in the car with all the windows down while we went inside to order; then I let him out of the car and led him to a table on the patio where Charlie was already seated. The combination of our patio heater and the sun shining down through intermittent clouds scudding across the sky warmed things up surprisingly well, at least on the outside. After imagining what Bodie Erickson had gone through, my insides still felt a bit frosty.

No sooner were we settled than my phone rang. I glanced at the screen hoping it might be Jon, but it was Devon. I thought he might be calling me with an update on what he'd dug up about Charlie, so I let it go to voice mail.

Charlie waited until I set the phone aside and then said, "You felt it out there by Pine Lake and by the Hotchkiss place, didn't you? Something was in those woods, watching us."

Her words, spoken barely above a whisper, sent a chill down my spine. I was about to suggest what we'd felt was nothing more than the result of the setting, circumstances, and our own imaginations getting the better of us when Charlie's eerie little smile turned into a look of surprise as her gaze caught sight of something behind me.

"Hello, there, ladies," came a deep, male voice from over my shoulder.

A tall, slender man with dark hair silvered at the temples appeared on my right, a choice no doubt dictated by Newt being stretched out on my left. He had a handsome, slightly grizzled face and the hat he held in his hand looked like a prop he'd stolen from an Indiana Jones movie. He was dressed in blue jeans with a khaki shirt beneath a vest. I half expected to see a whip curled up and hung at his side. I knew who he was before I saw him because I recognized the voice even though I'd only heard it once before.

"Hans Baumann," I said, forcing a smile.

He grinned broadly at me. "Ah, I see my reputation precedes me."

It most certainly did, though probably not in the way he hoped.

He squinted at me, bending down closer. "Oh, wait. We've met, haven't we?" he said.

"Indeed, we have," I said, certain he'd recognized me and knew exactly who I was.

After waiting long enough to be sure I wasn't going to fill in the blanks for him, thereby setting myself up as the lesser-known quantity, he added, "You're the gal the police thought killed her parents. And you're a cryptozoologist, too, right?"

I managed to maintain my smile, but it took everything I had to keep it there. I knew Baumann was being intentionally obtuse, pushing my buttons in hopes of getting a rise out of me, and I wasn't about to give him the satisfaction. I looked around, my expression puzzled, my movements exaggerated.

"Are you saying there's another cryptozoologist here? Where? I'd love to meet them."

"Ha, ha," Hans said, flashing a mouth full of perfect, white teeth.

"What sort of cons are you running these days, Hans? Are you still bilking widows out of their life savings?" I managed to get the words out between my nearly clenched teeth. My cheek muscles ached from the effort to keep smiling.

"Not nice," Hans said, wagging a chastising finger at me. "I expected more professional courtesy from a colleague, but I suppose that's asking too much from a suspected killer."

"If you were a colleague, I would happily extend you every professional courtesy," I countered. "But it takes more than printing up a business card with the word 'cryptozoologist' on it to actually become one."

"Such as?"

"A relevant college degree, for starters."

"Really?" Hans said, sticking out his lower lip. "What relevant degrees did your parents have?"

Well, hell. He had me there. My father had gone to college, but his degree had been in business management, and my mother had obtained a two-year degree in accounting.

"They had a lifetime of experience between them," I said. "They were dedicated researchers who followed facts and science and kept meticulous records and notes. And I have degrees in both biology and zoology, so when it comes to qualifications, I think I have you easily beat. Not to mention I conduct serious, scientifically based searches whereas you simply try to find ways to con gullible people out of their money."

Baumann's smile returned, but there was a smug, self-satisfied quality to it, making me realize I'd played right into his hands. Fortunately, the waitress arrived with our sandwiches, providing me with an opportunity to mentally retreat and think through my next move. Hans Baumann had proven his ability to get under my skin. I was determined not to let him get any deeper.

Charlie must have sensed my discomfort, or maybe she just had good timing, but either way, she came to my rescue. "Are you interrupting our lunch for a specific reason, Mr. Baumann?" she asked.

Baumann shifted his gaze toward her, his smarmy smile still firmly in place. "Just trying to be friendly, warden," he said, donning his hat and giving the brim a sociable tug. "I'll leave you ladies to your little tea so I can get back to business." With this not-so-subtle insult, Hans Baumann spun around and left.

"What an absolute jerk," I muttered as soon as he was out of earshot. Though why I thought he shouldn't hear what I said was beyond me. Politeness is overrated at times and as far as I was concerned, the usual social niceties didn't apply to Hans Baumann. I watched him go and wasn't surprised to see him drive off in a silver Land Rover.

"He is quite nice-looking, though," Charlie said in a wistful tone. I gaped at her, and she burst out laughing. "Gotcha," she said.

"Good one," I acceded. "You almost had me there."

We ate in silence, Charlie making short work of her sandwich and chips, me sharing my food with Newt, who sat beside us with long strings of drool hanging from his jowls. I loved the beast, but his table manners were truly appalling at times.

"I suppose I should explain the thing about my parents," I said to Charlie when we were done eating and sipping our coffee, which really was perfection. "It's true they were both murdered, and it's also true I was a suspect—maybe I still am for all I know."

"I appreciate you offering," Charlie said, "but after Buck's comment yesterday I did a little digging of my own and read up on the case. To be honest, I'm not worried about you. I have a good sense when it comes to people and the vibe I get from you isn't that of a killer. If you decide you want to tell me your version of events at some point, I'll be happy to listen."

"Thank you," I said, honestly grateful but also appreciative of the irony of her being concerned about *my* background.

In a voice much too chipper for the words that went with it, Charlie said, "For a change of pace, how about we head back to

Bayfield and pay a visit to a lady who claims a Bigfoot tried to kill her dog two weeks ago?"

Newt's head shot up to look at her.

"Cripes, does he understand what I'm saying?" Charlie asked, eyes wide.

I had to smile. "He might. He's the smartest dog I've ever encountered, and he seems to understand anything I say to him. Heck, there are times when I think he can read my mind."

"Have you had him since he was a puppy?"

I shook my head. "Nope, he just appeared on my doorstep a year ago all beaten and bruised. The vet said he thought someone might have tried to use him in illegal dog fights because of his size, but he clearly doesn't have the temperament for it. I was feeling rather beaten and bruised myself at the time because of what happened to my parents, and the two of us just bonded. I took him in and cared for him, healing his wounds, and it started me on the road to my own healing emotionally, psychologically, even physically. We've been inseparable since then and I don't know what I'd do without him."

"Wow, that's quite a story. I'm glad the two of you found one another. I'll try not to upset him anymore with stories about m-o-n-s-t-e-r-esses that attack dogs."

Newt whined at her.

"Good God," Charlie said, leaning back in her chair. "He can spell, too?"

Her phone rang then, negating my need to answer. "Let me get this," she said, excusing herself from the table and walking away. Despite her distancing attempts and the lowering of her voice, I was easily able to overhear her end of the conversation.

"I don't know yet," she said to the person on the other end. "She seems legit and interested, so I guess we'll see." She cast a glance over her shoulder at me and I smiled. "Not tonight, but maybe later in the week. Let me see how this goes and I'll let you know."

After she said goodbye and disconnected the call, she returned to our table and said, "Shall we go?"

I don't know if she suspected I'd overheard her end of the phone conversation or she simply felt compelled to explain herself for another reason, but as soon as we piled back into the car and were on the road she said, "That was Kyle who called. He wanted to know how things were going with you."

"Kyle, as in Buck's son?" I said. "Your ex-fiancé?"

"Yeah." She made a face and sighed. "We've remained friends, though I'm not sure we should. He wants to get back together and insists I was just going through one of my phases when I broke things off this time. I've tried to break up with him twice before."

"That sounds controlling," I said, concerned.

"I suppose it does, but he's not. He's good to me, and he's thoughtful, and sweet . . . just an all-around nice guy despite the man who raised him."

"So, why do you want to break things off?"

"There's just no spark," Charlie said with a sigh. "It's hard to explain. I always thought when I met the man I'd spend the rest of my life with there would be more of a spark, a fire, maybe even an inferno." She glanced over at me with a bemused expression. "Am I being stupid and unrealistic?"

"No, I get it," I said. "Though a spark isn't always the answer. The man who murdered my parents was my fiancé, and we definitely had a spark. Or at least I thought we did. But it turned out he wasn't who he said he was—he'd actually stolen the identity of a dead man—and he wasn't interested in me for anything other than my money. When my parents found out and confronted him, he murdered them."

Charlie shot me an appalled look. "Geez, how horrible."

"It was. It still is. And as you now know, I was the primary suspect. We were all on a trip together camping in the Pine Barrens of New Jersey because my parents and I wanted to look into reports of deaths attributed to a cryptid known as the Jersey Devil. When my father told me he'd done a background check on David and discovered disturbing irregularities, I was furious with him because he'd recently promised me he wouldn't do background checks on my dates anymore after he'd scared off a couple of guys I really liked. But David had proposed to me earlier on the trip and we'd only been dating for six months. Apparently, that was more than Dad could take." I paused, squeezing my eyes closed as I felt a familiar wave of guilt wash over me.

"I can understand why your father did what he did if you're really wealthy."

I shot her a look, hesitant to confirm or deny. I don't like to advertise my wealth to people because it tends to cause problems. Then again, as Charlie pointed out, I'd let the cat out of the bag already and Buck had strongly hinted at it yesterday. Plus, the Carter name was well known in Door County even before the murders. If Charlie wanted to dig around, there was a wealth of information on my family's history and fortunes to be found.

"I'm definitely comfortable financially," I said. "Though I don't like to talk about it or advertise it."

"I get it," Charlie said. "Particularly in light of what happened. They never caught this David guy?"

A tiny thrill of panic raced down my spine and settled in my gut, squirming. "Nope, he's still out there somewhere."

"How awful," Charlie said. "And scary. I can't imagine what that must have been like for you."

A weighted silence filled the car until I said, "Sorry. I hadn't planned to ruin the day by sharing my story."

"It's okay. I'm glad you told me. Does Jon know about your past?"

Her question struck me as odd, but I answered anyway. "He does. In fact, his uncle was the lead detective on the investigation."

"Oh my God, really?" She gawked at me. "That sounds awkward as hell."

"It was at first, but we've managed to deal with it. We work well together. In fact, he's coming up tonight to help me over the weekend with this investigation."

Charlie perked up with this news. "Does he need a place to stay? It will be nigh onto impossible to find something on such short notice, particularly on a weekend, but I have a guest room at my place."

"That's very generous of you," I said, "but he's going to stay with me."

Charlie's face clouded over. "Oh. Okay."

"He'll be sleeping on the sofa," I added, feeling compelled to clarify the sleeping arrangements for reasons I didn't fully understand.

"Of course," Charlie said with a clearly forced smile.

Another heavy silence permeated the car's interior, and I found it ironic how this subject was somehow more polarizing and upsetting than the deaths of my parents and my potential role in their murders. Eager to change the subject, I said, "Hey, thanks for recommending the bistro near my suite. I got dinner there last night and it was delicious. While I was waiting for my order, I had an interesting discussion with a man named Lloyd Mann. Do you know him?"

"Oh, sure. His brother, Trip, is a good friend of Kyle's."

"Yeah, the brother was there, too, but he never said anything. The quiet type, I gather."

"He can be. He and Kyle both attended the U of W at the Superior campus and they roomed together. Back in those days they were a dynamic duo, a couple of pranksters and troublemakers, but they've both settled down in their middle age. Trip got an accounting degree and went to work with his brother managing their stores, while Kyle went on to law school in Chicago. They don't hang together as much anymore, though they still like to hit up the Bad River casino once or twice a year to test their latest system."

"System?"

Charlie smiled and shook her head. "Yeah, the two of them came up with some crazy system for playing the slot machines back when they were in college. It was a project for a statistical analysis class they took, and it actually worked for a while, well enough to pay for Trip's last year of college. By the way, you should know Lloyd Mann and Buck are pretty tight, so be careful what you say if you run into him again."

"Yeah, Buck showed up last night before I was able to get away. Apparently, I had unknowingly hijacked his seat at the bar."

"I'm surprised he didn't toss you in jail for that infraction. Buck likes his booze."

"No jail time, but he did remind me that he doesn't like me

investigating these deaths. He pretty much told me to get out of town, like it was the wild, wild West or something."

Charlie laughed. "I'm sorry Buck's being such a hard-ass. He's always acted like a buffoon and been full of himself, but he can also make your life miserable if he wants to, so don't push him too hard. He gets off on the power. I think he believes my breakups with Kyle are all because of him and I let him think that because as long as he feels superior over me, he leaves me alone, for the most part. Except he ribs me constantly about my fascination with Bigfoot, and he's not alone. Nearly all of the LEOs are skeptics when it comes to the topic. That's why they kick the reports down to me all the time."

"Your interest has caused you a lot of grief, hasn't it?"

Charlie sighed. "Yeah, I get it, though. To be honest, if I hadn't seen it with my own eyes, I'd be a skeptic, too."

I studied her for a moment. Her steadfast conviction was exciting but also a smidge worrisome. "Charlie, your childhood experience had to have been terribly traumatic for you. And the age you were at the time isn't a particularly stable stage of human development. All those hormones can really mess with you. Do you think it's possible you—"

"Absolutely not! I know what I saw."

No equivocating there, so I decided to let the matter drop and embrace plausible existability. For now.

CHAPTER 18

⌒

Minutes later, Charlie pulled up in front of a house at the end of a street on the northeast side of Bayfield. The road was steep, and the house was positioned on a hillside in a way that put the back entrance of the structure on level ground while the front had a flight of precipitously steep concrete steps to climb to get to the main entrance. Fortunately, we were able to park at the rear of the house, where we were quickly met by a short, pleasantly plump, white-haired woman who scurried out the back door. Charlie introduced her as Freda Becker.

Freda greeted me with a hearty "Good day!" and then immediately turned her attention to Newt. "And who is this handsome fella?" She leaned forward and gave Newt's ears a hearty rub.

"That's Newt," I told her. "And I'm Morgan Carter." I got the sense she couldn't have cared less what my name was once she set her eyes on Newt.

"Who's a good boy, eh?" she murmured, massaging my dog's neck. Eventually, she looked up and acknowledged my presence. "Can I get a treat for him?"

"Sure."

"Wonderful!" She clapped her hands, said, "Come along, Newt," and then disappeared into her house. Newt had dutifully followed on her heels, though he did stop just past the threshold to look back at me as if to ask permission. I nodded and off he went.

Charlie and I looked at one another. "I suppose we can go in, too," she said with a shrug.

We entered the house and walked through a living room furnished with two big recliners and a large-screen TV mounted over a brick fireplace. Two bookcases on either side of the fireplace were filled with DVDs. A quick scan of the titles revealed multiple episodes from *Unsolved Mysteries* and *The X-Files*, as well as an assortment of sci-fi movies ranging from *E.T.* to *Independence Day*.

We found Newt in the kitchen happily drooling over a dog treat Freda was holding out to him.

"He's very well behaved," Freda said as Newt gently took the treat from her hand.

"Yes, he's a sweetheart and wicked smart. Do you have a dog?" I asked, looking around curiously even though I knew the answer.

"I do," Freda said, grabbing another of the treats and giving it to Newt. "But she's not here right now. My little Poppy was injured and she's at the vet recovering from her latest surgery. It's the third one she's had to have. That creature messed her up bad."

"I'm so sorry," I said. "How awful for you and Poppy."

Freda nodded, her face contorting as she tried not to cry.

"That's why we're here, Freda," Charlie said. "Tell Morgan what you told me about what happened to Poppy."

"That damned Bigfoot got her," Freda said irritably. "It was last Friday night and I heard noise out back near where the trash cans are. Poppy started barking like crazy at the back door and I grabbed a broom and went outside to investigate, figuring it was a possum or a raccoon because I see them out there all the time. The frigging raccoons like to get into the trash and strew it all over the place, making a big mess I then have to clean up." She shook her head in disgust. "Anyway, my little Poppy went into protective mode, running out to the cans ahead of me, barking like crazy. She may be a little bugger, but she's fierce and she always looks out for me."

Freda started to say something more but clamped her mouth shut, her eyes glistening with threatened tears. My heart ached for her. I couldn't imagine losing Newt or even knowing he was hurt. Eventually, Freda looked back at us with a pitiful attempt at a smile.

"Anyway," she said with a big exhale, "before I could catch up to Poppy and get around the corner of the shed, I heard her yelp, and then I saw a huge critter run off and disappear into the ravine back there. It spooked me good, I'll tell ya, and when Poppy didn't come to my calls, I went looking for her. Found her on the ground just beyond the trash cans, bleeding."

Her eyes went wide with remembered fear, and I had to swallow down my own anxiety at Freda's mention of the creature disappearing into the ravine. "I'm so sorry, Freda," I said again, my empathy genuine. "How awful."

Newt let out a tiny whimper I suspect was his not-so-subtle way of letting it be known he wanted more treats, but the timing made it seem as if he, too, was commiserating over Poppy. Heck, maybe he was. Maybe he did understand everything we humans uttered.

"Did you get a good look at the animal?" I asked Freda.

"I sure did! I saw it even though my eyesight isn't so great these days and I wear glasses so thick they make my eyes look twice their normal size." She looked away then, as if recalling a different memory. "Shocking to realize it," she said. "We get this image in our heads of what we look like and then reality kicks in and it's not so pretty. I saw a picture my son took of me when I was reading. I happened to glance up just as he snapped it, and my eyes came out looking like some kind of alien space bug!" She paused and shuddered, as if shaking off the memory. "But I wasn't wearing my bug-eyeglasses when I saw the Bigfoot because I always take them off as soon as I get up from my chair. Walking in them is like being on a bad drunk."

"What, exactly, did you see?" I asked, hoping to get her to home in on the description. It worked.

"Something dark and hairy," she said. "It stood up on two legs. And it was *big*."

I estimated Freda was a tad shy of five feet tall on a good day and figured a garden gnome might look big to her, but I decided to give her the benefit of the doubt for now. I started to ask more, but she stopped me with a raised hand and an I-won't-hear-it tilt of her head.

"Now, before you go suggesting it might have been a bear, I've seen bears in these parts before and I know what they look like. It wasn't full dark yet when this happened, and this critter looked tall when I caught my first glimpse of it. Taller than a bear, I'm sure.

And it wasn't built like a bear. It looked more like a man. But different." She gave me a frustrated look and made a shooing gesture with her hand. "It's hard to explain. Wish I could draw it and show you, but I can barely render a decent stick figure."

"You saw it run away?" I asked.

She made a face. "Not exactly. The shed kind of blocked my view when it first took off and by the time I got to the edge of the ravine and looked down, it was out of sight. But I sure as heck heard it. That thing made all kinds of noise crashing through the trees. That's how I know it was big."

While Freda's narrative did little to convince me the perpetrator hadn't been a bear, her story did have some astonishing similarities to my own experience the night before at the old soccer field, enough so that gooseflesh raised on my arms.

"I didn't have time to get a picture of it," Freda said. "I was more concerned with Poppy. But I did get a picture of a footprint it left behind." She patted her pants pocket and looked around the room. "Now, where did I leave my cell phone?" She scurried off into an adjoining room, muttering along the way, leaving me and Charlie standing in the kitchen. "Quite the character, isn't she?" Charlie said sotto voce.

I gave her a wide-eyed nod of agreement just as Freda returned and handed me a cell phone. On the screen was a picture of hard, dry ground covered with leaves and twigs. I held the phone closer, studying it, and played with zooming in on certain areas, but couldn't find anything resembling a footprint.

"I'm sorry, Freda. I don't see it."

She grabbed the phone from my hand impatiently and pointed to a spot in the middle of the picture. "There. See?" she said. Her finger traced an area of bare dirt. "See how all the leaves and stuff got pushed out, making this bare spot here in the shape of a big foot?"

I looked again and thought the bare spot of ground vaguely resembled the shape of a Bigfoot print. In Picasso's world.

Freda must have sensed my skepticism because she grabbed the phone from me again, swiped at the screen, and handed it back. This time the picture on the screen was of a little white poodle mix that looked like it was sleeping. There was a smear of blood at the corner of its mouth and a large open wound on its side.

"That's my poor little Poppy," Freda said, her voice thick with grief.

I stared at her, momentarily speechless, too astonished by the picture of her poor injured dog to be able to think of what to say. I handed the phone to Charlie, only later realizing she'd most likely seen this picture already. She took the phone anyway and uttered a few appropriately commiserative remarks.

I said, "Freda, the injuries to Poppy could have come from a bear, coyote, wolf, or mountain lion, though I'd expect bite marks if it had been a cat of some type."

"It wasn't any of them," Freda said with an obstinate jut of her chin. "I'll admit I don't know for sure what the hell it was, but I damned sure know what it wasn't."

"Fair enough," I said, realizing I wasn't sure what I'd seen last night either, but like Freda, I felt reasonably certain about what it hadn't been.

"You know," Freda said, slipping the phone into a pants pocket after Charlie handed it back to her, "if you really want to catch the Bigfoot you might want to talk to this handsome fella who's been sniffing around by the name of . . . Hank? No, Harry?" She shook her head. "Hold on, I have his card here somewhere." She spun around and started shuffling the papers she had piled on her countertop.

"It wouldn't be Hans Baumann, would it?" I asked.

"That's it!" Freda said with a snap of her fingers.

I looked at Charlie and rolled my eyes. Her cell phone chimed then, and she took it out and started swiping at the screen.

"Do you know this Hans fella?" Freda asked me.

I turned back to her, smiling. "We've met before."

"He came by here yesterday and asked about what happened to Poppy. I told him pretty much what I told you. He said he's been hunting Bigfoots for a decade or more. Said he nearly caught one last year down in Mississippi."

"The only thing Hans Baumann was likely to have caught was a load of bull crap," I said, shooting Charlie a knowing look.

"Did you know this Hans fellow can communicate with dead animals, too?" Freda challenged. Before I could answer, she added, "He offered to come back here and do a séance thing for me if Poppy doesn't make it so I can talk to her one last time."

I placed a hand on Freda's arm. "Freda, please don't give Mr. Baumann any money. He's a huckster just trying to make a buck off you."

Freda reared back, looking offended. "He said he'd try to establish contact for free and not charge me unless we made a real connection."

"Which he will fake," I told her.

"Fake how?" Freda sneered irritably.

I thought back to the living room we'd just walked through.

"He'll say something about how Poppy misses you and her favorite yellow pillow," I said.

Freda's mouth dropped open and her eyes grew big. "Do you talk to dead animals, too?"

"No, Freda. Besides, Poppy isn't dead and hopefully won't be. But when we came in your house, I noticed a yellow pillow on one of your recliners was covered with white hair. I thought it might have been from a cat at first, but now I know what Poppy looks like and it's easy to figure out she spends a lot of time on that pillow."

Freda folded her arms over her chest and set her lips into a firm line, scowling at me. "I'm sure you think you're quite clever," she said, her tone confrontational. "But I'll tell you this. That Hans fellow looked a whole lot more professional about this Bigfoot hunt than you do. He had binoculars, a big fancy camera, and a whole backpack full of other stuff. He even had a dart gun he said shot tranquilizers. And he was dressed for traipsing around in the woods, not citified like you are."

I smiled at her while wishing I had a tranquilizer dart gun, too, so I could use it on Hans Baumann. Then I pondered how the blue jeans, hiking boots, and plaid flannel shirt I was wearing qualified as citified. Then again, we were in northern Wisconsin.

"Well, I have something Mr. Baumann doesn't have," I said in my defense.

"What?" Freda said, looking skeptical.

"I've got Newt and his very excellent nose."

At the mention of his name, Newt perked up and whined a little. Freda stared down at him and her stern expression softened. "Fair enough," she said. Then she gave him another treat.

CHAPTER 19

"Sorry, but I can't put much stock in Freda's story," I told Charlie as we walked to the back edge of Freda's property and gazed down into the ravine running alongside her house. "If her DVD titles are any indication, she clearly has a case of confirmation bias. I think Poppy was most likely attacked by a bear."

"I know. Sorry if this was a waste of time, but I thought it might be worth hearing her out. I suppose I feel a little sorry for her because of her dog and all."

"Of course, and I hope little Poppy does okay. There's no need to apologize. It wasn't a wasted trip. You never know when something might turn out to be more important than it seems at first blush."

The two of us stood side by side for a minute, staring down into the ravine. The sides were steep, angling down to a small, dry creek bed forty feet below that I imagined might sport a healthy flow of water in the spring when the snow melted. Getting down there wouldn't be easy for man or beast as the sides were covered with deadfall, bushes, exposed roots, and an assortment of vines.

"Does this ravine run through the entire town?" I asked Charlie.

She nodded. "It does."

"It's the same ravine you can see from the dog park you told me about, the one on the outskirts of town?"

"It is. And it runs all the way down to Lake Superior."

I nodded contemplatively. "It's quite lovely in an ominous, menacing kind of way," I said. Once again I considered telling Charlie what I'd seen in the ravine last night and once again I decided to wait. Instead, I said, "Where are we off to next?"

We turned in unison to head back to the car. "We're going to chat with Walt Kendall. I sent him a text yesterday asking if we could come by and I got an answer from him while we were at Freda's. He said he's willing to talk to us, though he doesn't want to do it in front of his coworkers. He works on the docks at a marina loading boats onto the lake in the spring and unloading them this time of the year to prepare them for dry dock. The guys who work down there are a tight group. They party together as well as work together and they're quite the testosterone factory, so you might want to gird your loins."

Her comment made me chuckle. "Got it. My feminist armor is firmly in place."

The drive took less than five minutes, and Charlie parked on the street. As we walked toward the small marina Charlie pointed to an area where several boats were perched on stanchions and a giant lift ran out over the lake water. Two men were scrubbing the hull of a dry-docked boat.

"That's Walt," Charlie said, pointing to the left half of the duo, a fellow who was slender and quite tall, with a flaming-red head of hair. He looked like a matchstick. "Walt doesn't want the other guys to know he's seriously claiming to have seen a Bigfoot," Charlie said, her voice just above a whisper. "They'll all joke about it but whenever anyone gets serious on the subject the straitjackets start coming out. Walt's trying to sell the car he drives to work, that little red number parked over there, so if you don't mind, we're going to pretend you're an interested buyer. That will give us a way to pull him aside."

"Got it."

Charlie hailed Walt with a wave and hollered, "Hey, Walt! Sell your car yet?"

"Not yet."

"Got a potential buyer for you here. Have you got a minute?"

"Sure."

The fellow working with him turned around and waved at us. "Hey, Charlie," he said. "How are things?"

"Can't complain. How are Bonnie and the kids?"

"Complaining all the time," he said with a laugh.

I leaned in toward Charlie. "Do you know everyone around here?"

I was kidding, but Charlie answered with, "Pretty much. It's a small town with only four hundred or so year-round souls. My office is only a block away. I grew up here and now I work and live here, so . . ." She shrugged.

We met Walt at his car, a 2018 Hyundai parked curbside about fifty feet from where he'd been working. There was a FOR SALE sign in the rear window with a phone number.

"Walt, this is Morgan Carter and her dog, Newt. Morgan is a cryptozoologist and she's looking into a rash of recent sightings in our area as well as those two men who were killed. Tell her what you saw last week by your house."

Walt scrutinized me as a multitude of emotions flitted across his face: doubt, curiosity, perhaps a hint of condescension, something akin to anger but not quite there, and finally, suspicion. "I changed my mind, Charlie. I don't want to talk about it," he grumbled.

He started to turn away, but Charlie stopped him with a hand on his arm. "Come on, Walt. Morgan studies this stuff for a living, and she'll keep your information private." Charlie turned and gave me a questioning look. "Right?"

"Of course. I have no need to make anything public. I'm doing private research and I'd appreciate anything you can tell me."

Walt looked back toward his workmate, clearly hesitant. Newt seemed to sense the man's anxiety and he walked over to him and nudged his hand, his tail wagging. It never ceased to amaze me what a calming influence Newt could have on people, and Walt was no exception. The man began to stroke Newt's head and as he looked down at the dog, I saw his body tension ease away.

"I promise you I won't discuss what you tell me with anyone else," I said again, eager to reassure him.

"You looking to write a book or do some kind of podcast thing?" Walt asked.

I shook my head and started to explain more but Charlie beat me to it.

"She's here at my request, Walt. I have questions about those two men who died, and I'm just trying to gather all the facts I can and use Morgan's expertise to help answer those questions."

Walt shifted his attention to Charlie, still stroking Newt's head. "I thought they said those guys were killed by a rogue bear. You think a Bigfoot killed them?" His expression and tone suggested he didn't find the idea ludicrous.

Charlie raked her teeth over her lower lip before answering. "I don't know, Walt. But like I said, some things in the official reports don't quite fit. We're talking to several people who claim to have seen something like what you saw."

Walt considered this as he scouted out his surroundings. Apparently satisfied no one was within hearing distance, he swiped his free hand over his face and looked at me. "I live out near the school on the northeast side of town. There's a trail running behind my house that folks like to hike. I get bouts of insomnia from time to time, and walking helps, so sometimes I go out there late at night. I wear a head strap with a light on it so I can see where I'm going. Since it's usually quite late when I go out there, I almost never see anyone else on the trail."

He paused, taking a deep breath. "Last Thursday I went out around two in the morning, and I was about a hundred feet or so in when I heard something moving through the bushes off to my left. It sounded big, crashing, and crunching through the brush, and I thought it might be a bear. We get a fair number of them prowling around these parts, so I always carry bear spray with me. I took out my cell phone and used the flashlight on it to better light up the brush and when I aimed it toward the area where the noise was coming from, it stopped. I didn't see a bear or anything else, so I took a couple more steps toward the edge of the trail, moving the light back and forth. Then I saw it."

He paused again, swallowing hard, his Adam's apple bouncing up and down like the weight on a strongman's game at a carnival.

"It was dark, hairy, but with oddly human eyes. And it was big. At first it just stood there looking back at me but then it bared its teeth and started moving." Walt cast me a worried look. "This is where it gets weird," he said then, as if his story wasn't strange enough already. "It tried to fly. I think it did fly."

"Fly?" I said, jerked out of my fascination with his story.

"Yeah, I know. It sounds crazy, but I swear the thing went up from the ground and just disappeared."

In my mind's eye, I tried to envision what Walt might have seen, playing with various impediments to his view and clarity, such as darkness, tree limbs, shadow, light play, and his overwrought imagination. And then I decided it might have been a bear that had climbed up a tree.

I shared this theory with Walt and was repaid for my brilliance with a look of disappointment mixed with utter disgust. I knew I'd screwed up. Whatever the man had seen, he'd convinced himself it had been a Bigfoot. Aside from Charlie, who had a reputation in town for believing, or at least being openly interested in such things, I was probably the only person Walt had told his tale to. And what had I done? Dismissed his story, normalized it, denied his truth. I saw it in Walt's face when he made the decision to shut down and wasn't surprised when he spun around to leave without so much as a goodbye.

"Damn, I'm sorry. I totally botched this one," I said to Charlie as we watched Walt walk away. "The realist in me is always leaping to the forefront and trying to find more scientific, rational explanations for the things people claim to have seen. Playing the devil's advocate is my default mode."

"I get it. It's the only smart and honest way to do what you do," Charlie said. "Go with the evidence."

I shot her a grateful smile. "Yeah, but I could have been a little more tactful with Walt. To be honest, he threw me when he mentioned it tried to fly."

Charlie nodded but said nothing.

"Could you show me where Walt was when he saw this . . . whatever it was?"

"Sure."

We walked back to the car, drove to the northeast side of town, and parked on yet another steep, hillside street. I cringed thinking about what it must be like to drive around this town in the wintertime. I imagined the stop signs at the ends of some of these streets would end up being suggestions rather than rules.

Newt and I followed Charlie to the start of a well-marked trail. "That's Walt's house over there," she said, pointing across the street.

It looked ordinary enough, much like the other aging but reasonably well-maintained two-story homes in these hilly neighborhoods. The trail was easy to walk and heavily lined with trees on both sides. We hadn't gone far when Charlie stopped and said, "Here's where Walt said he saw it. Right over there."

She pointed into a thick growth of trees, a mix of pines and hardwoods amid an even thicker growth of viny bushes I estimated ranged in height from a foot high to well over six feet. It was easy to imagine the tangles of long, thin branches waving in a night breeze, creating an illusion of solidity and intent. Yet even as I stared into those woods, something about them changed, as if the perspective had shifted. It was like one of those Magic Eye pictures where a 3D image appears if you stare long enough.

"How far back do these woods go?" I asked Charlie.

"Not far. Maybe a hundred yards straight back, two hundred if you count the downhill and uphill parts. Just beyond the trees you see here is the ravine that runs up through town, the same one we saw behind Freda's house." That little detail sent a chill down my spine. "Another great spot to view the ravine is from the parking lot of the Old Rittenhouse Inn," Charlie continued. "It butts right up to it."

I knew the place she was referring to as it's a hard building to miss in Bayfield, a huge, beautifully maintained, and elaborately adorned Queen Anne Victorian resting proudly on a bluff overlooking much of the city and Lake Superior. Built in 1890 as a summer residence, it currently served as a bed-and-breakfast and a popular wedding venue.

"I think I'm ravined out for now," I told Charlie. "Though I have to say, it provides a convenient avenue for wildlife to make stealthy entries into the city. I suppose if I were a Bigfoot, I'd use it."

As if to add drama to my statement, a cloud obscured the sun overhead, casting us into semidarkness and making it feel as if the temperature dropped ten degrees. Then, just as suddenly as it went away, the sun reemerged. With the intermittent cloud cover and sunshine dribbling down through the treetops, the shadows in the woods around us undulated and moved even more than before.

I reached down and stroked Newt's head for reassurance. "Frankly," I said, "it's not hard to see why Bayfield is such a hotbed of Bigfoot legend. There's so much about this little town that makes it perfect Bigfoot territory."

I was aware of Charlie shooting me a look, but I continued to watch the shadows in the trees. The urge to tell her what I'd seen the night before at the dog park was strong and I'd made up my mind to go ahead and do it when she said, "Let's get you back to your suite. It's been a long day and I'm sure you're eager to get things ready for Jon's arrival."

"Not much to get ready other than dinner. I promised to feed him when he got here."

"Do you want me to run you by the grocery store?"

I shook my head. "I'm getting takeout. Jon sent me a text while we were chatting with Walt, and he said he's getting out of town earlier than he thought. He should arrive around nine thirty or ten and I thought I'd give the lemon garlic fettucine dish at the bistro a try. Lloyd Mann recommended it, and pasta reheats well in the microwave."

"I've had it and it's excellent. I'm sure he'll love it," Charlie said. "What are your plans for Saturday?"

"You know, I'm not sure yet. I want to think things over and do a bit of research. How about I give you a call on Saturday if I need you for something? I don't want to take advantage of your time."

"Nonsense. Call me for anything. I can open doors for you around here and I want to help as much as I can."

"Any idea when you'll get access to the ME's report on Pete Conrad?"

"No." She frowned as she answered. "I wonder what's taking so long. I'll check in with Bruce and let you know."

"Thanks. You've been a huge help today, Charlie."

"Happy to oblige."

It took only minutes to drive back to my suite and as I climbed out of the car, Charlie's parting words had a desperate, almost pleading tone to them. "Please call me, Morgan. I'm available all day tomorrow."

I gave her a noncommittal smile, thinking her eagerness might be related to a certain chief of police who would be with me tomorrow. I had no doubt she was attracted to Jon and willing to explore things with him, should the opportunity arise. And if I was honest with myself, this was one opportunity I didn't want to see come to fruition.

As I walked up to my door and inserted my key in the lock, a gust of wind followed me, creating a tiny whirlwind of dead leaves on the porch. A stronger gust followed, and I heard an odd howling noise come from somewhere toward the back of the house. It was definitely colder than it had been only minutes before, and the blue sky was rapidly giving way to thick, gray cloud cover.

There was a storm predicted for that night and I could already feel tension building in the air. I hoped it wasn't a portent of things to come.

CHAPTER 20

I took Newt for another walk along the waterfront and let him get his fill of splashing, smelling, and romping. Then we went back to the suite, and I told him to stay there until I returned. I walked the three blocks to the bistro I'd gone to last night and rather than going inside, I used the to-go window on the enclosed porch and ordered two of the lemon garlic fettucine dishes, both with a roasted chicken add-on. The waitress, who proved to be an excellent sales-person, managed to talk me into two slices of their lemon rasp-berry cake, as well, which she swore was "to die for."

No one else was on the porch and after being told my wait would be about twenty minutes, I also ordered a glass of wine and settled in at one of the empty tables, hoping to enjoy some peace and quiet. I felt bad leaving Newt back at the suite, but even though

I was allowed to have him with me in this part of the bistro, a wet dog is about as unappetizing as they come. I'd feared there might be other diners eating on the porch area, but as it turned out, I had it to myself, at least at first.

I'd been waiting about five minutes when the door to the porch area opened, and Trip Mann, Lloyd's brother, the one who had hardly acknowledged my presence the evening before, walked in. He was doing something on his phone and didn't see me at my table in the corner. He walked up to the window, placed an order for a burger to go, and then looked around for a place to sit.

That's when he spotted me. I saw recognition in his eyes, but he immediately looked away and I figured it would be a repeat of last night's antisocial behavior. He did something on his phone screen, handling it awkwardly with the fingers on his cast arm, and then tucked the device away in a pocket.

"You're Morgan, right?" he said, finally acknowledging my presence.

"I am. And you're Trip. I met you here last night along with your brother, Lloyd."

"Yes, I remember. Sorry if I was a bit antisocial, but I've learned to shut up and lay low when my little brother is flirting with someone."

"Is that what he was doing?"

Trip grinned. "It was. Couldn't you tell?"

"Honestly, I just thought he was being polite. It wasn't like he asked me out or even offered to buy me a drink."

"Oh, he would have if Buck Weaver hadn't shown up and made it clear you were persona non grata. What did you do to get under his skin?"

"He doesn't want me looking into some deaths in the area because they're considered closed cases."

"Deaths? I thought I heard you say last night you were hunting for a Bigfoot?"

"Well, yes, I am. There are those who think these deaths I mentioned might have been caused by a Bigfoot. I'm trying to find out if it's true, or even possible."

"Let me guess," Trip said. "Charlie Aberdeen has something to do with it." He chuckled and shook his head. Then he pulled out the chair across from me and slid onto it. "Charlie has been chasing Sasquatches since she was old enough to spell the word."

"You know Charlie?" I figured he did after what Charlie had told me about Trip and Kyle being best buds but had pegged it as more of a casual acquaintance. If he knew Charlie on a deeper level, I'd love to hear his take on her.

"Heck, yeah. Her fiancé, Kyle, and I go way back."

"Yes, Charlie told me you and Kyle were roomies during your college years."

"Yeah, those were the good old days," Trip said with a wistful smile. "We still hang every so often. In fact, I'm meeting him tonight at the casino for a little fun. Don't tell Charlie if you see her. She doesn't like it when Kyle gambles."

"I thought she and Kyle broke up."

Trip kiboshed this idea with a wave of a hand and a dismissive *pfft*. "Those two are on-again, off-again all the time. Kyle adores Charlie and he's determined to marry her, even if she is crazy obsessed with Bigfoot. Did she tell you she saw one when she was a kid?"

I wondered how Trip knew this. "What makes you think that?"

"Oh, Buck told us. He was there when Charlie's father died. It was one hell of a mess, apparently, though I kind of think it was a blessing in a way. Rumor had it the guy beat on Charlie and her mother a lot because Charlie was always coming to school with bruises everywhere. Everyone knew he drank, and Buck said his blood alcohol when he fell out of his tree stand was in the three hundreds, meaning he was a very practiced drunk." Trip paused, shook his head, and rolled his eyes. "Scary to think the guy was out there with a loaded rifle, isn't it? Anyway, Charlie told Buck she and her father saw a Bigfoot out there in the woods and it startled her father, making him lose his balance and fall out of the tree stand."

It seemed Buck had a big mouth as well as the personality of a bully. I wondered if his lack of discretion had anything to do with his lack of promotions over the years.

"Sounds like an interesting story. I'll have to ask Charlie about it."

Trip looked surprised. "Would have thought you knew about it already." He shrugged. "Maybe Charlie's hooked up with the other fellow who's in town looking for a Bigfoot. He came in here the night before you did."

I sighed. "Hans Baumann."

Trip shrugged again. "Don't know the fellow's name but he was tall, nice looking, and dressed like an Indiana Jones wannabe."

"Yep, that's Hans," I said. "Watch out for him. He's a con artist."

Trip appeared nonplussed. "And you're not?" he said. I must have looked offended because he quickly added, "I mean, I just assumed anyone looking for a Bigfoot is a con artist of some sort. No one in their right mind would think such a creature actually exists."

I stared at him, unsure what to say.

His eyes narrowed and his lips curled into a funny little grin. He leaned toward me, the cast on his arm scraping along the ceramic tabletop with a noise like fingernails on a blackboard. His voice dropped to just above a whisper. "Are you saying you think there really is a Bigfoot out there?"

I considered my answer carefully. "I believe in something my mother called plausible existability, though admittedly a Bigfoot is lower on the list than most other cryptids. Too many loopholes in the theories folks put forth to try to explain their existence."

"Your mother looked for Bigfoot, too?" Trip appeared amused by the idea.

I nodded. "Both her and my father. They traveled all over the world looking for cryptids. It was something of a family business."

Trip leaned back in his chair and tipped his head to the side, his expression softening. "You refer to them in the past tense."

"They were killed two years ago."

He gave me a curious look. "Both at the same time?" I nodded and he let out a low whistle. "I'm sorry. Do you have any siblings?"

I shook my head. "Nope, I was their only child."

"It must have been hard for you. I hope they weren't killed by one of the monsters they were hunting."

I knew from his tone that this was Trip's well-intentioned attempt to inject a bit of levity into the conversation, but it fell painfully flat. "They were killed by a monster, all right, just not the kind they typically went looking for."

Seeming to realize his gaffe, Trip mumbled an apology, and we were then saved from any more awkwardness by the waitress sliding open the window and announcing our respective orders were ready.

Trip grabbed his container and started to leave, but then set it on a nearby table while I grabbed the bag containing my two containers of fettucine. "Look," he said, reaching into a back pocket and digging out his wallet. Something fell to the floor, and I bent down to pick it up. It was a token with a number ten on it.

"Here, you dropped this," I said, handing it to him.

"Oh, thanks. It's my good luck charm. Wouldn't want to lose that." He switched the wallet to his cast hand and shoved the token back into his pocket. Then he removed a business card from his wallet. "Don't let Buck Weaver intimidate you," he said, dropping the card into my bag.

"He doesn't."

This won me a broad smile. "Attagirl. And if there's anything I can help you with while you're here, please give me a call. Since my little brother didn't beat me to it, if you're free one evening while you're here in town and want to go out to dinner with me, let me know."

"It's very sweet of you to ask," I said. "But I'm not really dating right now."

"Fair enough. But you can still call me if you think I can help you with anything. I've lived in Bayfield my entire life and I promise, no pressure."

"Thanks."

"I best get going," he said, grabbing his order from the table. "Don't want to keep Kyle waiting. You have a good night."

"You, too."

I started walking back to my suite and watched as Trip got into an older model Honda sedan and drove away, giving a little *toot-toot* of his horn as he passed. I hit up a small store around the corner for a couple bottles of Chardonnay and stashed them in the fridge when I got back to my suite. The aroma of the fettucine as I unpacked it was maddening. Even Newt was drooling grossly, though I warned him I wasn't going to be able to share because it had garlic in it. Luckily for Newt, there were a couple of plain, buttered rolls wrapped in foil and I tossed one of those to him.

I had every intention of waiting until Jon arrived to eat, but I was hungry, and the smell of the garlicky sauce and roasted chicken was practically making me drool like Newt. I finally caved and opened one of the containers, intending to take just a bite or two. Before I knew it, I'd finished off half the dish. I could have eaten the rest of it right then and there but managed to stop myself. I put it and the other full order into the fridge—out of sight, out of mind.

Before tossing the bag out, I pulled Trip's business card from it. On the left side of the card was a picture of a duck in flight with reeds around it, and across the middle of this picture was a white banner with MANN BROTHERS OUTFITTERS embossed on it in black letters. On the right side of the card was Trip's name at the top with a phone number, a physical address for the store, an email address, and a website. The card was nicely done, printed on heavy card stock with the duck picture also embossed.

I didn't think I'd have a need to contact Trip while I was in Bayfield and was about to toss his card in the trash when an idea came to me. I tucked the card into my jacket pocket, plopped down on the couch, turned on the TV, and prepared to await Jon's arrival, trying my darnedest to ignore the lingering aromas in the room.

CHAPTER 21

Jon knocked on the door to my suite at a little after nine thirty and the sight of him cheered me to a surprising degree. It was raining out, steady but not a downpour, and he had water droplets in his hair. He greeted me with a kiss I think he meant to place on my cheek, but I thought he was coming in for a hug instead and in the awkward little dance that followed, his lips managed to land on mine and those rain droplets ran down both of our faces.

It startled us, and we both backed away quickly, swiping at our faces and busying ourselves with other things. Jon wheeled his overnight bag over toward the far end of the sofa while I got out the Chardonnay and food I had in the fridge.

"I'm famished," Jon said. "What did you end up getting us for dinner?"

Grateful to have the elephant pushed out of the room by more mundane tasks, I said, "I got a chicken fettucine dish someone at the local bistro swore would be wonderful. I just need to zap it in the microwave. Why don't you go freshen up while I get it ready? The bathroom is through there."

By the time we settled in at the dinner table and dug in, the comfortable camaraderie we typically shared had returned. I filled Jon in on my day while we ate, including a colorful replay of Hans Baumann's antics.

"You know this guy from before, with your parents?" Jon asked.

I nodded, chewing a mouthful of fettucine and noticing how the food tasted even better now because I was sharing it with Jon. "Baumann's a con man," I said once I'd swallowed. "He claims to have this ESP connection to animals, including cryptids, and he convinces gullible folks to pay him money to go on cryptid hunts or to connect with a dead pet the person has lost. He's handsome, garrulous, and charming enough to baffle people with his bullshit. I'm sure he's claimed to have found or contacted other cryptids in the past—all without any real, scientific proof of course—but his specialty has always been Bigfoot. My parents suspected him of salting sites ahead of time with fake footprints and other things, but they could never prove it."

"You think he's handsome?" Jon said, a hint of concern in his voice.

I stared at him, holding another forkful of fettucine inches from my mouth. "That's your takeaway from everything I just told you?"

"Not the only one. Do you?"

"Sorry to burst your bubble, Jon, but Hans Baumann would be characterized as handsome by anyone's standards. He has movie star good looks."

"Hmph," Jon said around a mouthful of fettucine.

"Fortunately, I'm not swayed by good looks."

Jon frowned and I belatedly realized how what I'd said must have sounded. "Wait, that's not what I meant," I blurted out. "Well, it was what I meant, but it doesn't mean you aren't handsome, too. You are. Very much so." It was my turn to blush, and I shoved the fettucine in my mouth to shut myself up.

Jon set his fork down on his empty plate and said, "Relax. I'm not insecure about my looks." He leaned back and patted his stomach. "Though if this thing between us works out and you continue to feed me like this, I hope you'll still find me attractive when I get fat."

I winked at him and swallowed. "I hope you saved a little room for dessert because I also have some lemon raspberry cake."

He groaned and licked his lips. "Give me about twenty minutes and we'll see. We might have to save the cake for a breakfast treat. In the meantime, I did a little digging today and I have information to share with you."

"Do tell."

"I went ahead and asked Charlie to send me the info relevant to both men's deaths and noticed there was a delay for some reason on the final report from the ME on the second victim, Pete Conrad. I called the medical examiner who did the autopsy to find out why it was taking so long and learned something interesting."

"He was willing to talk to you?" I said, surprised.

"Yeah, well, I don't think he wanted to but he kind of owed me a favor. I pulled his son over on the island this past spring for driving under the influence. His father called and begged me to let the kid off with just a warning because he was applying to Harvard in the fall and a DUI on his record might disqualify him."

I knew Jon's wife and three-year-old son had been killed in a tragic accident involving a drunk driver. I couldn't imagine a worse person to ask for such a favor, but Jon surprised me. "You said no, right?" I said.

"Au contraire. I let the kid off with a warning and drove him the rest of the way to the house where he was staying."

"What? No. Why?" I stared at him in disbelief.

"Because he was genuinely remorseful and appeared honestly surprised when he blew a one-point-two. I could tell it scared him. He wasn't an asshole about it; I think he'd resigned himself to losing out on Harvard because of it. Plus, he wasn't counting on daddy to help him out. He didn't want me to call his father at all. I only did so because the kid was seventeen and a minor."

"Wow," I said. "That must have been hard for you."

He gave me a one-shouldered shrug and a brief half smile. "Just in case the kid wasn't scared enough already, I told him about what happened to Bjorn and Natalie. He cried and then he hugged me. Perhaps it was a gamble to let him go, but it was one I thought worth taking. And look how it paid off. I ended up getting useful info for you out of the deal."

I leaned forward, eager to hear what he'd learned. "Okay then. Don't keep me in suspense any longer."

He rubbed his palms together and smiled. "Well, it seems the injuries to Mr. Conrad were significantly different from those found on Mr. Erickson. The neck wounds on Erickson were ragged tears like you'd see with bites or claw marks. The doc said the wound in Conrad's neck suggested there might have been an initial deep cut, a slice of about two inches that appeared oddly clean in a few tiny spots. It severed the carotid artery, which would have caused a major arterial bleed with a loss of consciousness in a matter of seconds and death in a minute or two. Because of the quick bleed-out, he thought there were secondary, tearing injuries on top of the original neck injury that may have been inflicted either extremely close to death or postmortem."

"Meaning what?" I said, struggling to follow the logic of his explanation.

"Well, the ME said he couldn't rule out an initial, ultimately fatal injury that was inflicted with a knife and then further damaged by an animal afterward."

"He thinks Pete Conrad might have been murdered?"

Jon shrugged. "He said he couldn't be sure. Could an animal have inflicted a relatively clean slice across Conrad's neck and then done additional damage to the same spot after the guy was dead? He thought it was possible. Couldn't rule it out anyway. But he's bothered enough by the injuries to be hesitant about issuing his final determination, particularly since the postmortem damage was largely superficial. Those secondary injuries didn't extend down into the musculature of the neck like the first wound."

My eyes grew wide. "You're saying Conrad might have been killed by some*one*, not something."

Jon gave me a slow, sagacious nod. "Maybe. Possibly. Probably. There's something else. The fatal wound, which was on the left side of Conrad's neck, was angled upward, an unusual presentation for an animal attack. Not impossible though, particularly if he was knocked down before the fatal injury was inflicted. But Pete Conrad was a short man, only five-five. And an up-angled wound makes perfect sense if someone came at him from behind with a knife, particularly someone taller." Jon mimicked drawing a knife across his own neck.

"Okay, this certainly changes the way I'm looking at things. So, when is the ME's final report going to come out?"

"Well, probably tomorrow, but don't get your hopes up too much. The doc didn't feel comfortable making an official declaration either way. It's most likely going to say the cause of death was from exsanguination, but the means of death remains undetermined though highly suggestive of animal predation."

"I don't understand," I said. "How can the ME put that out given what you just told me?"

"Because he can't be sure. Some of Conrad's injuries were consistent with those seen in other animal attack victims. Plus, there were two hairs found in Conrad's wounds and they appear to be from a bear, though the DNA analysis is still pending."

I winced as I imagined how awful Conrad's death must have been, though at least it had been swift. The way he'd died—bleeding out from a catastrophic neck wound—was also how my parents had died. With that thought an image leapt to mind, one of my parents lying sprawled inside the mobile home they'd rented, their throats slashed, their life's blood everywhere but where it should have been. It hit me like a slap in the face and made me gasp.

"Are you all right?" Jon asked.

I nodded, swallowing hard. "I will be. Just a bad flashback." I grabbed my wineglass with the last of my Chardonnay in it and gulped it down.

"Those can be tough," Jon said, nodding knowingly with the barest hint of pain in his voice.

I wondered what kinds of flashbacks, if any, he had. Maybe one day I'd ask him.

"One other thing about Conrad," Jon said, "though I'm not sure how useful it is, and Charlie might have told you already. He doesn't live around here. His home is in Milwaukee."

I shrugged. "So, he was up here for a vacation."

"Yeah, maybe." Jon didn't look convinced, and I sensed his police antennae were twitching. It was enough to stoke my curiosity.

"Remind me again, what did he do for a living? I think it's in the folder Charlie gave me, but I don't remember the details."

"He worked as an accountant for a large firm in Milwaukee providing corporate tax and finance management to individuals and companies. On a whim, I called and tried to bluff my way into getting a list of clients he managed but they told me to get a subpoena. And with his means of death being ambiguous but consistent with animal predation, odds are I'd never be able to get one."

"Do you think it's possible he was killed because of something work related?"

Jon shrugged. "Stranger things have happened. You work in this business long enough and you learn to follow the money and the heart. Nine times out of ten, one, or sometimes both of those, is the motive."

"Speaking of stranger things . . ." I told him about my first night here walking Newt at the site of the old soccer field and what I saw in the ravine. "I never got a really good look at it because it moved too fast and there were so many trees and bushes. Plus, I'm not used to the night vision binoculars. Even so, it wasn't any typical animal. Nor was it a human." I hesitated but then took the plunge. "It seemed to be a mix of the two."

Jon gave me a sympathetically skeptical look. "Do you think it's possible your own biases and predeterminations might have influenced what you saw?" he asked gently.

I started to come back with an immediate denial but forced myself to stop and consider his question honestly. "Is it possible my brain fooled my eyes into seeing something different than what was really there? Of course. But my gut says there's something odd out there, and I don't think it's a rogue black bear."

"Fair enough," Jon said, and I adored him for not making more attempts to convince me I was imagining things. "So, what's on our agenda for tomorrow?"

I held up my left hand and ticked off the items on my list by folding down a finger for each one. "First, I want to call Pete Conrad's wife to see if she can shed any light on what he might have been working on at the time of his death and how he came to be up here when he died. His phone is missing, but I'd also like to ask his wife if he ever worked from home and used a laptop computer."

"Smart," Jon said with an approving nod.

"Second, I want to call Bob Keller. He was the witness to the Erickson attack. Charlie said he's been reluctant to talk with anyone, but I want to try anyway.

"Third, I want to see what Devon digs up on Buck Weaver. Weaver made it clear to me he doesn't want me looking into these deaths and I want to know why. Plus, there's just something off about him, something I can't put a finger on.

"Fourth, I'd like to talk to Bruce White, the conservation warden out of the Washburn station who was the lead investigator for both of these cases. I'd like to see what, if anything, he can add to these reports."

I was left holding up just my thumb, like a hitchhiker. I folded it in and said, "Finally, there are those bone piles Charlie said she's found. There is a deliberateness to them, in the way the bones are cleaned and stacked. It strikes me as curious, and I want to look at one Charlie said she found several days ago."

"Sounds like a full day," Jon said with a weighty sigh.

"It will be. And if we have any time left over, I'd like to go shopping in Washburn."

"Shopping?" Jon's expression was one I'd expect if I'd suggested we go digging for corpses.

"Yes, just to chat with the locals about these deaths and find out what the current gossip is. I did something similar here in Bayfield and got a strong sense there was something underlying all the jokes and fun rumors. I'm curious if we'll find the same thing in Washburn."

"Ah, okay," Jon said with a tired smile.

I had other things I wanted to do, but I kept those to myself for now, suspecting Jon might not approve. No sense rocking the boat too soon.

And if the sound of the rain coming down outside was any indication, we'd be needing a sturdy boat before too long.

CHAPTER 22

My phone rang then and, when I saw it was Devon, I answered, told him he was on speaker, and let him know Jon was there. "Got anything good for me?"

"Maybe. I dug around in some old newspaper stories and found an article referencing what happened to Charlotte Aberdeen and her father. It wasn't particularly informative or helpful, though. It simply said her father died as the result of a fall from a tree stand while hunting with his daughter."

I saw Jon raise his eyebrows in question and made a stalling hand gesture to let him know I'd fill him in later.

"Charlie's mother is still alive and living in Duluth," Devon went on. "I've forwarded you her email and phone number in case you want to contact her."

"Good work, Devon. Anything else?"

"Of course. I did a little sleuthing into the social media accounts for the two victims and found something interesting on the second fellow, Pete Conrad. He and his wife come up to Bayfield every year for the weekend of the annual Apple Festival and they stay the week after. Looks like his wife comes for the festival while Pete typically goes fishing."

"His wife was here?" I said, confused.

"No, she wasn't. According to her Facebook account, she was going to come with him but had to cancel at the last minute because of something work related. Her post asked for people to cross their fingers for her because something big might be happening."

"Where does she work?" I asked.

"She's a Realtor. Owns her own brokerage."

"Interesting," I said. "Did you find anything work related in Conrad's Facebook posts? Or anywhere else?"

"Not really. His profile says he works for a firm called Teach and Springer. They're a large financial management company in Milwaukee."

"How about Erickson?" I asked. "Find anything interesting on him?"

"Nothing we didn't already know," Devon said. "He was single, worked in construction, was an avid bow hunter, and lived just outside of Bayfield."

"Any family in the area?"

"Nope. He's from New England originally. Maine to be exact. He got a liberal arts degree from the U of Dub but then got certified as a welder. I guess he liked Wisconsin and decided to stay. He's lived in Madison, Rhinelander, Waukesha, and Bayfield."

"Okay. Not much to work with there."

"Perhaps not, but I'm not done," Devon said in a smug tone. "I discovered something interesting about Bob Keller, the witness to Erickson's attack." He paused dramatically and I couldn't help but smile. Devon loved to create suspense around his discoveries.

"Come on," I urged. "Tell us before I reach through the phone and strangle you."

Devon laughed. "Turns out, the guy's eyesight is terrible. He wears glasses with such a heavy-duty prescription he claims he's one step away from legal blindness, though he apparently still drives and maintains an online presence. Some of his recent online posts have been about technologies created to help the visually impaired use computers and access the internet."

"Wow," I said. "And he was out bowhunting? That's a little unnerving."

"Isn't it though?" Devon agreed.

Jon asked, "What does he do for a living?"

"He was a self-employed corporate headhunter until his diabetes cost him the better part of his eyesight three years ago," Devon said. "He did a lot of online posting advocating for reasonable insulin prices prior to that, and then blamed the loss of his eyesight on being unable to adequately control his diabetes. Not sure what he does for a living now, but the bank foreclosed on his house last year and his current online posts come from an IP address located in a public library. He still maintains an online presence on social media, though his participation has fallen off significantly and most of his posts these days are political rants, though nothing extremist in nature."

"Did he post anything about the incident with Erickson?" Jon asked.

"Nope, not a word," Devon said. "Kind of curious, don't you think?"

I did. "What about Buck Weaver? Did you find anything on him?"

"Does the proverbial bear sh—" I heard him suck in a breath. "Never mind. That would have been inappropriate under the circumstances. And yes, I found a little bit of info on the Buckster though not as much as I would have liked. There was a newspaper article about a family suing the county because their son, who was a musician, was injured by a county sheriff and the son's arm suffered a permanent loss of function as a result. They claimed the cop used excessive force. They ended up settling. Buck Weaver was the sheriff involved. I found two other newspaper articles about claims against the sheriff's office for the use of excessive force by one of their officers and while neither article named the sheriff involved, one named the victim and the other provided enough details about the incident to allow me to determine who the victim was. With that info, I was able to access the arrest records for the victims and saw Buck Weaver was the arresting officer for both. That's it for now, but I'm still digging."

"Devon, you're a miracle worker."

"Yeah, I know. I should probably get a raise."

"I just gave you one," I protested. "How are things at the store? All okay?"

"Well, Rita's talking about rearranging the taxidermied animals again. I tried to talk her out of it, but you know how she gets. She keeps insisting the eyes look at her too often and she wants them more toward the far side wall so they can't see her when she's behind the desk. And we caught someone trying to shoplift three decks of tarot cards. Otherwise, all is well. It's been busy."

I smiled at Rita's obsession with the taxidermied animals we sold. Her tolerance of the non-book inventory in my store has always been arbitrary. Bodies or parts of them floating in jars filled with formaldehyde don't faze her in the least and she'll happily wear jewelry and other adornments made from various animal parts. But she's never liked the dead, stuffed animals and, based on the way she looks at him, I think Henry gives her the heebie-jeebies, too, though she's always denied it.

"Let Rita rearrange stuff if she wants," I said. "It's a small price to pay to keep her happy."

"Gotcha. How are things going up there?"

"Slow. Interesting. Keep digging and let me know if you turn up anything else of interest."

"Will do."

I ended the call and was about to ask Jon if he was ready for dessert when he said, "What's this incident you two were talking about with Charlie and her father?"

"Ah, now, there's an interesting story." I picked up the wine bottle, added a little more to both of our glasses, and then told him what Charlie had told me, though I didn't share any of my suspicions about the full circumstances surrounding her father's fall. Let him draw his own conclusions.

"You're right," Jon said when I was done. "It's quite a story. It helps to explain her interest in all of this, I suppose." He reached for his wine glass and drained the last little bit from it. Then he stretched his arms overhead and yawned loudly. "I hate to be a party pooper, but it's been a long day for me. Would it be okay if we call it a night?"

"Of course. Let me get linens for the couch."

I found an extra set of sheets, two pillows, and three blankets in a closet in my bedroom. I returned to the sitting room and set them on one end of the couch. Jon was unpacking things from his overnight case.

"Are you sure you don't want some dessert before you go to bed?" I asked. "The cake looked quite good."

Jon rubbed a hand over his stomach and shook his head. "I'm stuffed. The pasta was fantastic but filling. Save the cake for tomorrow. I've always loved something sweet for breakfast."

"Right. I seem to recall a delicious coffee cake you had at your place when I was there on our last case."

"Don't get me wrong," he said. "I love a good omelet and would sell my soul for bacon at times, but I prefer eating breakfast food for lunch or dinner. Makes me rather odd, I suppose."

"Certifiable," I said with a wink.

He smiled and gestured toward the bathroom. "Mind if I use the facilities first? I promise I'll be quick."

"Of course. Have at it."

While I waited for Jon to finish, I went ahead and made up the couch for him. He was true to his word, spending maybe five minutes in the bathroom before emerging in a pair of sweatpants and a T-shirt.

"All yours," he said. He waved a hand toward the bathroom door, and I carried my pajamas in there and closed the door. When I emerged about ten minutes later, Jon was reclined on the couch with the lights off. Thinking he was already asleep, I tiptoed toward the bedroom, where Newt was stretched out beside my bed. Just before I slid between the sheets, I heard Jon say, "Good night, Morgan."

It made me smile. "Good night, Jon. Thanks for coming up here."

"Thanks for inviting me."

I settled in, feeling oddly content and hoping for a good night's sleep. Instead, I found myself fighting for my life mere hours later.

CHAPTER 23

⌐

I struggled for air as David Johnson held me down by pushing on my shoulders and forcing my body underwater. Desperate, I flailed my fists at him. Bloodred water swirled around me as my parents' lifeless bodies floated by.

"Morgan! Morgan!"

My eyes shot open to a softly lit room and the sight of Newt's face near mine. He was panting hard, and hot doggy breath washed over my face. My own breath came in gasps, and I was covered in a cold sweat that made my damp pajamas cling to me as if I really had been underwater.

"Morgan, are you okay?" I instantly recognized the worried voice behind those words as Jon's rather than David's, but my heart continued to race like a well-trained thoroughbred in the Kentucky Derby. Jon's pale face peered down at me alongside Newt's.

My arms were pinned beneath Newt—one under his chest, the other under a leg—because he was half draped over my body. I managed to wriggle an arm loose so I could stroke his furry head. "I'm sorry, buddy," I said. "You did good. I'm okay."

With those words, Newt carefully backed off, settling alongside me in the middle of the bed. He rested his big head on his front paws and stared worriedly at me with those dark, soulful eyes of his. My breathing and heart rate began to slow to a more normal pace.

"*Are* you okay?" Jon asked again, peering down at me, one hip perched on the side of my bed.

I pushed up to a sitting position and nodded. "Yes, I will be." I let out a slow breath. "Sorry if I woke you. I haven't had one of those in . . . well, in months now. I'd hoped I was done with them, but apparently not."

"What exactly is 'them'?"

"Nightmares. Dreams triggered by the PTSD I've developed since the murder of my parents." I swiped a hand down my face, feeling the sweaty slickness on my palm. A shiver shook me, making Newt whimper, and I gave him a reassuring pat on the head. "I think this one was triggered by our talk about how Pete Conrad died. It brought back images . . . memories I keep trying to forget."

"You scared the hell out of me," Jon said, running a hand through his hair and making the front of it stick up in an adorable cowlick. "I came running in here when I heard you yelling, and when I flipped on the light, I saw Newt on top of you. You were hitting him, and at first, I thought he was attacking you, but then I realized you were the one attacking him."

I stroked Newt's head. "I'm so sorry, buddy," I whispered near his ear. "You're such a good boy." His tail thumped on the mattress several times, and I leaned down and kissed him on his snout. "Newt helps me whenever I have one of these nightmares," I explained, continuing to pet my dog's head. "He lays on top of me and the pressure of his body calms me. It doesn't always work right away, and sometimes I hit him because I think I'm hitting David until my mind fully wakes. Fortunately, Newt just takes it. He seems to understand."

"Was he trained to do that?"

I smiled and shook my head. "Nope. He just took to it instinctively. I think I'd had him maybe a month before the first one happened, and he knew what to do."

Jon placed a hand on my arm. "Are you sure you're okay now?"

I nodded and sighed. "I will be. It always takes a little time for me to fully relax and calm down again, but I'll get there." I looked over at the alarm clock on the bedside stand and when I saw it was a little after two in the morning, I groaned. "I'm sorry I woke you."

"Don't be. I'm glad I was here. Can I get you anything? A glass of water? A piece of cake?"

My heart was still doing its clippety-clop thing, albeit slower now, and a lingering pall of anxiety hung over me. I didn't want Jon to leave. Not yet.

"You know what?" I said, managing a smile. "Cake does sound good."

Jon sprang up from the bed. "Be right back." He dashed out into the main area of the suite, and I heard the clatter of plates and the sound of a drawer being opened and closed. "Want anything to drink?" he hollered. "Maybe a little wine?"

I smiled. "Sure."

Over the next hour, Jon and I sat side by side on my bed eating cake—which was as delicious as the waitress had promised—and sipping chilled glasses of Chardonnay while Newt stretched out between us like some canine version of a chaperone. Even though Jon knew what had happened with David, me, and my parents, I told it all again, providing a bit more detail this time . . . and a lot more emotion. The talk proved cathartic, though the wine might have helped. It calmed me, even as a furious rainstorm rolled in, bringing with it bright flashes of lightning, deep rumbles of thunder, and sheets of rain slapping hard against the windows and outside walls. The storm made Newt nervous; he cast a wary eye toward the windows with each flash, but to me the storm had an odd calming effect and, eventually, my eyelids grew heavy.

I don't remember saying good night to Jon again, nor do I remember settling back down to sleep. I simply awoke sometime later to the sound of hard knocking on the door to my suite. I sat bolt upright in bed as Newt hopped down from his spot alongside me and headed for the door with a low growl. Weak daylight eked its way between the slats on the window blinds and a glance at the bedside clock told me it was a quarter past seven. I tossed back the covers and swung my feet over the side only to have them collide with something both hard and soft. I looked down, surprised to see my feet on Jon's shoulder. He'd fixed up a makeshift bed alongside mine by placing his pillows and blankets on the floor.

"Did you order room service or something?" Jon muttered,

swiping a hand over his face as I pulled my feet back. He stood, scooped up the sheets and blanket and tossed them onto the small bedroom chair. Then he picked up the pillows and flung those onto the bed.

I climbed out of bed and pulled a robe on over my pajamas, staring at Jon in disbelief. "You slept on the floor?"

"I was worried about you."

My heart give a little hitch and I wanted more than anything to kiss him, but another hard knock came, and I went to the door instead. "Who's there?"

"Morgan, it's me, Charlie."

What the hell?

I unlocked and opened the door. "It's kind of early, Charlie. Did we agree to get together this morning?" My hazy, half-awake mind wasn't sure.

"No. Sorry. I know it's early, but I didn't think this should wait. There was a Bigfoot sighting this morning, over on Madeline Island. It left behind some evidence and if we hurry, we can catch the eight o'clock ferry."

Jon came stumbling out of the bedroom in his pajamas and when Charlie saw him, her face went dark for a second. "Good morning, Charlie," he said, rubbing at one of his eyes.

Charlie acknowledged him with a nod, and a terse, "Jon," before turning back to me.

"Okay, then," I said blinking hard to get the sleep out of my eyes. I went into action, starting a pot of coffee and then going back to the bedroom to get dressed. Jon used the bathroom to change, so I had to wait my turn. I passed the time prepping a couple of travel mugs. Charlie paced back and forth in the sitting room, glancing at her watch every few seconds and looking decidedly impatient. The ferry landing was only three blocks away, a quick and easy stroll and only a minute's drive, if that.

A little over half an hour later, we all climbed into Charlie's SUV, Newt and I in the back seat, Jon up front. We drove to the ferry landing, arriving with ten minutes to spare. Charlie got us in line without having to pay by flashing her badge and telling the ticket lady we were going over on official business.

Once we were situated on the boat, we all got out of the car and went upstairs to one of the passenger decks. Newt was captivated with the sights and smells, and once the boat got underway, he stayed near one of the side rails, fixated on the water passing by down below. It was a brisk but lovely morning with a cloudless, azure sky and little to no breeze other than what the ferry's movement created. We were situated at the back end of the boat, which wasn't crowded, and had the deck to ourselves. We sipped our coffees and watched the mainland recede as Charlie filled us in on the specifics.

"Nearly all of the Apostle Islands have sea caves carved out by wind and water erosion. Madeline Island is no exception, though there are more impressive ones on some of the other islands. Still, they're a sight to behold. More about the caves in a sec.

"This morning, a young man was walking a trail in Big Bay Park when he heard grunting noises, followed by the sound of something big crashing and thrashing through the brush alongside the path. When he looked toward the sound, he saw something large and dark moving away. He tried to follow it but couldn't get far in the thick underbrush. However, he did find something interesting."

"Let me guess, a Bigfoot footprint?" I said, stifling a yawn.

Charlie nodded. "He snapped a picture and then looked around hoping to get another glimpse of whatever might have made the print, but he didn't hear or see anything more."

"Do you have the picture?" I asked her.

She took out her phone and pulled up a photo. The print was surprisingly clear, left in a patch of open mud bordered on both sides by leaves and other forest debris.

"The fellow also said he heard a sound like a cross between a scream and a howl. He thought it came from somewhere deep in the woods in the direction where the creature had disappeared."

"Creature," I repeated. "His word or yours?"

Charlie flushed, blending the rest of her face with the red on her cheeks from the morning chill. "Mine," she admitted. "The witness referred to it as an animal."

"Is this witness available to talk to us?"

Charlie nodded. "I have the address of the house he's staying at. He and a couple of his friends are here for the weekend. The family of one of the friends owns the house and he and his buddies come up whenever they can. The witness said he likes to walk the park trail every morning to catch the sunrise whenever he's here."

I gazed out over the growing expanse of water between us and the dock from which we'd departed. "Thing is," I said, gesturing toward the mainland, "I find it highly unlikely a Bigfoot would swim to an island from over there. In all the Bigfoot lore out there, I don't know of anyone who has reported seeing one swimming. And this is a significant distance."

"True," Charlie said. "But remember, the waters between here and Madeline Island freeze over in the winter, creating an ice bridge. People drive on it, so surely a Bigfoot could walk on it. Maybe one came over and didn't mean to stay on the island. Maybe it got caught by an unexpected early thaw and couldn't go back."

I could practically smell Charlie's need to believe.

"And it's been living on the island for the past, what, six months?" Jon asked, the incredulity clear in his voice. "Madeline Island is the only one of the Apostles allowing personal ownership of land, isn't it?" Charlie nodded. "And how many people live on the island year-round?"

"Around four hundred," Charlie said.

"And how many tourists and visitors come to the island each year?" Jon went on.

"A couple thousand, give or take." Charlie grumbled. She must have guessed what Jon was getting at because I could tell she didn't like him quashing her enthusiasm.

"Do you think it's reasonable to think a Bigfoot has been living on Madeline Island for the past six months and no one has seen it until now?" Jon said.

Charlie scowled. "There have been other sightings. And remember those caves I mentioned? It would be easy for a creature to hide out in them and avoid detection by only coming out at night. There are kayakers who visit the caves during the summer months, but they typically come only in July and August because of the frigid water temperatures."

I couldn't fault Charlie's logic, not yet anyway, but I needed to see the footprint for myself. The ferry ride was only twenty minutes long and we were nearing the landing on Madeline Island, so Charlie said we should head back to the car. Newt appeared as reluctant as I was to return to the vehicle. The brisk morning air and warmth of the sun made for a pleasant way to start the day.

Ten minutes later, Charlie drove us off the ferry and onto the main road to La Pointe, a picturesque village filled with boutiques, art galleries, cozy eateries, and coffee shops. We headed away from town, however, and the homes we passed once we left the village proper were separated by heavily wooded acreage similar to what I'd seen surrounding houses in Bayfield and Washburn.

"The hike is even terrain, so it shouldn't be a problem," Charlie said. "You can bring Newt, but you need to keep him on a leash."

"Of course."

Minutes later, we pulled into a small paved lot where another conservation warden sat parked in an official car. He nodded at us as we drove by but gave us little attention otherwise. As soon as we were parked, we all got out and headed for a lakeside trail that turned out to be an absolute delight.

Charlie led us along a section of high, rocky shoreline marked by steep banks of rust-colored sand alternating with giant, stacked slabs of sandstone jutting out into the water. The tops and edges of these bluffs had been smoothed and sculpted by centuries of wind and wave action and while some hugged the shoreline, others extended out into the lake, their surfaces covered with green moss, yellow lichen, or the occasional scrub tree that had somehow found purchase in the rock. Most had underlying sea caves, everything from small, domed crescents to dark holes extending too far back to fully see from where we stood. Waves flowed in, around, and out of these hollows, crashing, splashing, and sometimes exploding in

sprays that caught the morning sunlight and glittered like dia-
monds.

On our left was a forest of trees displaying the reds, yellows,
and oranges of fall mixed in with the green of conifers. To our right
was the vast expanse of Lake Superior, her waves shimmering in
the morning light. Red squirrels scampered about, collecting food
for the upcoming winter and attracting Newt's eager attention. A
minute or so into our walk, a bald eagle soared by over the water,
hanging on an updraft for a moment as it eyed us with curiosity.
The setting was an exquisite example of Mother Nature at her finest,
utterly breathtaking. It was the kind of awe-inspiring place where
one could forget about the problems of life for a while and simply
revel in the glory of Earth's bounty and beauty.

Unfortunately, about ten minutes in, Charlie steered us away
from the shoreline and onto an inland path called Woods Trail. As
the name implied, it meandered through dense woods, occasionally
forcing us to sidestep fallen trees and large mud puddles left behind
by the night's storm. This was never an easy detour as the ground
on either side of the trail was often boggy or thick with roots, bushes,
and foot-snagging vines.

While the trees were lovely with their colorful, wet leaves glistening in the filtered morning light, there was little in the way of a
breeze at ground level and lots in the way of gnat-like bugs hanging
about. It wasn't all bad, though. The morning was utterly quiet
aside from birdsong, our breathing, the distant sound of lapping
waves, and the rustling of leaves in the treetops as a high, light
breeze made them dance. Sunlight peeked down through the
overhead canopy, creating glimmering light mosaics on the ground.

And while the air was humid, still, and buggy, it was also heavily perfumed with the piney, earthy smells of nature.

After we slogged along single file for a way, me endlessly waving my hand in front of my face to keep gnats from flying up my nose, Charlie finally stopped and pointed at a single yellow flag stuck in the ground. I told Newt to stay, and Jon and I went up to look.

In front of us was a large, muddy portion of the path. Smack dab in the middle of it was the prize we'd come for: a huge, humanlike footprint with five distinct toes.

CHAPTER 24

W hat do you make of it, Morgan?" Jon said as the three of us
stared down at the footprint.

I chewed the inside of my cheek, my thoughts churning as I
studied the impression. It was quite distinct, with the first or big
toe somewhat separate from the others. Closer inspection revealed
a faint line running down the center of the print from what would
have been the ball back to the heel, like a foot crease. There was
faint blurring around the outside edges, suggestive of movement,
and the direction of the footprint indicated the creature had been
moving perpendicular to the path and heading into the woods. I
took a tape measure out of my pocket and carefully measured the
length—eighteen inches—and width—ten inches.

I let Jon's question hang in the morning air for the time being
and ventured deeper into the woods in the direction the footprint

was pointed, studying the ground and the surrounding vegetation intently.

"Tell me how the young man who witnessed . . . whatever this was, described what happened," I said to Charlie.

"He said he likes to come out here early before things get busy and while it's still dark. He uses a small headlamp to help him see the trail, and he entered the park from a different direction than we did, from a parking lot about half a mile ahead of us. His goal was to reach the shoreline and the sandstone outcroppings about the time the sun would be coming up."

Charlie paused and pointed farther down the trail. "He was around the bend up there coming our way when he heard something grunting ahead of him. Worried it might be a bear, he stopped to look and listen. He heard more grunts followed by heavy, slow, rhythmic footsteps and then he yelled out, thinking if it was a bear, the sound might scare it off."

"Did he say what it was he yelled?" I asked.

Charlie shook her head. "No, but it had an effect, apparently, because the next thing he heard was crashing and thrashing sounds as if something large was moving through the underbrush. In the dim light he thought he saw a tall, dark figure running through the trees and it appeared to be staggering at times. Since it looked and sounded as if it was moving away from him, he stayed where he was. Once it got quiet again, he cautiously continued forward along the path. Then he found the print. He took a picture of it, high-tailed it back to his car, and called the La Pointe police, who put him through to me."

I nodded and studied our surroundings some more. When I

looked back at Jon and Charlie, I saw the two of them watching me expectantly. Newt wagged his tail when I looked his way, but he remained where he was on the path.

"Okay," I said. "I have a problem with this scenario, and I'll tell you why. It makes no sense for any creature to charge off through this heavy tangle of trees and bushes when there's a perfectly good, mostly clear path to run along. What's more, the imprint of the full foot is a little too . . . perfect. If the creature made the print while running through the trees, I would expect to see two things I don't. One, there would be more blurring from the movement of the foot as it hit the ground and then pushed off again. And two, I would expect to see greater depth in the impression near the toe end of the print indicative of the way the ball of the foot pushes off during walking or running. This print appears flat and even."

"You're assuming the creature's foot operates like ours and it runs the same way we do," Charlie said.

Hope dies hard for some, and this seemed particularly true for Charlie. Still, I welcomed her challenges to my logic.

"Well, yes," I said. "Basic primate anatomy is assumed to be the basis behind most theories regarding Bigfoot. There's also the issue of the difference in size and shape from the print we found at the scene of Conrad's death. While I didn't personally measure the Pine Lake print, the dimensions suggested by the ruler in the file picture indicated a foot longer and wider than this one. So, either we're talking about two of these creatures, or there's something hinky going on here."

Jon nodded; Charlie pouted.

"Another thing bothering me is the lack of another print or

two—even a partial—somewhere nearby. Thanks to last night's rain, the ground is soft and muddy enough to easily take an impression if something big stepped on it. Yet this is the only one."

"There's a lot of heavy ground cover," Charlie argued, though I could tell she was having a tough time even convincing herself.

"One more thing makes me suspect this print isn't real," I said. I pointed at my dog, who was still sitting where I'd told him to, watching us. "Newt has had no reaction to anything in this area except the occasional squirrel. Look at him over there, patient but bored, sporadically sniffing the air but showing no particular interest in anything. Remember how he behaved when we were at the spot near where Bodie Erickson was killed?"

Charlie's brows drew together. "I do," she said uncertainly, "but maybe he was simply reacting to how someone had died a horrible, bloody death there within the past couple of weeks. You know, the lingering smell of human blood."

"Yet he didn't react when we were at the spot where Pete Conrad died," I pointed out. "And his death was just as bloody *and* more recent."

Charlie rolled her lips inward and shook her head with annoyance. She folded her arms over her chest, looked off into the trees, and shifted her weight from one foot to the other with irritated impatience.

Jon said, "Charlie, there's something about Pete Conrad's death you should know, and it won't be in the official ME report when it's released." Charlie shot him a questioning look. "Based on the microscopic examination of the wounds, it's possible Pete Conrad's death was at the hands of a human rather than an animal."

Charlie dropped her arms to her sides and gaped at him, her

expression rapidly changing from disbelief to confusion, and then to denial before finally settling on reluctant acceptance.

"Tell me more," she said, and Jon did, giving her all the facts he'd shared with me except for the reason why the ME owed him a favor. Luckily, she didn't push him on this point.

"And Erickson?" she asked when he was done.

"No indication of any human involvement there," Jon said. "Particularly since there was a witness. But the evidence in his case does suggest a bear attack."

"But . . . the hair," Charlie said, then she turned away. I felt bad for her just then; she looked so dejected and . . . broken.

"Look, Charlie," I said. "I know you believe this creature exists. Maybe it does. But I want . . . I *need* truth, science, and facts. And the facts here don't support it."

"Then what do you think this guy saw here this morning?" she asked. "What made this print if it wasn't a Bigfoot?"

"I think I know," I said. "But I need to check on something first. And I want to talk to the young man who found this print."

"Then let's go do it," Charlie said irritably. She pushed past Jon and marched back down the path in the direction we'd come, not bothering to look back to see if we were following.

I used my phone to snap a couple of quick pics of the print, and then Newt, Jon, and I followed in Charlie's wake. Her angry, rapid stride got her to the parking lot well ahead of us and she was leaning against her vehicle waiting, looking like a kid who'd just been told Santa Claus isn't real.

The ride to the rental house where the young man was staying took only about five minutes, but it felt like an eternity as Charlie's disappointment and unhappiness spread through the car like a rabid virus. Even Newt sensed it. He whimpered and hunkered down on the back seat with his head in my lap, looking up worriedly at me. I felt bad for Charlie, but I saw no benefit to coddling her or feeding her need to believe with unwarranted speculations.

The rental house was a large, older home with across-the-road access to Lake Superior. Our witness, whose name was Allen Lawson, was a twenty-something graduate student at the University of Wisconsin. He told us he was enjoying a weekend escape at the house, which was owned by one of his friends.

"We come up whenever we can," Allen told us. "We all love it up here, especially this time of the year, and Chris's parents—they're the ones who own the house—don't come up much anymore. There's a hidden key we know about so we can come up anytime we want. Chris's parents are talking about renting the place or selling it, but I hope they don't."

Allen's story about what had happened on the path earlier matched what Charlie had already told us. I had a couple of questions for him, though.

"Can you better describe the build of the animal you saw going through the trees?"

Allen shrugged and scrunched up his face. "Not really. It was still pretty dark, and my headlamp didn't penetrate very deep into the woods. I could tell it was tall. Taller than any animal I'd expect except maybe a bear, but only if the bear was on its hind legs. And this thing stayed tall as it ran through the woods, whereas a bear would've dropped to all fours."

"What about smell?"

"Smell?" Allen looked perplexed by the question.

"Yes, did you notice any odd or strong odors in the area?"

Allen thought briefly. "No, I didn't. I heard it, and saw it, or got a glimpse of it anyway, and there was the footprint. But I didn't smell anything unusual."

"Yes, about the print, did you see the animal run across the path at any point?"

Allen shook his head. "No, I only found the print by accident after it had already run off into the woods."

I thanked him and sidestepped his question when he asked if I thought there was a Bigfoot running around the island.

Our car ride back to the ferry landing was quiet and tense. We pulled into line for the next boat and Charlie turned the car off since we had a fifteen-minute wait. After a couple of minutes enduring the uncomfortable silence, I said I'd be right back and got out. I went up to the man who was selling tickets and pulled up a photo of Hans Baumann on my phone.

"Any chance you remember seeing this man come over on the ferry in the past day or so? He would have been driving a silver Land Rover."

The gent studied the picture but then shook his head. "Can't say I do," he said. "And I'd remember a Land Rover. But then I've been off duty for the past couple of days. Today's my first day back."

I thanked him and went back to the car.

"What was that about?" Jon asked.

"I wanted to know if he'd seen Hans Baumann come over at all."

"And had he?" Jon asked. I shook my head.

"You're convinced the print is a fake, aren't you?" Charlie said.

"I am. For the reasons I mentioned at the site but also for one other reason I'll explain a little later. I need to check on something first."

We fell back into the uncomfortable silence until Jon, bless his heart, started telling us about a wacky call he'd gotten while on duty the day before. This led to Charlie sharing one of her more bizarre calls, and then the two of them began chatting amiably, swapping stories in the front seat until it came time to drive onto the ferry. Once we were aboard, Jon and Charlie climbed out of the car to go up to one of the open decks.

"You guys go on ahead," I said. "I'll be up in a minute. I need to make a phone call first."

Charlie looked delighted at the prospect of time alone with Jon, however brief it might be. I knew it bothered Jon not to be on top of whatever I was thinking, but he'd just have to make do. As soon as the two of them were out of earshot, I placed a call to Devon, told him what I needed, and asked how the store was doing.

"We're busy," he told me. "We've been open for a little over an hour and it's been bustling. A handful of customers have asked for you and they were quite disappointed to learn you weren't here. I think the news coverage of the case you worked on with Jon has turned you into something of a local celebrity. One lady even said she wanted to get your autograph."

I suspected he was right about my sudden celebrity. There had been a small write-up in the local rag and, ever since the article appeared, the store had seen a significant uptick in the number of customers. I couldn't help but notice how many of them stared or pointed at me while whispering to their companions. I wasn't wild about the attention but figured it would fade eventually.

"I hope to be back soon," I told Devon. "In the meantime, if you find what I asked you about, shoot the info to my phone, would you?"

"Sure."

I waited until we drove off the ferry and then asked Charlie if she would let me out of the car so Newt and I could walk back to my building. At first, she seemed delighted by my request, but when Jon wanted to come with me, her attitude took a nosedive. Once again I found myself feeling bad for her, so before she drove away I stuck my head down by her window and said, "Why don't you join us for lunch? I might need your help with things I want to do this afternoon. Can you recommend a place?"

She perked up, quickly accepted the invite, and then offered to bring lunch with her. "There's a great little deli here in town that makes basic but delicious sandwiches and salads. Turkey and roast beef clubs sound okay?"

"Sounds great. Meet us at my suite at twelve thirty?"

"Will do. I'll grab a couple of side salads, too."

I watched her drive away and then turned to see Jon staring at me with a quizzical expression. I grinned and crooked a finger at him. "Follow me, copper."

I walked over to the ferry's ticket booth, brought up the picture of Hans Baumann on my phone, and asked the woman there the same question I'd asked the gent on the other side.

"Heck, yeah," she said without hesitation. "I'd remember this fella anywhere. He parked in line and then got out of his vehicle to go into the terminal. Probably to use the facilities," she added in a hushed aside. "Anyway, he kind of stood out because he was quite tall and had on one of them long coats like the cowboys in those old Western movies, you know?

"A duster?" I said.

She shrugged. "Don't know what you call it, but it was black and kind of flapped in the back, and he had on black boots, too.

Looked like he'd stepped right out of a Wyatt Earp movie. He sure is a real nice-looking fellow." She sighed dreamily, and I shot Jon a smug grin. "Figured he's probably got money, too," the woman went on, her eyes big. "He was driving some gas-guzzling Land Rover."

"When did you see him?" I asked.

"Yesterday afternoon. He went over on the three o'clock, or maybe it was four. You know him? Is he single?"

"Have you seen him come back?" I asked, ignoring her questions.

She shook her head. "I worked till five and then mentioned him to Suzette on account of she's single, too," she said with a saucy wink. "Told her to watch out for him. But when I talked to her this morning, she said he didn't come back last evening. Must have spent the night on the island somewhere and I'll bet you dollars to doughnuts he's still there."

I thanked her and turned to Jon. "Let's head back to the suite." As we walked, I said, "Too bad you don't have jurisdiction up here. I'd love to find an excuse to pull Baumann over when he returns to the mainland and search his Land Rover."

"For what?" Jon said.

"I'll tell you over lunch."

CHAPTER 25

Since neither of us had had a chance to shower yet, Jon and I agreed to take turns in the bathroom once we got back to the suite. Jon went first and I used the time to review the items in Charlie's folders again, focusing harder on Pete Conrad since we now suspected his death had been a homicide rather than an animal attack. If we were right, it raised several questions. Why had Conrad been killed? What was the motive? And of course, who could have done it?

I kept coming back to Conrad's job and the nagging feeling it might have something to do with his death. I figured it was a place to start anyway. But if the cops couldn't get any client information from the company Conrad worked for, I figured I wasn't going to have any luck either. Then I got an idea. I looked through Charlie's folder until I found the name of Conrad's wife, Joanne, and a cell number for her. After a moment's hesitation, I made the call.

"Hello?"

"Hi, is this Mrs. Conrad?"

This was answered with a weary sigh. "Look, I'm not taking calls right now because—"

"I know why," I said quickly. "That's the reason I'm calling. My name is Morgan. I'm a wildlife biologist looking into the circumstances surrounding your husband's death." Technically, this was true; I did have a degree in biology, and I was looking into her husband's death. I hoped this would be unusual enough to give her pause. When she didn't hang up on me, I hurried on. "I'm looking into whatever animal attacked your husband and I have some questions I thought you might be able to answer."

"What do you mean by whatever animal it was? The policeman I spoke to said it was a bear attack."

"It might have been," I assured her. "But we want to rule out other potential animals, like wolves or cougars." I felt her hesitancy radiating over the airwaves. "In the interest of public safety," I added quickly, hoping an appeal for the greater good might sway her. "We wouldn't want to point the finger at a bear and then discover it was a different animal after someone else gets attacked."

"Exactly how do you think I can help?" I heard the skepticism in her voice and envisioned her making little finger circles beside her head to someone else in the room. But at least she was still talking to me.

"Did you speak to or exchange any text messages with your husband on the day he died?"

"No. The last time I spoke to him was the evening before. We go up for a week every year during the Apple Festival so I knew he'd be spending all his time fishing and would likely head out at the butt crack of dawn every day. Since I didn't get to go this year, Pete used most of our last phone call trying to convince me I wasn't missing out on anything because the trees had already dropped their leaves and the weather was colder and wetter than usual. It was sweet of him, but I knew he was lying."

"Why didn't you come with him?"

"Funny story," she said in a decidedly unfunny tone. "I'm a real estate broker and I've been struggling to stay afloat lately. I recently picked up a great listing for a very high-end home on the lake and the day before we were supposed to leave, I got two calls for showings on the place from what sounded like serious buyers. As luck would have it, both callers wanted to see the place in the days after we were supposed to leave. I could have had another agent cover for me and show the house in my absence, but on such a big-ticket home, I didn't want to hand it off. No one knows the house the way I do. Plus, the commission on a sale would have set me up nicely for a time. So, after a discussion, we decided Pete should go to Bayfield alone this year."

"Did you get an offer from either of your potential buyers?"

"Hardly. Neither one of them showed up," she said, her voice laden with bitterness.

"How awful. Is that unusual?"

"It's not unheard-of, though the more common scenario is people who do show up but are only lookie-loos with no intention of buying. They waste everyone's time. These guys both sounded serious. Clearly I was pranked, and I was not amused," she said sourly.

"Did you get names and phone numbers for either of them?"

"I did," she said tiredly, letting me know I was reaching the end of my tether with her. "The names they gave me were bogus, though they matched up to some bigwigs at a couple of large corporations. I did my due diligence ahead of time and researched the names. It's why I was so convinced the inquiries were legit. But when I called those people afterward, they had no idea what I was talking about, and the voices were different. As soon as I heard them, I knew I'd been had."

"I'm so sorry," I said, and I meant it. It never feels good to be duped.

"Both calls initially displayed as unknown, and the numbers might not have come up at all except I have a special dedicated toll-free number for this listing because these high-end places attract buyers from all over the world. Since calling a toll-free number basically creates a collect call, I as the owner have a right to know who's calling and generating a charge to me. So, those blocking tactics, like dialing star-sixty-seven first, don't work."

"Would you mind giving me those phone numbers?"

"Why?"

I scrambled for an answer. "Um, well, I have a lot of connections with law enforcement and maybe they can find the persons behind the prank." I held my breath, waiting for her reply.

She sighed. "Yeah, whatever. I don't suppose it matters at this point. Give me a second." I heard the click of her shoes as she walked and then the sound of papers being shuffled about. Finally, she rattled the numbers off to me.

"Did either of these clients provide you with any other identifying information?"

"No. Like I said, once I realized the names they gave me weren't their real ones, I came up empty. That, too, isn't uncommon with wealthy clients who may want to hide their true identity. Actors do it all the time, checking into hotels under false names and such. But this was different. Either there were no clients in the first place, or they changed their mind and didn't have the courtesy to call and let me know. I suspect it was the former and not the latter."

I was inclined to agree with her, but I found the whole story disconcertingly convenient, particularly in light of what I then knew about Pete's death. I debated how to segue into the next part of my call.

"Mrs. Conrad, I'm really sorry about what happened, and I can't imagine how difficult it must be for you. I lost both of my parents two years ago and it still makes my heart ache. I can tell you it does get better. Not quickly, and maybe not all the way, but it gets easier with time."

"Thank you. I'm sorry about your parents."

"Thanks." I hesitated before launching into the next part. "Listen, I know this isn't the best time to ask, but my parents left me with a chunk of money I need to invest, and I haven't been able to deal with it until recently. I see your husband did investment work at one of the firms I was considering using and I know wives often know a fair amount about what their husbands do. I wondered if you could give me the name of any clients whose accounts he managed. I'd really like to talk with people who have dealt with Teach and Springer before I put my money with them. I tried to get references from the company directly, but the people I spoke to said they couldn't because it was confidential information. Of course, they assured me they were trustworthy, upstanding, and blah, blah, blah." I sighed for emphasis, and heard Joanne let out a sympathetic chuckle.

"I know these places will tell me anything to get my business," I went on, "and I want to make sure I'm not handing my money over to a reckless operation. I realize it's inconsiderate of me to ask you so soon after your husband's death, but if you'll help me, I promise it will remain our secret. And I'll be happy to make a generous donation in Pete's name to a charity of your choice as a way to say thank you."

I paused, nearly out of breath from talking so fast, and squeezed my eyes closed, praying my ruse would work. I knew Joanne hadn't hung up on me because I could hear her breathing, but I had no way of knowing what she was thinking or might be about to do.

After an interminable amount of time, during which my hopes sagged and my shame grew with each passing second, Joanne said, "I suppose you'll want the names of individuals rather than companies."

"Yes, please," I said, nearly breathless with genuine gratitude. "Anything you can give me would be fabulous. I'll take small company names, too. I don't suppose you know of any up here in the Bayfield area?"

"I do. Pete does business everywhere we go." Silence for a beat, then she amended her statement with, "He *did* business." Her voice cracked and I let her have a moment to collect herself. "Pete kept a notebook in his desk drawer," she said finally. "Hold on."

I heard more footsteps, and by the time she spoke again, I had my pen at the ready and scribbled down the two names she gave me. "Those are the only individuals I know of in the Bayfield area," she said. "But he managed funds for three small businesses there, too." She then gave me the names and contact info for these, concluding with, "Do me a favor and don't tell them where you got the info from?"

"I promise; it's our secret," I said. "And thank you so, so much, Joanne."

"St. Jude's, the kid's cancer hospital."

"Sorry, what?"

"It's where you can make the donation, if you're really going to do it." Clearly, her bullshit detector was starting to buzz.

"Oh, I will," I promised. "You'll see. And thanks again for helping me."

"Yeah, okay. Can you tell me when the cops are going to give me back Pete's personal effects? I'd really like to get his phone and laptop back."

Her mention of a laptop turned on a light bulb in my head. "My understanding is they were unable to find his cell phone," I told her. "It might be at the bottom of the lake where he was fishing."

Even as I said this, I realized how little sense it made if the animal attack scenario was applied. Conrad had never actually gone out on the water. He'd been fishing from shore and there was no evidence he'd even gotten a line in the water. Had his killer taken the phone? Or tossed it out into the lake? I tucked those questions away for later contemplation.

"As for a laptop," I said, "did he bring one with him?"

"He did. He always takes . . . took the damn thing with him. We never went on a vacation together where he wasn't working for part of it."

"I'll check with the primary officer in charge of his case and see what I can do," I said, thinking if there was a laptop, I wanted to get my hands on it first.

"Great. Bye." Apparently, Mrs. Conrad had reached the limits of her patience because the call abruptly ended.

I winced as another wave of guilt washed over me. Then I hopped on my laptop and made a generous donation to St. Jude's Hospital in the name and memory of Pete Conrad with notification to go to his wife. When I was done, I waited with toe-tapping impatience for Jon to get out of the bathroom. When he finally emerged trailing a cloud of steamy air behind him, I jumped right in with no preamble, telling him about my phone conversation with Joanne Conrad.

"The names she gave me might be a bust, but we should try to find out if Conrad's laptop is here," I said. "His wife said he always traveled with it. If we could get a peek at it . . ."

"You mean if *Devon* could get a peek at it, don't you?" Jon said.

I grinned at him.

"If I recall, you said this sheriff, Buck something or other, wasn't too keen on you looking into things. I doubt he's going to be willing to share evidence."

"With me," I said. "But what about with a fellow law enforcement officer who just happens to be the chief of police in another jurisdiction?"

Jon frowned. "I'm not sure I'd be comfortable doing something like that."

"It's not official evidence if the case is closed. Once the ME report comes out, it shouldn't be a problem, should it?"

Jon's frown deepened and before he could put another kibosh on my idea, I added, "Plus, it's not Buck Weaver's evidence anyway.

Charlie told me a conservation warden in Washburn is the lead on both cases."

A knock sounded at the door, saving me. It was Charlie, carrying a box full of lunch, and once again arriving earlier than expected, though this time I was willing to forgive her.

"I know I'm early," she said, bustling in and setting the box on the table. "But I finally got a copy of the official ME's report on Pete Conrad." She removed a sheet of paper from the box and handed it past me to Jon. Apparently, my involvement on the case had been supplanted.

Jon looked it over and then gave it to me. "Just what we expected," he said.

"We were talking about Pete Conrad's laptop right before you arrived," I said to Charlie. "His wife said he brought it up here with him. Do you think we can get a look at it?"

"I don't see why not," Charlie said with a shrug. "All of Conrad's belongings should still be in an evidence locker at the Washburn office since Bruce was the LEO in charge of the case. I don't think he'd mind if we took a look at any of it. This ME's report means the case will now be considered closed."

"Great," I said.

"We can go now, if you want," Charlie offered.

"I was just about to hop in the shower," I said, beginning to suspect Charlie's middle name might be Impatience.

"Go ahead," she said with great magnanimity. You would have thought it was her suite we were in, and I was the interloper. "I'll give Bruce a call and let him know we're coming. And don't worry about the food. It's just sandwiches and salads. Nothing hot." She turned to Jon, effectively dismissing me.

I went into the bedroom to get some clean clothes and my shower supplies and stopped short. The bed was still unmade from this morning, but my suitcase was sitting on top of it. I was sure I'd left the suitcase on the luggage rack across the room and thought back to this morning, trying to recall if I'd moved it at all. I was certain I hadn't. Heck, I hadn't even opened it. In the rush to leave and catch the ferry, I'd simply put on my clothes from the day before, which had been draped over a chair.

The suitcase was unzipped, and I opened it, tensed as if I expected to find a bomb inside. In a way, I did. Sitting on top of my clothes, was a note, computer printed in all caps on plain white paper. The message was simple and clear: GO HOME AND MIND YOUR OWN BUSINESS.

CHAPTER 26

I picked up the note and carried it out to the kitchen table. Charlie was just finishing her phone call to Bruce White. "We're all set to get Pete Conrad's personal effects," she said. "I told Bruce I was heading down to Milwaukee this coming week and could deliver the items to his widow in person and express our sympathy at the same time."

"She was quite convincing," Jon said. Charlie beamed beneath his praise.

"Well, I hate to be a party pooper, but someone came in here and left me a present." I dropped the paper on the table.

"What the—" Jon slid it toward him. "Where did you find this?"

"In my suitcase, which was on the bed. Which was odd because I didn't put it on the bed this morning."

"Someone came in here while we were out?" Jon said, his eyebrows twisting into an angry scowl.

"Yes, and I think I know who it was. Buck Weaver made it clear he doesn't want me looking into these deaths, and he mentioned he knew the woman who owns this place. I'm betting she let him into my room, probably on some trumped-up pretext he gave her."

"Not acceptable," Jon grumbled. "I need to have a chat with this Weaver fellow."

"Mm . . . not such a good idea," Charlie said, grimacing. "Buck has a lot of pull around here and he can make life real miserable for us if he wants to. If he does, we'll never get access to anything. It might be best not to antagonize him any more than he already is, at least for now."

"Much as I hate it, Charlie is right," I said. "Plus, we can't know for sure it was Buck."

Jon frowned, clearly unhappy with this hands-off approach.

"At least let's wait until we have Conrad's laptop in hand," I said. I looked at Charlie. "One other thing. I got some names from Conrad's wife, clients of Pete's who are in this area. Do you know any of these people or companies?" I showed her the notepad where I'd scribbled them down.

Charlie looked over the list and said, "I know both of the individuals. Sarah Meyers owns a couple of artisanal bakeries and coffee shops, one here in Bayfield and the other in Washburn. And George Zander runs a fishing charter out of Bayfield. As for these company names, I believe Olander Fisheries Inc. supplies seafood to area restaurants. The owner doesn't have much to do with the business anymore because he's older than Methuselah. I think his grandson manages things these days. I can't recall their names right off the bat, but we can probably find it online. Parker's Parcels LLC is a string of bed-and-breakfast inns owned by Becky Parker. She owns places in several lakeside towns and one on Madeline Island. As for this last one, Berryman Industries, I don't recognize it."

"I'll put Devon on it," I said. "In the meantime, let's go get this laptop. Maybe we can find the answer there. I'll take my shower later."

We opted to let Charlie drive again and Newt and I took the back seat while Jon sat up front. During the drive, I called Devon and asked him to dig around to see if he could find anything of interest on the names and companies Conrad's wife had given me. When I was done relaying the information to him, he said, "I found the other thing you asked me to look into this morning. I just sent a photo to your phone."

I thanked him, ended the call, and then checked the picture he'd sent me. "Check this out," I said, handing my phone to Jon.

He looked at the picture, brow furrowed. "It looks like another big footprint," he said.

"Exactly. It's one Hans Baumann found in a Mississippi marsh area two years ago."

"Ooookay," Jon said. "What am I missing?"

"Scroll to the next picture in my gallery. It's a shot of the footprint we found on Madeline Island this morning."

Jon did so while Charlie did her best to try and peer at my phone and stay on the road. I watched as Jon swiped back and forth from one photo to the other, studying each one for a few seconds. "Aha!" he said so suddenly it made Charlie jump. "I see it."

"See what?" Charlie said, her curiosity piqued.

"There's a vertical line running down part of the footprint in both photos," Jon said.

"Yeah. So?" Charlie said.

"The lines are vague, but they appear to be identical in length, angle, and shape," I explained. "As is the size and outline of each print, in two different footprints found years and hundreds of miles apart. I suspect the line we can see is due to a slight defect in whatever cast Baumann is using to create the footprints."

"Oh." Charlie slumped a little in her seat, clearly disappointed. "Maybe they migrate?" she suggested weakly. I shot her a look. "Yeah, I admit it's a reach. So that means the sighting on Madeline Island this morning..."

"Was Hans Baumann getting caught in the act," I said. I reiterated what the ticket agent at the ferry landing had told me earlier. "In thick, shadowy woods with hardly any early-morning sunlight, a man as tall as Baumann dressed in a long, black duster running through the trees could easily be interpreted as a Bigfoot, particularly once our witness saw the footprint. And we've long suspected Baumann has a recording of some sort on his cell phone that he uses to mimic the sound of a Bigfoot, or at least what he thinks one might sound like. The grunting noises our witness heard were most likely the sound of Baumann's efforts to make the print. My guess is he jumps up and down on the cast or pounds it with something to give it depth."

I saw the disappointment on Charlie's face in the rearview mirror and realized how badly she'd wanted the morning's sighting to bear out. "I'm sorry, Charlie, but it appears to be a classic case of confirmation bias."

My phone dinged, indicating another message, and Jon handed it back to me. "Devon just sent you something else."

I took the phone and read Devon's message and the attached documentation. "I knew it!" I said. "Devon found out when Hans Baumann flew from his home in Connecticut to here. Baumann made it sound to Charlie like he was at home when she called him, but he was already in the area. In fact, he was here when Pete Conrad was killed. If he'd heard about Erickson's attack and the rumors swirling about, he might have hightailed it here way back then to see how many people he could scam." I paused, my mental wheels turning faster than those on the car. "Heck, I wouldn't put it past him to have staged Conrad's death to further his cause."

Jon looked skeptical. "I mean, I know you said the guy's a slimeball and a con artist, but do you really think he's capable of murder?"

"I wouldn't put it past him. There's something off about the man."

"Okay, let's say your theory is right. How did he know Conrad and how was he able to get the drop on the guy while he was out on a fishing trip in the Chequamegon National Forest? Where's the connection?"

"I don't know," I grumbled, cursing Jon's damnable logic. "But I'm going to try to find out. Maybe he just picked a guy at random and befriended him."

Jon's expression told me what he thought of that idea.

"Yeah, okay, maybe I'm reaching." I snapped my fingers, my eyes growing wide as an idea came to me. "Or maybe Baumann knew Conrad. Conrad might have provided financial services to him. Maybe we'll find him in a list of clients on Conrad's laptop."

As if he was reading my mind from hundreds of miles away, Devon sent me a third message saying he'd looked at trying to hack into the company database at Teach and Springer and it didn't look promising. I wasn't surprised. Devon was often a miracle worker, but even he had his limits. I had to put my hopes on the idea of Conrad's computer containing a client list and being accessible. I feared both were long shots.

When we arrived at the Washburn DNR station, Charlie parked in the small lot and turned to us. "You guys should probably wait here. Seeing you trailing behind me might make Bruce suspicious."

"Smart thinking," Jon said, and once again Charlie glowed beneath his praise. I swear she had a bounce in her step as she walked across the lot.

Once we were alone in the car, Jon said, "Are you feeling a little less anxious about Charlie at this point? She's been helpful, hasn't she?"

"She has," I said hesitantly. "Though I don't know if we can trust her motivation."

"Because of what happened to her when she was a kid?"

"Well, yes, but also because I sometimes think she wishes I was out of the picture."

"What?"

"Oh, come on, Jon, surely you've realized she has a huge crush on you." He shot me a look of skeptical disbelief. "I'm serious. First, there are all her frequent early arrivals, something I find annoying, by the way."

"It's just her enthusiasm for the case."

"It's her enthusiasm for something, all right. Did you see the look on her face this morning when you came out of the bedroom in your pajamas?"

"*Pfft*! It's not like we slept together."

"She doesn't know that. Think about how it must have looked to her."

His gaze drifted off to the side for a moment, brow furrowed, and I knew when he saw it. I expected a serious response from him but instead he grinned at me and said, "I can't help it if I'm devilishly handsome and irresistible."

I rolled my eyes at him but smiled. He had a point. Our conversation was cut short by the return of Charlie carrying a leather laptop bag and a suitcase. She loaded the latter into the rear of the SUV and brought the laptop bag up front with her and handed it to Jon. I peered over his shoulder as he looked inside and saw it contained a small laptop computer and electrical cord. Newt, apparently thinking there might be something edible and tasty in the bag, also looked over Jon's shoulder, drooling on it for good measure.

"I want to park somewhere else before we start looking at those," Charlie said. "I don't want someone inside to look out a window and see us snooping." She started the car, pulled out onto the main road, and a minute later drove into the parking lot of an auto parts store.

As soon as she shifted into park, Jon took the laptop out and turned it on. Fortunately, the battery had enough of a charge left to start it up. Unfortunately, it revealed only three icons on the screen, two of them bearing a T&S logo I assumed was for Teach and Springer. One of these icons was labeled as portfolio management and the other was clearly Conrad's work email account.

The third icon was simply two computer monitors tethered together. Not surprisingly, all of these programs prompted for a password when Jon tried to open them, though the username lines filled in automatically.

"Well, this is a dead end," Jon muttered.

Silence, other than the sound of Newt panting, filled the car, and I wondered if anyone else was thinking about the pun in Jon's comment. I shook off the macabre thought and as I stared out my side window, an idea came to me.

"Let's go back to the suite," I said. "I think we may be able to come at this from a different angle."

CHAPTER 27

I didn't share my idea with anyone because I wasn't certain it would work and needed to check with Devon first. As soon as we got back to my suite, I grabbed clean clothes from my suitcase—no surprises in it this time—and headed for the shower, leaving Jon and Charlie at the kitchen table eating the food Charlie had brought earlier. While I was in the bathroom, I sent a text to Devon telling him what we'd found with the laptop and asking him if my idea had any chance of success.

I knew what the icon with the two connected computer monitors was because I'd once had it on my own laptop. It was a program to allow remote access, and I'd first used it when I needed Devon to help with something on my computer while he was in his home state of Louisiana on vacation. I hoped the same icon appearing on Conrad's computer meant Devon could access it remotely.

By the time I got out of the shower I had his answer—a somewhat disappointing one. Devon thought he could probably establish remote access with my help, but because the laptop was a work computer the odds of being able to guess a password to the other programs on it were slim to none. Ever hopeful, I told him I wanted to try anyway.

When I emerged from the bathroom amid a rolling cloud of steam, I nearly tripped over Newt, who was stretched out in front of the bathroom door.

"He whined the whole time you were in there," Jon said.

"Sorry. He's not used to being separated from me. I typically don't shut the door to the bathroom when I shower at home."

"I think it's sweet," Jon said with a smile. Charlie tried to smile, too, but hers didn't fully form. Jon's next comment didn't help the situation any. "I love the curls in your hair when it's wet," he said, gazing up at me from his seat. "You look lovely."

"Tell us about this idea of yours," Charlie said quickly, sharply, all business. "I'm feeling restless. We need to do something."

"Devon is going to do a deep dive on Pete Conrad and see if he can come up with a list of possible passwords to try when I give him remote access to Conrad's computer. In the meantime, there's something else I want to do."

"Such as?" Charlie asked. She appeared to be sulking.

"I want to have a chat with Bob Keller, the man who witnessed the attack on Erickson. I know you said he's refused to talk to anyone, but I still want to try."

Charlie shrugged, still looking mildly annoyed. "We can give it a shot, I guess. I'll dig out his number."

"I'd rather pay him a visit and not let him know we're coming,"

I said. "It's easier to ignore a ringing phone than it is someone pounding on your door."

Charlie didn't look hopeful, but she shrugged. "Your call."

"Great! I'm going to take Newt out for a quick walk first."

At hearing the word "walk" Newt was up and wagging his tail. I grabbed his leash and headed out the door, noticing how Charlie's mood had abruptly improved. Surely Jon could see how the woman was fawning over him. Granted, he'd been married for years before his wife and son died, but had it been long enough for him to have forgotten how to recognize the signs? Then again, I'd been blind to things I should have seen when I was dating David so who was I to judge? Man, this romance stuff was complicated!

Newt, oblivious to my mood, surprised me by pulling me in a different direction for our walk. Instead of heading across the road to the waterfront, he was leading me down the narrow alley between the house where my suite was located and another building that held an art store and a small grocery. Nose to the ground and sniffing like crazy, he entered the backyard behind my building. There was a large pile of lumber stacked near the back of the property, most of it marred by burn marks. Newt pulled hard toward it, and I knew he was on the scent of something, probably a critter hiding out or living in the discarded wood.

Newt sniffed vigorously all around the stack, sticking his nose in little nooks and crannies, tilting his head at times, whining on occasion. I heard the scrabble of little feet from within the pile and told Newt, "You're never going to get to whatever's in there, so you might as well give it up."

He let out one last whine, lifted a leg, and peed on a board near the ground, thereby marking the territory as his. Then he turned back toward the house. The lingering smell of smoke and burnt wood hung with me, tickling at my brain. What was it about that smell?

Despite a valiant effort, I wasn't able to pull it out by the time we got back to the suite. Not surprisingly, Charlie looked disappointed by my return, but I was too famished to be concerned with her feelings at the moment. I went to the fridge, grabbed a bottle of water and one of the sandwiches Charlie had brought earlier, and then I plopped into a chair at the table and began to eat, Newt, drooly as ever, sitting beside me and watching every bite go into my mouth. Newt's tactics weren't subtle by any means, but they were effective. I ended up giving him at least a quarter of my sandwich even though his food bowl was full.

While I ate, Jon and Charlie discussed various approaches we could try with Bob Keller. As I watched the two of them talk, sharing ideas in their work-related jargon, I experienced a tiny twinge of jealousy. Jon Flanders had managed to worm his way into my heart, and I didn't want to lose the way he made me feel whenever he was around. I found his presence uplifting and enjoyable. Plus, the way he'd comforted me, staying with me after my nightmare and then sleeping on the floor next to my bed once I'd finally managed to fall asleep made my heart do a little hitch whenever I thought about it. Flatfoot Flanders had a strong soft side, a vulnerability I found appealing. It was my own vulnerabilities that frightened me.

I watched Charlie twirl her hair and cast her eyes down before looking back up coquettishly as she talked to him and realized I couldn't blame her for being attracted to him. If I wasn't careful, he might slip away. It had been three years since his wife had died and based on our conversations, he was ready to look for love again. Was I? Could I let down my guard enough to get past my fear of making another soul-crushing, life-altering mistake? He'd said he would wait, but for how long?

Now wasn't the time to worry about it, I decided. Things to do, places to go. I slid the laptop off the table and carried it into the bedroom, where I turned it on and followed Devon's texted instructions. When I was done, I went back to the kitchen. While Jon and Charlie hadn't seemed to notice me leaving the room with the laptop, they did notice my return. They both turned and looked at me expectantly.

"Let's go visit this Keller fellow," I said.

"He lives up on the tip of the peninsula near the federal lands," Charlie said. "Are you sure you want to spring a surprise visit on him? It might tick him off if we simply show up."

I looked over at Jon, eyebrows raised in question. "What do you think?"

"We surprise him," he said without hesitation.

"Okay," I said with a decisive nod. "Let's do it. But first, let's go through Pete Conrad's suitcase to see if there's anything helpful in it."

The suitcase proved to be a bust, nothing but clothes and toiletries. We left it in the back of Charlie's SUV and the four of us hopped into the vehicle, Jon in front, me in the back seat with Newt. The drive to Bob Keller's place took twenty minutes, during which time Charlie and Jon continued their work talk, never once including me. It gave me time to think, and I used it to mentally review what I knew so far, which wasn't much when it came right down to it.

Bob Keller's home was a rusted trailer sitting on a parcel of heavily wooded land. Given the location and isolation, I doubted the place had electricity—I certainly couldn't see any lines coming into the place—and wondered if it had indoor plumbing. One answer was provided as we approached the door, and I heard the hum of a generator running somewhere.

Parked beside the trailer was a rusted Chevy pickup that looked to be a relic from the nineties, its body a mix of rust, primer, and a few faint remnants of a sickly looking, yellow paint. The yard, which was dirt with a handful of determined clumps of scrub grass, sported several pieces of outdoor furniture—a rusty metal patio table; three lawn chairs, two of which had broken streamers of webbing hanging below the seats; a firepit filled with ash; a rickety, worn gas grill; and a relatively new looking picnic table.

We'd agreed during the ride, or at least Charlie and Jon had agreed to let Charlie approach Keller first since she'd met him before. I left Newt in the car, figuring his intimidating size might frighten the man, and Jon and I hung back and watched as Charlie climbed the two wooden steps to the trailer's door and knocked.

I half expected Keller to look out a window and decide to ignore us, but he came to the door seconds later. His face sported at least a week's worth of beard growth, his clothes looked like he'd slept in them, and his hair had a greasy sheen to it suggesting he hadn't washed it in a while. Most importantly, I noticed he wasn't wearing any eyeglasses.

Charlie cleared her throat before speaking. "Hi, Mr. Keller. I don't know if you remember me, but I was helping with—"

"I remember you," he said with obvious displeasure. "I've already told you guys everything I know."

He stepped back and started to close the door, so I took two quick steps forward and in a loud voice said, "Not everything, Mr. Keller. Why aren't you wearing your eyeglasses?"

He froze with the door halfway shut and squinted at us.

"Please, Mr. Keller," I pleaded. "We just want to ask you a couple of questions about what you saw that day in the forest. Some things aren't adding up right."

"You saying I lied?" he challenged, closing his hands into fists.

"No, not at all." I moved closer. "I think you described things the best you could, but I also think your visual acuity isn't great and some of what you saw might be open to interpretation."

"Christ on a cracker," he muttered, sliding a hand through his greasy hair. "Are you all cops?"

"I'm not," I said, hoping he wouldn't realize I was circling around his question. "I'm a cryptozoologist. Do you know what that is?" He shook his head, so I gave him a quick explanation. "I look for creatures rumored to exist even though there's no proof to support the idea. Like Bigfoot or the Loch Ness Monster. I'm trying to get to the bottom of what happened out in those woods." I gestured toward Jon. "This is my assistant, Jon, and Warden Aberdeen here kindly offered to bring us to your place so we could chat with you."

Keller stared at us with squinty-eyed indecision.

I needed to up the ante. "I'm willing to pay you for your time."

His eyes widened. "How much?"

"A hundred bucks for ten minutes."

"You can pay now?"

I thought quickly, calculating what I had on me for cash. "I can."

"Okay, then." He stepped outside and closed the door behind him. "Why don't we sit outside." Fortunately, he pointed to the picnic table. Had he not, I feared we would have had to engage in a dicey version of musical chairs. Outside seemed like a wise idea, also. I suspected the inside of Mr. Keller's trailer might have been a little ripe, a worry I became convinced of once I got close enough to catch a whiff of the man. Charlie didn't sit; she paced instead. Jon and I lucked out by ending up in positions upwind of Keller and close to the firepit. The lingering scent of burnt wood once again triggered a niggle in my brain, but there were too many distractions for me to pull it out.

I slid five twenties over to Keller and he snatched them up and tucked them away somewhere below the table. He didn't examine them to make sure the amount was right, and I wondered if he'd be able to tell what denomination they were with his eyesight being what it was. I began by letting him know I was aware of his visual limitations.

"To be honest, I was a little surprised to learn you were out in the forest bowhunting," I said.

"I hunt for food," he said defensively. "And I can see shapes, colors, enough to tell if I'm shooting at an animal rather than a person, as long as folks wear their bright orange."

I saw Charlie roll her lips inward and briefly look skyward, and I gave her a subtle shake of my head. The last thing I wanted was for her to shut Keller down by saying the wrong thing.

"Describe for me what happened," I said. "What first drew your attention to Mr. Erickson?"

"Well, I hadn't seen any deer where I was, so I was going to try a different spot. I was working my way back toward the road, trying to focus on what little bit of a path there was when I heard the sound of something moving through the underbrush. I figured it was something small because the noise didn't sound big, you know? And I'm good with sounds on account of my sight not being so hot. But then the sound got bigger, and I froze." His eyes grew huge as he said this and, for a moment, he froze right there at the table.

He swiped the back of his hand over his mouth before continuing. "I was looking all around, trying to see something in the trees when I heard a bolt getting fired and hitting something fleshy. Then there was this god-awful keening screech off to the left." He paused, shuddering as the memory washed over him.

"I've never heard anything like it in my life. It spooked me and I started moving again as fast as I dared, but I hadn't gone maybe ten steps when I saw there was a man up ahead standing by a tree. I saw his blaze orange."

"He was just standing there when you first saw him?" I asked.

Keller nodded. "For maybe . . . five seconds? I don't know. Time was kind of slowed down, you know? Suddenly something big and dark and moving on two legs burst out of a bush and went after the man. It attacked him in this frenzy, fast and furious. The poor man tried to fight it off but to no use. He even tried bear spray on it—I heard it and smelled it—but all it did was make the beast crazier. The guy hollered and screamed something awful." The words spewed out of Keller fast and furious until he was forced to pause and take a breath. Then he squeezed his eyes closed, as if this could somehow stop him from seeing what lived in the haunted halls of his memories.

"Did you see him use a knife at all?" I asked.

Keller's horror-stricken expression turned contrite, and he shrugged. "I wasn't close enough to tell and everything happened so fast. It was hard for me to see. I could smell it, though."

"What do you mean?" I asked.

"There was this pungent, animalistic odor emanating from it. It was really strong. My sense of smell is good because of my poor eyesight, but I think anyone would have noticed this. Even as far away as I was. Even over the smell of the bear spray."

"You didn't try to help Erickson?" Charlie asked, her lips pursed.

I shot her an irritated look and quickly said, "I wouldn't have. I would have been hightailing it out of there." I didn't know if this was true or not; I couldn't imagine being in a situation like the one Keller had faced with his visual limitations, but then it was also hard for me to imagine watching an animal rip another person apart and doing nothing about it.

"I . . . I froze," Keller said, his voice hiccupping. "I wanted to run but I didn't know which way to go. I thought it might come after me and I didn't know how many of them there were."

I started to say something more when these last words registered with me. "I'm sorry, what do you mean you didn't know how many there were?"

"That's the thing, you see," Keller said, a haunted look in his unseeing eyes. "That hunter fella shot at something off to my left. Shot at it and hit it, whatever it was. I'm certain of it. I heard it hit and heard the beast scream. But the thing that attacked him? It came out of the trees to my right."

CHAPTER 28

We spent half of the ride back from Bob Keller's place in a contemplative silence. After the man's revelation about how there might have been more than one animal involved, we'd listened as he told us how he'd carefully approached Erickson's body once the attacking animal had disappeared, constantly looking over his shoulder in case it came back for him. He explained in heart-wrenching detail how he'd managed to discern enough of Erickson's anatomy—feeling the man's chest for the rise of a breath and palpating the one remaining wrist for a pulse—to know he was too far gone for Keller to help him. It was a horribly grim series of events, and it was no wonder Keller didn't want to talk about it. Surely he must have PTSD as a result of his experience. I practically had it simply from hearing the tale.

It was Charlie who finally broke the silence on our ride back to town. "What a waste of time," she said testily. "Clearly, Keller is an unreliable witness."

I shot her a surprised look. "What makes you say that?"

"He lied to us by withholding key information about his vision issues when we initially questioned him. And he shouldn't be out there hunting, for God's sake. I mean, he couldn't even keep his directions straight." Charlie shook her head ruefully. "His story made no sense."

"Hard to say," I said.

Charlie looked askance at me via the rearview mirror. "What's hard about it? The guy can't see worth a damn, his description of whatever attacked Erickson could have been anything, and he was clearly so freaked out he got himself all turned around, making him think there were two animals."

"Maybe there *were* two of them," I said, curious as to why Charlie found it so hard to believe in two creatures when she'd spent most of her life steadfastly believing in one. "Maybe Erickson shot at a bear cub, hit it, and the mother bear was angered by it and attacked him."

Jon turned sideways in his seat so he could look at us both. "Mr. Keller seemed certain it wasn't a human attacking Erickson," he said. "He was adamant about the sound and the smell, and I don't see either of those making sense with a human attacker."

"Agreed," I said.

"So we need to look at Erickson and Conrad as two separate, unrelated cases," he said.

"Not totally unrelated," I muttered.

Before anyone could ask me why I thought this, Charlie let out an exasperated sigh and asked. "So, where do we go from here?"

"I'm going to see what Devon has dug up on the names Conrad's wife gave me," I said. "And then I'm going to do some more local shopping, try to get a better feel for what the townsfolk think about all of this." I caught Charlie's eye in the mirror, knowing she wasn't going to like what I was about to say next. "I don't think we'll need you for anything else for now, Charlie. We've already taken up too much of your time."

"I don't mind," she said quickly, an objection I'd anticipated. "I know most of the locals and the business owners. I can introduce you."

"It's kind of you to offer, but to be honest, I think they'll be more likely to talk freely with us if there isn't a member of law enforcement present."

"Jon's a cop," she pointed out.

"Yes, but they won't know that."

This earned me a scowl. I could practically feel Charlie's unhappiness radiating off her and into the back seat. Newt felt it, too, if the nervous side-eye he gave me was any indication.

When we got back to my suite, I thanked Charlie profusely for her help, told her I planned to leave in the morning, and then went inside to let her have time alone with Jon to say goodbye. It didn't take long and, judging from the way Charlie peeled off down the road five minutes later, it hadn't gone the way she'd hoped.

Jon came inside looking mildly unhappy. "Everything okay?" I asked.

He shrugged. "I think I may have dashed Charlie's hopes. She asked if we could see one another for a dinner or night out and I told her I wasn't in a position to be dating or seeing people romantically right now."

"I take it she didn't receive the news well?"

Jon gave me a pained smile. "She came back at me with a snippy comment, something to the effect of how I was obviously lying because I'm sleeping with you and if I wasn't interested, why didn't I just say so. Then she got in the car and left in a huff."

"Yeah, I heard her drive off. Sorry, Jon."

"It's okay. I feel bad about hurting her feelings, is all. She seems like a nice enough person." He sighed, shrugged again, and smiled meekly. "And I'm afraid I have some bad news for you, too. I got a call from my office while I was out there. My officer who was on vacation had his flight canceled, and he can't get back until Monday. I need to head home tonight so I can cover the day shift tomorrow."

My dismay was obvious. "Oh no. What crappy timing. I was looking forward to more time alone."

"I know and I'm really sorry, Morgan. Believe me, if I could stay, I would." His expression softened and so did his voice with his next words. "I was looking forward to more time alone, too." He clearly felt awful about having to leave so I tried to swallow down the majority of my disappointment.

"No worries," I said. "I understand the obligations you have. I've revamped my list of things to do because the remaining ones won't be particularly helpful. I think I'm going to head home tomorrow. I'll use my time tonight to go over the facts some more because I feel like I'm missing something obvious and haven't quite figured out what it is yet."

Jon narrowed his eyes at me. "Just don't do anything reckless or stupid."

"Of course not."

I hadn't been lying when I told him I'd rethought my approach to things. I'd abandoned what was left on my original checklist of things to do and the line I'd given Charlie about spending time chatting with more local folks had been a ruse. What I planned to do instead that night—plans I had originally intended to include Jon in on—was neither reckless nor stupid, I decided. Still, I was glad I hadn't yet told Jon of my new plan because I suspected he'd disapprove if he knew I intended to go it alone. Though technically I wouldn't be alone. I'd have Newt.

Jon still looked doubtful, so I added, "I'll be fine. I'd go home tonight, too, except I think it will do me good to have one more evening of time away from the store to think. And I'd rather drive when it's light outside."

Jon nodded slowly and I saw suspicion lingering in his eyes. I think he sensed I wasn't being 100 percent honest with him and I realized he'd learned to read me well rather quickly, a fact I found both unsettling and titillating. Or maybe it was simply his skill as a cop.

I helped him load up his SUV and gave him a bottle of water and a couple of the leftover sandwiches from lunch to take with him.

"Don't do anything I wouldn't do," he said as he prepared to leave. "And stay away from Buck Weaver. That guy sounds like trouble."

"I have no intention of dealing with Buck," I said honestly.

I sent Jon on his way a little after two in the afternoon. Our parting kiss was a good deal more involved than the casually friendly pecks we'd shared in the past, and I found myself missing him before he was out of the driveway. Newt and I watched him go and already the world seemed a little less bright, a little less vivid.

Now that the emotional stuff was out of the way, I focused on making the necessary preparations for my evening plans. I opened the back of my car and inventoried the items I'd brought from home, including my blaze orange vest, a cap with a pocket for a small, battery-operated LED light, and the blaze orange halter I had for Newt, which also had reflector strips on it. Then I went inside and loaded what I thought I'd need into my backpack. Finally, I made a pot of coffee and filled my thermos, grabbed Newt's bowls and a day's worth of his food, and loaded a dozen bottles of water into the car.

The last thing I did before leaving the suite was stash Pete Conrad's laptop, plugged in and turned on, behind the couch in the sitting area. In case my note-writing visitor decided to return, I didn't want the computer to disappear.

I drove to Washburn, where my first stop was a grocery store. After getting what I needed there, I pulled into the lot for Mann Brothers Outfitters and went inside to finish off my mental list of needs, leaving Newt in the car with the windows cracked. I didn't bother to lock the doors, not because I thought petty crimes don't happen in small-town Wisconsin, but because Newt was the best theft deterrent device I could have hoped for.

I was inside the store staring at a creative sales display set up like a campsite consisting of four brands of tent with all the accessories and a stuffed black bear standing on its hind legs, when a familiar voice spoke behind me.

"Can I assist you with anything?"

I turned around and saw it was Lloyd Mann.

"Oh, hi," he said, looking as if he wanted to rethink his offer of help.

"Hello, again. And yes, you can help me," I said, deciding not to let him off the hook. "I need a few things. I'm going to camp out in the Chequamegon Forest tonight, and I didn't bring all of my own gear with me. It's kind of a spur-of-the-moment decision."

Lloyd's eyebrows raised. "The Cheq isn't for the uninitiated. It can be dangerous if you don't know what you're doing."

"I'll be fine," I assured him. "I've camped lots of times before, in places much scarier than the Cheq." This was true, though on those other occasions I'd had my parents with me, and their presence had made the prospect less intimidating. With their larger-than-life personalities, insatiable curiosities, and overall joie de vivre, it was hard to believe in real danger when they were around. They'd always seemed so strong and invincible to me. How wrong I'd been.

Lloyd shrugged, "Your funeral," he said.

Lloyd needed to work on his salesmanship. "I need a tent," I told him. "Nothing fancy. Just something to get me through the night. I already own a nice one but it's at home."

Lloyd tilted his head to one side. "And where is home?"

"Door County."

Looking unimpressed, he pointed toward a tent. "For an easy one-nighter, I'd recommend this one. It's a supereasy pop-up. Once you unpackage it, the thing will erect itself. Easy to take down, too." He demonstrated by collapsing and securing the one in the display in about a minute and a half. When he was done, he tossed it back toward where it had been, and the thing sprang open into a perfectly erect tent.

"Nice," I said, duly impressed.

Lloyd nodded his agreement. "It's in the mid-price range,

certainly sturdy enough for one night but not high end." He paused and pointed toward a much pricier tent. "However—"

"This one will do fine," I said, grabbing a box containing the one he'd just demoed from a nearby shelf and hoisting it into my cart.

"Will it be just you or will others be with you?"

The question struck me as odd because the box stated the tent was large enough for two adults. Did he think I was planning a party?

"Just me," I said with a smile.

"Okay. What else do you need?"

I rattled off my mental shopping list and followed him around the store as we collected each item: bear spray, flashlight and headlamp batteries, a kerosene lamp, kerosene, hand and feet warmers, a map of the Chequamegon National Forest, and a pad for the tent floor. I already had my good down sleeping bag and a parka in the car. I'd brought them from home, thinking I might want to do a bit of nighttime surveillance—though I hadn't really planned on camping out—and knowing the sleeping bag made for a cozy wrap on cold nights. With it unzipped and opened all the way, it made a nice coverall for me and Newt, whose body warmth worked like a furnace.

With my list complete, Lloyd steered me to the sole cashier on duty, who was currently ringing up someone else. He then hurried away, seeming glad to be rid of me. It was rather ungrateful of him, if you ask me, considering the amount of money I was spending in his store.

As I waited in line, I saw Lloyd's brother, Trip, filling items in an endcap a couple of aisles away, his progress slow thanks to the cast on his right arm. He saw me, waved, and came over to talk as I waited for the cashier to finish ringing up the person ahead of me.

"Wow, you've quite the haul there," he said. "Did Maureen kick you out of your suite?"

"No, I'm going camping in the Cheq tonight to hunt for a Bigfoot."

I saw the cashier shoot me an amused look. The man she was ringing up had no visible reaction at all. Trip, on the other hand, looked highly concerned.

"You're going to camp out in the Cheq? Is Charlie going with you?"

"Nope. I'm going alone. I'll be fine. I've done this sort of thing plenty of times before."

"Do you have any blaze orange? It's bow- and duck-hunting season out there."

"I do. Thanks for checking, though."

"No problem." He tilted his head much the same way his brother had earlier. "You've got guts," he said. "Just be careful out there, okay? There's little to no cell service in the Cheq." He snapped his fingers. "That reminds me, do you have a first aid kit?"

I didn't, and while it was something I should have thought of, I was willing to do without one. "I'm only going overnight."

Trip wagged a finger at me. "You can't be too careful. We have complimentary ones in the back we give out to our best customers. They're basic but it will do the job for most things." This garnered him an odd look from the cashier and an affronted one from the male customer ahead of me, who I'm guessing hadn't been offered a free first aid kit.

"Sure, okay," I said, sensing Trip wasn't going to let the matter drop. At first, I'd thought his offer had been a sales pitch but if he was willing to give me one for free, what the heck.

"I'll be right back," he said, and then he took off at a gallop down a nearby aisle.

The cashier had me fully checked out and was printing my receipt by the time Trip returned, slightly out of breath and with a first aid kit in hand. "Here you go," he said, slipping a cardboard box with a big red cross on top of it into one of my bags. "Sorry it took me so long. We must be running low because I had a tough time finding one. This one has been opened but I checked the contents, and everything is there. I taped it shut, so it's nothing fancy but it will do the job if you need it." He gave me an apologetic smile.

Hard to complain since it was free. "Thank you."

"You're very welcome." He tipped an imaginary hat and then added, "Would you have dinner with me some night while you're here?"

I stared at him, momentarily stymied. Hadn't we done this dance already?

"What?" he said, looking worried. "You aren't married, are you? You're not wearing a ring."

"No. No, I'm not married," I said, finally finding my voice. The cashier watched me with amusement.

"Then what do you say?" Trip asked with a smile.

"It's sweet of you to ask but I live in Door County, and I find long distance things don't work well. Besides, I'm kind of seeing someone else right now."

Trip flushed, smiled, and said, "Understood. My loss, but I had to try. Nothing ventured and all that." He turned away and hurried off, disappearing into the depths of the store.

As I wheeled my cart out to my car, I felt bad for Trip's obvious awkwardness at being turned down, but I also felt good about claiming I was seeing someone else. Yes, I'd said 'kind of seeing' but still. For me it was progress.

It took me several minutes to load my new purchases into the cargo area of my car and I ended up moving some of the more sensitive toys, like my drone and night vision binoculars, up front to make room for the new stuff. I added the grocery items I'd bought to my backpack and moved it up front, too.

Newt, who had been dozing on the back seat, didn't bother to get up. As I pulled out of the store lot, I noticed a sheriff's department cruiser parked alongside the building. And standing beside it, glaring at me, was Buck Weaver.

CHAPTER 29

I pulled into the empty parking lot of a church near the edge of town and took out my map of the Chequamegon National Forest so I could study it and figure out exactly where I wanted to go. Part of the reason I'd pulled over was to consult the map, but another part was to look for Buck Weaver's cruiser. I'd half expected him to pull me over after I'd left the store, but after several minutes with no sign of him, I relaxed and focused on the map.

I found the spot where Bodie Erickson's attack had occurred and the nearby lake I'd spotted on the other map. The lake, a freshwater source, was where I wanted to be. Studying the roads and trails on the map, I took a few minutes to memorize the way there. I hadn't paid close attention to all the turns Charlie had taken the other day when we'd visited the Erickson site, but even if I had, our rapid getaway route when we were trying to lose Hans Baumann's tail had definitely clouded things for me.

The lake was in an isolated spot, but it appeared to be reasonably accessible with a short hike. Whether or not there would be a good place to set up camp remained to be seen. I marked a spot where I could park and I figured if the terrain turned out to be more than I felt I could comfortably manage, I'd go back to the drawing board. I folded the map so it would be easy to consult again if necessary, setting it on the front seat beside me.

It took me half an hour to get deep into the forest region, and it was nearing five in the evening by the time I reached the spot I had in mind. The sun hung low in the sky and the horizon was painted in glorious shades of gold, red, pink, and orange. I found a small clearing of dirt along the side of the road to park on and checked my map again. Once I was certain of my orientation, I geared up, making sure both Newt and I were decked out in our reflective, blaze orange gear.

The shadows grew long as Newt and I navigated our way into the woods, heading in the direction of the lake. We hiked up and down hills, across a small ravine, and over downed limbs and protruding roots. After fifteen minutes, I stopped long enough to turn on my headlamp and check my compass headings before continuing. Five minutes later I was starting to doubt myself, but then we crested a small hill and there below us was the lake, its surface dappled with sparkling remnants of daylight.

I was lucky enough to find a flat, relatively clear spot with soft ground cover about a hundred and fifty feet up from the lake and I stopped and slid my backpack off. I lit the kerosene lamp and hung it from a tree branch, turned off my headlamp, and then set up the tent in less than a minute. After putting down some kibble and water for Newt, I settled onto a nearby log and munched on one of the protein bars I'd grabbed at the grocery store.

Our world rapidly diminished to the small circle of light cast off by the kerosene lamp, and I eventually extinguished it and let my eyes adjust to the dusky light. Newt sat beside me, nose to the air, nostrils working overtime, his head turning first one way then another in response to the sounds of rustling critters all around us. I draped an arm over his neck and slowly stroked his shoulder to keep him calm. Despite his interest, he made no effort to go after any of the scurrying noises, as if he understood he was a guest in their home now.

The temperature dropped quickly as the sun finally slipped below the horizon, and the golden surface of the lake turned inky blue, then black. I slipped on my parka, poured a cup of coffee from my thermos, and sat on my log again as the shadows claimed the last vestiges of light, spreading like an oil spill through the trees. Within minutes the darkness was nearly absolute, and stars started popping out overhead—so many stars!

After testing my knowledge of the constellations, I turned on my headlamp and took up the bowl of dry food I'd put down for Newt—I didn't want to attract any woodland critters, big or small— repacking the kibble in a plastic container and stashing it in my backpack. I dug my night vision binoculars and my flashlight out of the backpack and leashed up Newt. Then the two of us ventured off into the surrounding trees.

We worked our way around the lake slowly, flashlight to the ground most of the time, though I occasionally studied nearby trees for evidence of antler rubbing. Every few minutes I stopped, turned off my lights, and used the night vision binoculars to scan more distant surroundings, spotting a rabbit, a pair of raccoons, and a possum, but nothing bigger. More importantly, I saw no evidence of human presence or activity.

The lake sat nestled in a bowl of land, a natural hollow surrounded by hills and ridges. It wasn't a big lake, but it took us the better part of three hours to circle the entire perimeter thanks to blockades created by trees and bushes, and deceptive areas along the shoreline that appeared solid but were actually boggy land obscured by plant growth. The going was further complicated by heavy undergrowth. I looked for any indication of pathways or trails leading down to the water but found nothing. Nor did I spot any scat. I planned to look around some more come daylight, but by the time I completed our circuit of the lake, all I wanted to do was crawl into some warmth.

I snuggled beneath my sleeping bag inside the tent. Newt stretched his warm body out beside me and I pulled the down sleeping bag close around us both. I didn't expect to sleep much, if at all, but I dropped off almost instantly, only to be abruptly awakened by Newt's low growl sometime later.

It was pitch black inside the tent and I felt around for my cell phone to see what time it was: just after midnight. Blinded by the light of my phone's screen, I set it down and felt around for my night vision binoculars and the flashlight. I was able to make out the door of the tent and, rising onto my hands and knees, I reached over and carefully undid the zipper, letting the flap fall open. I hung the binoculars around my neck, told Newt to stay, and crawled out of the tent, the flashlight tucked into my coat pocket.

A quarter moon faintly illuminated the lake's surface and I stared into the darkness, barely able to make out the shapes of the nearby trees. I turned on the binoculars and the attached infrared light, and my surroundings sprang to life in the viewfinder. I scanned the area closest to the lake first, but when I saw nothing there, I looked at the woods on either side of me and then behind me. Seconds later I froze as something moved about a hundred yards away up the hill toward the road where I'd parked the car. The crunch of distant footsteps, tentative and halting, carried to me over the night air. I briefly caught glimpses of a distinctly human shape making his or her way through and around the trees, but the woods were too dense, and the tree trunks spaced too close together to ever get a full view. Still, I saw enough to be certain it was a person and not a bear or any other animal skulking around.

I turned off the infrared light, knowing it could be seen, and closed my eyes to listen. There were a few more tentative steps with twigs snapping and leaves crunching. I looked through the binoculars again without the infrared on and made out a hooded parka much like my own. What I didn't see was a bow or a rifle, making me think the person wasn't a hunter.

I heard the low rumble of Newt's growl inside the tent and did a quick palm pat on my hip, letting him know he could come out and sit beside me. He was at my side in an instant and after a brief sniff of the night air, he was laser focused on the human figure above us. On the off chance it was a hunter up there, I whispered to Newt to stay. The last thing I needed was some trigger-happy poacher shooting Newt because he looked like a deer.

I sat frozen, like a trapped animal, my thoughts whirling. Who the hell was up there skulking around? And *why* were they up there skulking around? Should I shout out to them?

My instincts screamed at me to stay put and keep quiet, and I decided to listen to them. Then a scary thought came to me. Could it be David? Had he finally decided to track me down? Had he followed me out here into these secluded woods to kill me and finish the job he'd started two years ago when he'd murdered my parents?

The air seemed to drop ten degrees suddenly, and I broke out in a cold sweat. My breathing turned rapid and shallow, creating tiny clouds of mist in the night air. I forced myself to hold each breath for a second or two and let it out slowly. My heart refused to follow suit, however, and it went from a quick canter to a full-out gallop.

I'd lost sight of the human interloper when I'd briefly looked down at Newt but knew he was still close by when Newt decided to turn his low-throated growl into a menacing, snarling series of barks. In an instant, the occasional crunch of those distant footsteps became a frantic thrashing. I hastily scanned the area with the night vision binoculars, cursing when the mist from my own breath briefly fogged the glass. The rapid footsteps continued, and I couldn't tell if they were coming at me or moving away. The narrow field of vision I had with the binocs made it hard to scan quickly, and I turned the infrared light back on just in time to catch sight of a retreating human shape seconds before it disappeared over a ridge. Knowing the person was retreating eased my panic some, but something I saw in the last second before the figure disappeared had my heart racing again. There'd been the glint of something in one of the hands. A knife, perhaps? Fine. I had a hunting knife with me, too. In my backpack. In the tent. *Great thinking, Morgan.*

This prompted action, however belated and illogical, on my part.

"Who's out there?" I yelled, my voice trembling from fear, anger, and adrenaline. Angry with myself for letting my fear show even a little, I braced myself and yelled out again, happy to hear solid determination in my voice this time. "I'm armed and my dog will tear you to shreds if you come any closer."

I looked and listened, still frozen to my spot, wide awake and with my senses on hyperdrive. An owl hooted. I inhaled the scents of pine, earth, dead leaves, and my own fear. Bits of mist curled and wound around tree trunks like wandering wraiths in the night. Newt calmed, and eventually I did the same. I swapped the binoculars for the flashlight, running the beam around my immediate area. I had a momentary start when I saw the glow of eyes looking back at me, but I quickly realized they belonged to a raccoon.

Then, carried upon the chill night air, I heard the distant rumble of a car being started and driven away. I breathed a sigh of relief and crawled back into the tent. Newt followed and I snuggled beneath the sleeping bag again, curling up next to his warm, furry body.

CHAPTER 30

There was too much nervous adrenaline pumping through my system to hope for any more sleep. It didn't stop me from trying, however, and I tossed and turned for several hours, listening to the sounds of the forest and Newt's breathing alongside me. Memories of my parents drifted in and out of my thoughts, good memories of fun and laughter and cryptid hunting adventures in woods much like the ones surrounding me. Inevitably, these fond reminiscences gave way to horrific flashbacks and thoughts of David Johnson.

In hindsight, I realized how silly it had been to think it might have been David out there skulking about. Had he wanted to, he could have found and killed me any number of times in the two years since he'd murdered my parents. I'd never made any effort to hide from him because I didn't think he had any reason to come after me.

I wondered where he was now. Probably hiding out overseas somewhere, living a low-key life. The smart thing for him to do was to stay disappeared and let the case turn colder than the night air outside my tent. But he was greedy and hadn't managed to score any real money from me, so perhaps he was already looking for or bilking his next victim and I'd merely been practice for him.

Sometime later I was once again startled by the sound of Newt growling and the sharp shock of cold air as he got up and left my side. He stood at the entrance to the tent, his head tilted as he listened, a menacing rumble emanating from deep in his throat. Had the skulker returned?

With a feeling of déjà vu, I opened the tent flap and crawled outside, taking the night vision binoculars and flashlight with me, though this time I also grabbed the hunting knife from my pack. Newt followed and sat at my side, staring fixedly off to my right. I looked through the binoculars with the infrared light on and slowly scanned my surroundings, starting with where the skulker had been earlier. I didn't see anything unusual, so I slowly moved the binoculars to my right, in the direction Newt was staring. Again, I saw nothing unusual and when I'd covered an arc of one hundred and eighty degrees, I raised the binoculars higher and came back over the same territory. Still nothing. I did one more sweep on that side of the lake, raising the binoculars higher still to catch the tops of the hills and a nearby ridge surrounding the hollow we were in.

Something big moved on top of the ridge in a grove of trees, but it was too far away to see clearly. I zoomed the binoculars and adjusted the focus, but this made my field of vision so small that even a tiny bit of movement on my part led to a huge jump in the area I was looking at. I'd lost sight of whatever it was, so I zoomed back out and slowly scanned up and down, back and forth, until I was focused on the top line of the ridge again. I zoomed in a little at a time while searching across the ridgeline, honestly expecting to see a deer any second. Finally, I saw movement again and zeroed in on it. Then I gasped.

For a fleeting second or two, I saw the animal clear as day, squatting at the base of a large, gnarly tree and then rising up to stand on two legs. I saw the slightly hunched posture, the thick fur covering it from head to toe, and I even caught a glimpse of oddly humanlike eyes as it turned to face me, staring in my general direction. I swore I felt a connection to it, as if a subtle, nonverbal form of communication had passed between us. The hairs along the back of my neck rose to attention and an army of chill bugs raced down my spine, making me shiver.

Beside me, Newt let out a loud bark and the response from the creature was instantaneous. It turned away, appeared to take a step or two, and then simply vanished. Belatedly, I realized I should have triggered the camera option on the binoculars and saved an image of the creature to the SD card, but I'd been so stunned, and things had happened so fast, it hadn't occurred to me.

"Damn," I muttered. Newt nudged my arm with his nose, making my field of view leap away from the spot where the creature had been. I lowered the binoculars, looked down at him, and sighed. Sensing my dismay, he whined and wagged his tail tentatively, unsure if he'd done good.

"It's okay, buddy," I said, stroking his big head. "I appreciate your efforts to protect me. I just wish you'd waited a smidge longer to do it." Newt's tail picked up the pace, letting me know he was happy with my faint praise.

The sky had a steely gray hue to it, and I took my cell phone out of my pocket to check the time. It was closing in on six in the morning and the sun would be coming up soon. When it did, I planned to hike up to the spot where I'd seen the creature. It had been doing something at the base of the tree and I wanted to know what. I studied and memorized a couple of nearby landmarks; then I went back into the tent and poured myself a cup of coffee.

Newt came into the tent with me, still wagging his tail excitedly as if he knew we were about to embark on another adventure. He watched me like a hawk, interpreting every movement I made, every facial expression I had, trying to figure out when we would go. I carried my coffee outside and sat on the downed log with my sleeping bag draped over my shoulders for warmth, watching the sun come up. Shards of sunlight shone down through a canopy of green and gold, highlighting the forest floor in an undulating mosaic of dark and light. Fog hovered over the surface of the lake, and I wouldn't have been surprised to see a ghost ship emerge from the mist. There was something magical and miraculous about watching the world awaken and doing it in a forest populated with all manner of flora and fauna. It made me feel privileged and special.

By the time I finished my coffee, there was enough sunlight to easily see without the aid of any devices. I shrugged off my sleeping bag and slipped into my blaze orange vest and cap. Then I grabbed my backpack and packed the flashlight in it, just in case, the bear spray, just in case, my hunting knife, just in case, and my phone, though this latter item was more for picture-taking than calling or texting since I had no cell service.

I put Newt's blaze orange vest on him, a task made difficult by his excitement, which had his entire body wagging, not just his tail. Then the two of us peed at the base of a nearby tree, a peculiar form of bonding. When we were done, I leashed Newt up and off we went, making our way toward that ridge, a trek requiring a couple of lengthy detours to avoid the marshy, orange-yellow tamarack bogs and land too steep or cluttered with downed trees to be traversable. I followed a path similar to the one I'd taken last night when I'd circled the lake, but instead of sticking close to the water, I steadily climbed to a higher elevation. Newt marked our path through and around brambles and thickets, and between groves of black spruce, maple, oak, and aspen trees. He pulled me along slowly, and I nudged him a couple of times in the direction we needed to go, gradually making our way up to the first of the landmarks I'd eyed earlier. By then I was nearly at the top of the ridge and Newt stopped and whined, his nose to the air. At first I thought he was picking up on a nearby animal or other intruder, but then I caught a distinctive whiff of decay and covered my nose. I recognized it immediately; it was the smell of death.

The stench intensified as we continued toward the final landmark—the large, gnarly tree—and as I approached it, I saw why the creature I'd seen earlier had seemed to simply disappear when Newt had barked. The tree stood on a narrow strip of land with a steep drop on the opposite side. Two steps back and the creature had disappeared over the edge. I looked back in the direction of my campsite and saw I had a clear line of vision to it but a prohibitively steep and cluttered hillside between the tent and where I stood. When I finally got within a few feet of the tree, I discovered the source of the foul odor. On the ground beneath it was a partially decomposed body.

I instructed Newt to sit and stay, knowing the smell, which was so off-putting to me, would be a lure to him. It's an instinctive behavior for dogs to roll in nasty-smelling stuff. They do it to mask their own scent, and given the chance, I wouldn't put it past Newt to flop and squirm in the mess.

I approached the body and saw it was in the advanced stages of decomposition with bones showing and maggots working on the still-soft parts. The recent cool fall temperatures, which had neared freezing on some nights, had slowed the process but nature was slowly reclaiming the body. Despite this, there was enough form left to make out the apelike features, the body-covering fur, and the bolt embedded in its chest, held upright by the two ribs it had gone between. As my eyes scanned lower, I let out a little gasp of shock and sadness when I saw its belly.

I took out my phone and snapped a dozen pictures. Then I knelt to examine branches laid out on top of the body in a manner suggesting purposeful placement as opposed to random droppage. The teeth of the animal were exposed, and a small stick protruded from between two of them. I understood then with a little hitch of my heart why the other creature had been here. I also felt certain the other creature had been the one that had attacked Bodie Erickson. Now I knew why.

I stood and looked down the steep hillside behind me, wondering where the animal had gone to. It could be anywhere within the more than 858,000 acres of land making up the Chequamegon National Forest. Was it alone now? Or were there others?

I took a moment to listen to the forest, to birdsong growing louder with each passing minute, to the scurry of tiny feet beneath the thick ground cover, to the distant splash of a fish surfacing on the lake, to the gentle susurrus of the wind rustling the treetops. After a look at Newt, I took a cue from him and put my nose to the air, closing my eyes and taking in the fetid smell of the body at my feet, but also catching whiffs of pine, water, earth, and moss. I could feel the warmth of the sun on my face as its rays filtered down through the overhead canopy. It was tranquil and serene, and for a brief moment, I envied the creatures of these woods, coveted the earthly sounds and smells, the feel of nature surrounding them, and the simplicity of life without all the strict social constructs we humans have to deal with.

Then I looked down at the body again and realized the simple life these creatures lived came with cold, hard realities, like the need to find food and water, the need to survive harsh weather conditions, the need to find shelter, and the need to avoid predators. Sadly, we humans were the deadliest predators of all.

A wash of guilt, of shame for my species, spilled over me. Newt whimpered and I thought he must have sensed my mood, so I turned to tell him I was okay, but then saw he was staring off into the trees beyond me, farther along the ridge.

I felt it then—eyes watching me.

Perhaps I should have been afraid, but I felt oddly calm. There was a dogwood bush about ten feet away and I walked over and broke off a small branch with green leaves, small white berries, and a red stem. Then I walked back to the body, knelt beside it, and gently laid the branch over the swollen belly, the skin of which had long ago split open to reveal the fetus beneath.

I stood and looked in the direction Newt was staring, not seeing anything at first but then catching the slightest hint of movement up in a tree maybe a hundred yards away. A dark form, the suggestion of fur, and . . . had it been the slow nod of a head? I felt the connection again and nodded back, thinking as I did so about Walt Kendall and how he'd said the creature had seemed to fly up and disappear. That's how it would have appeared given what agile tree climbers these animals were. The movements of the creature I'd seen in the ravine at the dog park made sense now, too.

Most of the puzzle pieces fell into place and so many things made sense to me now. The remaining question was, what should I do about it?

CHAPTER 31

The return hike to my campsite went a little easier since it was mostly downhill, and while packing up my campsite, I sent a mental thank-you to Lloyd Mann for recommending the pop-up tent. Just as he had promised, the takedown had been an easy two-minute task. I fed and watered Newt, and while packing up everything to haul back to the car, I reviewed what I knew in my head, tossing facts and theories around. Some pieces still didn't fit.

I gave the campsite one last look, to make sure I was practicing leave-no-trace camping but also to share a last commune with nature. The peace and beauty of the place made me reconsider leaving, but then I remembered there was a murderer on the loose and I had a job to do. Before hiking out, I stared at the gnarly tree on the ridge hoping I might get one last look at the creature I'd seen during the night, but if it was there, I couldn't see it.

On the drive back to Bayfield, I spotted a restaurant along the main highway in Washburn advertising all-day breakfast. After my camping adventure, a hearty breakfast sounded good, and my stomach rumbled its agreement. The restaurant struck a bell with me, and I figured Charlie must have mentioned and perhaps recommended the place at some point, but then my phone started dinging with notifications, my thoughts went in a different direction, and another piece of the puzzle fell into place.

I arrived back at my suite a little after eleven and found Charlie parked alongside the house waiting for me. I was annoyed to find her there because my phone had exploded with messages and voice mail notifications once I was within cell phone range, and I was eager to see who they were from and what they were about.

"Where have you been?" she asked irritably. "I was here early this morning, and your car was gone. I checked with Maureen, and she said you never came back last night and hadn't checked out. I was worried sick, especially after the note you found yesterday."

"I went camping," I said, walking to the door of my suite and unlocking it.

Charlie reared back and looked at me as if I'd just said I'd been to Mars. "Camping? Where?"

"Beside the lake closest to where Bodie Erickson was killed."

Charlie stared at me, mouth agape, clearly unable to formulate her next question. I let Newt out of the car, locked it, and headed into my suite. I didn't extend an invitation to Charlie to come inside, but she followed me anyway. After putting down my backpack, I sneaked a look at my phone, saw messages from both Devon and Jon, and a missed call each from the two of them, as well as one from Charlie.

"You went camping by yourself out there?" Charlie said with disbelief.

"No, I went with Newt," I said, smiling. Judging from Charlie's expression, she didn't appreciate my attempt at humor. "I'm not a novice when it comes to camping," I told her in a more serious tone. "I did it all the time when I was younger."

Charlie pursed her lips into a thin line of exasperation. She folded her arms over her chest and started tapping one foot irritably. "Why?" she asked. "What were you trying to find?"

"Proof of your theory that there's something out there. And now I have it." I'd be lying if I said I wasn't amused by the way her arms fell to her sides and her jaw dropped. I almost hated having to deliver the buzz kill. "Unfortunately, it doesn't answer all of our questions since I'm now certain one of our victims was killed by a human animal rather than a wild one."

Charlie's eyes grew wide as she stared at me, transfixed. "What did you find? What do you mean?" She propped one arm on her hip, rolled her eyes, and said, "Come on, woman. You're killing me here. Tell me."

"I'm sorry to torture you, Charlie, but I need you to bear with me just a little bit longer."

Charlie whipped her head around and stared off to the side for a moment before turning back to face me with a look of exasperated incredulity. "You have *got* to be kidding me!"

"Let me do my job," I said calmly. "My full job. There are several questions I need answers to first, and I think some of them may be in the messages I have waiting for me and haven't been able to check yet." I showed her my phone. "Give me until tonight, tomorrow morning at the latest, okay?"

Charlie gawked at me a little longer before spinning around and stomping out of my suite like a petulant child, slamming the door behind her. I couldn't say I blamed her. To be so close to an answer and then have it withheld had to be frustrating, but she'd have to deal with it. I wasn't about to put forth half-baked theories and wild accusations. My reputation was on the line.

My stomach growled so loudly Newt looked at me and cocked his head sideways. After making sure he had food in his bowl, I settled in at the table with one of the protein bars I'd bought and a cup of fresh coffee. I read the text messages on my phone first—the two from Jon were simple enough, one from last night letting me know he was back home and the other from early this morning asking me to let him know I was okay. The texts from Devon, the first sent during the wee hours of the morning and the second about an hour ago, were even simpler: Call me.

Next, I listened to the voice messages, doing Charlie's first, sent a little over an hour ago. I heard a hint of the panic I'd seen in her upon my arrival, and listened as she said she was at my place—where the hell was I? Next came a message from Jon asking me to call him, his voice notably more emphatic than his usual voice mails. His message had been left a little after Charlie's and I wondered if she had called him once she discovered me missing.

In contrast, Devon's message, left at the crack of dawn just before I'd made my discovery at the base of the gnarly tree, was an upbeat request to call and hear about all the "great stuff" he'd dug up for me. I was about to do so when Jon called me.

"Hey, Jon," I said, putting him on speaker.

"Thank goodness," he said with a huge sigh of relief. "I was getting worried when you didn't answer my texts or return my call."

"Sorry. I was camping."

This revelation was met with several beats of silence. "You were camping," Jon eventually repeated, his voice deadpan.

"Yep, I pitched a tent out in the Chequamegon National Forest, and Newt and I spent the night out there. And in doing so, I solved one of the deaths in question. I now know exactly what killed Bodie Erickson and why."

"You camped alone in the forest?" Jon sounded irritated now. "Why would you do something risky like that?"

"Risky?"

"You're a woman, camping alone in a big, isolated wooded area," Jon said.

"I was going to ask you to come with me but then you had to return home. Besides, I wasn't alone. I had Newt with me. And—"

"I know you think Newt is your great protector, but, Morgan, he's not some kind of superdog."

Says you. "I had a hunting knife with me. And bear spray. We were fine." Now it was my turn to sound annoyed. I didn't appreciate having to defend my choices and was frankly surprised he'd skipped right over my revelation regarding Bodie Erickson's death.

There were more beats of silence, followed by another sigh. "I'm sorry, Morgan, but I was really worried about you. Why the hell didn't you tell me you were planning to go camping out there?"

"Because once I knew you couldn't come with me, I figured you'd try to talk me out of it."

To his credit, he didn't deny this. "It scares me when you take risks," he said, his voice softer. "I care about you, Morgan. I don't want anything to happen to you."

Those last few words, spoken in his healing-but-still-wounded voice, instantly deflated my lingering balloon of resentment. After what had happened to his wife and child, it had been selfish and inconsiderate of me not to keep him apprised of my plans.

"I'm sorry, Jon. I should have told you yesterday before you left. To be honest, I didn't say anything on purpose because I knew you'd tell me not to do it and I didn't want to argue about it. It was something I felt I had to do. Can we hash this out later since you now know I'm safe and managed to solve part of this case? I really want to call Devon to see what he's found out for me."

There was a long pause, so long I thought maybe our call had dropped. "Wait, you solved part of the case?" Jon said. "What do you mean?"

There we were! Back on track. "I know the why and the what." I told him what had happened during the night and what I'd found on top of the ridge near my campsite.

"Chimpanzees? You're sure?" Jon's skepticism rang clear.

"Yep, and large ones at that. I think it was a couple, a male and a female. And Bodie Erickson shot the pregnant female while her partner was nearby. That's what provoked the unfortunate attack. It also explains why Bob Keller was confused about the location of the attacking animal. It hadn't come from the direction Erickson shot toward."

"How in the world did two chimpanzees end up living in the Chequamegon Forest?"

"That's the million-dollar question. What's more, I suspect it may be more than two. I have some ideas, but I need to do a little more research."

"More than two? That's crazy," Jon said. After a few seconds of silence, during which I assumed his brain was struggling to assimilate this information, he said, "And Pete Conrad? How does he fit into this picture?"

"He doesn't, technically. I'm convinced he was killed by a human, someone who knew enough about Bodie Erickson's attack to try to mimic the injuries. He or she did a decent job of it, too. Though perhaps not good enough."

"He or *she*?" Jon echoed.

"Just being politically correct," I said, but Jon wasn't fooled.

"Charlie is on your list of suspects?"

"Right now, the entire town of Bayfield is on my list of suspects. Let me see what Devon has dug up for me before you make me commit to anything, okay?"

"All right, but will you promise to be careful and to keep me posted?"

"I will. I swear. It was thoughtless of me not to tell you what I was planning for last night. I really, truly am sorry."

"Thank you." I heard yet another sigh, but this one had a ring of resignation to it. "And you're right, you know. I would have tried to talk you out of it."

"You realize I would have gone anyway, right?"

He chuckled and it was my turn to sag with relief, knowing the relaxed, easy-going character of our relationship had been restored. At least for the time being. I promised again to keep him updated and ended our call.

It was chilly inside the suite, and I wandered into the bedroom to get a sweater. As I went to my suitcase across the room, I caught a whiff of burnt wood, the same smell I'd noticed in the stack of wood in the house's backyard. Then I saw the window at the far end of the room was open several inches and since it faced the back of the house, the smell was indeed the same one I'd noticed before. But why was the window open? I felt certain it hadn't been before. I walked over and closed it, flipping over the lock. Had it been locked before? This, I wasn't so sure about. Could Jon have opened the window while he was here and then forgotten to close it?

Then I remembered the laptop and I hurried out to the main sitting area to look behind the couch. I sighed with relief as I pulled the computer from its hiding place. I set it on the table and then went back to my suitcase to grab my sweater. I experienced a tickle in my brain again as I smelled the lingering dregs of smoky, burnt wood. Something about that smell was trying to connect with an elusive bit of knowledge lurking inside my brain, but whatever it was, it kept doing a vanishing act.

The thought of vanishing acts made me think of magic and shows and then, in the blink of an eye, I finally made the connection.

CHAPTER 32

⌒

I grabbed my phone and hit the speed dial number for Devon, who answered on the first ring.

"Boss, you're going to be so happy with what I found out for you, you're going to feel compelled to give me another raise. A significant one."

I chuckled. "Tell me what you have first."

"Well, I got this brainstorm in the middle of the night last night. The place this Conrad guy worked for, Teach and Springer, is a huge company with several hundred employees, some of whom work out of remote offices in other cities. Plus, some of those employees manage financial portfolios requiring them to be on top of foreign stock markets in other countries, in other time zones. Those kinds of setups typically require having an IT department available twenty-four seven in case the employees have a problem, day or night."

"Okay," I said, not sure where he was going.

"And there's one thing I know about IT departments, or any department operating on a twenty-four-seven schedule. The weekend and night shifts have the highest rates of turnover. If you're going to try to bamboozle an IT department, you want to do it on a weekend night shift."

"You bamboozled them?"

"I sure did." I heard the pride in his voice and in my mind's eye I saw his face with its beaming, toothy smile. "I should win an Oscar for the performance I put on for this poor gal. I discovered the IT department Teach and Springer uses is located offsite in Texas. I called it in the middle of the night and pretended to be Pete Conrad, hoping no one would know I wasn't him or that he was dead. I told the woman who answered that I was away on vacation and had a client—a very big and important client—who needed me to do some emergency money transfers first thing Monday morning with the New Zealand Stock Exchange, which happens to be eighteen hours ahead of us. I told her I was unable to log onto my computer because I forgot to bring the booklet with my passwords with me on my vacation. I was appropriately frantic but also a little flirtatious with her. Basically, I charmed the heck out of her."

I had no doubt he had. "She gave you the password for Conrad's work stuff?"

"She reset it for me and gave me a temporary new one to get me into both his work files and his email."

"You *are* a genius," I said. "Let me get the computer and see if it works."

"No need. I already did it. I've been in there poking around for a while now."

"What? How? I have the computer here with me."

"And you left it on. I was able to access it using the remote app we opened earlier. You never shut it down."

I was duly impressed with his ingenuity. "Okay. You'll have a bonus on your next paycheck. And be sure to put these hours down on your time card."

"Happy to help," he said.

"Tell me what you found. Anything of interest?"

"Yes and no. I looked at spreadsheets and data for the names Conrad's wife gave you, but I'm no financial expert and have no idea what any of it means. It was all just a bunch of numbers, letters, and gobbledygook to me. However, when I went into Conrad's email account, I did find a handful of recent exchanges between him and a woman named Anna Perry indicating there were financial irregularities Conrad needed to clear up. This Perry woman seemed open to the idea at first but then started resisting. The last email they exchanged was two days before Conrad came up here for his trip and he told Anna Perry he planned to visit her when he was here."

"Do you know what kind of business this Perry woman operates?"

"Maybe but I need to run something by you first. In those names you gave me, the businesses Conrad's wife gave you, you mentioned a Berryman Industries. I wasn't able to find a company with that name in Conrad's files. But Anna Perry's company was mentioned in one of his emails. It was Perryman Industries."

I took a few seconds to sort out what he was saying. "You're thinking I misheard it when Conrad's wife said it."

"It did occur to me."

"You're probably right. I should have had her spell it out for me. B and P can sound alike, especially over a phone. Sorry."

"No biggie."

"Does this Anna Perry live in the Bayfield area?"

"I honestly don't know. I couldn't find anyone with that name in the white pages listings online, but these days those aren't very inclusive. Everyone has cell phones. I tried to trace the IP address the emails came from, but Anna uses a VPN, or virtual private network. And Teach and Springer uses one also, plus encryption, making it all a major headache to figure out."

"Okay," I said, massaging my temples. My lack of sleep was catching up to me and making my brain muzzy. "Let me see if I have this straight. You bamboozled the IT department at Teach and Springer and accessed Conrad's emails, where you found the name of a woman who had issues with Conrad that might provide a motive, but you have no idea who she is, where she is, or if she had anything to do with his death?"

"Oh, ye of little faith," Devon said, sounding wounded.

"Sorry. I'm just tired, physically and mentally. Is there more?"

"No, but there will be now that I've run the Berryman, Perryman thing by you. On a hunch, I did look into Perryman Industries. It's Germany-based, so records are a little harder to come by. I'm still digging."

"Good. Keep at it. What you've accomplished so far is amazing, as usual. Do you think you can squeeze one more project into your day for me?"

"Of course. What do you need?"

I told him about my experience out in the forest, describing the live animal I'd seen and the dead, pregnant one. I had an idea about where they might have come from, and I wanted Devon to see if he could find supporting evidence for my theory.

"I'll see what I can dig up," he told me when he was done. "You're sure they were chimpanzees?"

"Absolutely," I told him. "Despite the decay on the body of the dead one, the facial features and opposable thumbs on the hands and feet were clear and distinct enough to make identification possible. And while the live one I saw was admittedly from a distance and in the dark, these night vision binoculars I have are amazing. It was a chimpanzee, and a big one."

"Doesn't the behavior you described seem a bit odd?" Devon said, clearly not convinced yet.

"Not at all. Chimpanzees are very social animals and they've been shown to act in socially meaningful ways when they experience death, particularly if it's a chimp they've bonded with. Sometimes they react with frenzied emotions, jumping about and screeching. Other times they act with solemnity, curious prodding, or ponderous behaviors. They've been witnessed grooming dead bodies. It looked as if the male I saw—and I confess, I'm taking an educated leap here based on size and behavior because I wasn't able to verify the gender—brought plants to place on the female's body. And the stick in between her teeth could be indicative of a type of grooming behavior observed before in chimpanzees attending to a dead family member. This is going to sound gross, but they've been known to pick out food particles stuck in the teeth of a dead chimp and eat them."

"Ew!" Devon groaned. "I could have done without that visual. You've convinced me. No need to describe anything else. I'll start looking into this. Are you coming home anytime soon?"

"Maybe tomorrow. I'll let you know." Then I disconnected.

After my call with Devon, I leashed up Newt and took him for a walk so I could sort my thoughts. One of the things bothering me about this case, one of many, was the footprint at the Conrad site. It had been located a good twenty feet from the water's edge in that dry, dusty dirt and yet it had appeared nearly perfectly formed, its shape maintained over a period of days. I'd had Devon check on the rainfall statistics for this area when I'd first arrived, and he told me it had been an unusually dry year, with less than an inch of rainfall all summer. And what had fallen had been early in the season. The area had been under a serious drought for months.

The dryness helped explain one thing for me, but it complicated another. I'd been convinced the footprint at Conrad's death site had been a fake since day one. In order to get an imprint molded as well as that one had been, the earth would have needed to have a claylike consistency. Yet the dirt at the site was dry as dust, meaning water had to have been added to the spot where the impression had been made.

Something the drought helped to explain was the sudden increase in Bigfoot sightings in Bayfield and the surrounding areas. The summer drought had caused levels in the lakes and rivers to drop, and some bodies of water had turned brackish. This might well have forced all kinds of animals—including chimpanzees—into populated areas in search of fresh drinking water. It explained the creature Nathan Hotchkiss and his dogs had seen. It explained the creature Walt had seen. It even explained the one I had seen at the dog park my first night in Bayfield, though I still thought a bear was behind the attack on Freda Becker's dog.

Newt and I reached the waterfront park across the street from my suite, and I let him off his leash to frolic along the shoreline while I sat on a nearby bench. I thought about Conrad and how his wife had canceled her plans to come with him for their annual trip because of the interested buyers in her high-end house, buyers who had never shown up. Somehow, I didn't think it was a coincidence, but to prove it, I was going to need Jon's help. I took out my cell phone and called him.

Like Devon, he answered on the first ring. "Are you okay?"

"Yes, yes, I'm fine," I assured him. "I'm calling because I need your help with something."

"Such as?"

"The reason Pete Conrad's wife didn't come with him on this trip strikes me as a little too convenient. Is there any way you can trace the phones used to call her about the showings?"

"You mean the ones who didn't show up?"

"Yes."

I heard Jon sigh. "It's not my case or my jurisdiction."

"I have the phone numbers. Mrs. Conrad got the calls on a toll-free line she set up. Does that help?"

Another sigh. "It might. Give them to me."

"I'm outside walking Newt right now so I don't have them in front of me, but I'll email them to you as soon as I get back to my suite."

"Okay."

"One other thing. Did you by any chance open the window in the bedroom of my suite when you were here?"

"No. Why?" There was deep suspicion in his voice.

"Did you happen to notice if it was locked?"

"Morgan, what aren't you telling me?"

"It's probably nothing. I noticed it was open a crack when I got back today. It might have been open before and I just didn't see it." This sounded feeble as hell to my ears, so I wasn't surprised when Jon scoffed at my explanation.

"Why don't you head home now and finish this investigation from there?" he said. "I'm getting a bad feeling about all of this."

"I'm okay. I've got Newt, remember?" Even as I said this, I saw Newt running off down shore chasing after a taunting seagull. "And I think I'm going to head home tomorrow."

"You're not going camping again tonight, are you?"

"No."

"Promise?"

"Promise."

Another call was coming in and when I looked at the screen, I saw it was Devon. "Will it calm your nerves if I promise to call you this evening to let you know I'm okay?"

"It will."

"Consider it done. Now let me go. Devon's calling."

Jon ended the call without any further comment, and I picked up Devon's call. "Hey, kiddo. You're fast. What have you got for me?"

"Your mental itch was an interesting one," he said. "I looked into circus fires and learned there was a terrible one with the Ringling Brothers and Barnum & Bailey Circus in 1944. It occurred during an afternoon show under the big top and was attended by thousands of people. The tent caught fire and collapsed in a matter of minutes, resulting in at least 167 deaths and more than 700 people injured. However, the only animals in the tent at the time were the big cats and they were all removed safely, so no animals escaped or died in the incident."

"There was another fire two years earlier and it not only killed a number of animals, it allowed others to escape. The circus was a bit vague about the circumstances, something of a trend in those days. But both of these incidents occurred out of state, so while they're not relevant to what you found in Bayfield, they might be part of what triggered your brain itch."

"Most likely. My mind made a connection between fires and circuses, and I know Wisconsin has an extensive circus history. When I was younger and my parents were looking to buy some circus-themed items for the store, I visited the circus museum in Baraboo. I became fascinated with all things circus for the better part of a year. I remember reading about the first fire you mentioned. It was in Connecticut, wasn't it?"

"It was. One of the worst fire tragedies in U.S. history."

"What about escapes in Wisconsin? Maybe in Baraboo? It was the original home of the five Ringling brothers and the birthplace of the Ringling Brothers Circus."

"True, but they only wintered there up until 1918. Lots of other circuses holed up in Baraboo over the years. I called the museum you mentioned, and a nice lady there told me that while there have been incidents involving escaped animals, the most notable of which might be the elephant that got out in 2017 and took a leisurely morning stroll through a Baraboo suburb, there weren't any she knew of involving primates specifically. Of course, it doesn't mean they didn't happen."

"Precisely. Circus folks might not be too eager to admit it when any of their animals are on the loose."

"I have to confess, I found this research fascinating," Devon said. "I had no idea Wisconsin has been home to sixty circuses over the years in thirty different cities. Did you know P. T. Barnum's circus got its start in Delavan in 1871?"

I chuckled, knowing Devon had been bitten by the circus bug. "I do now. You should talk to Rita, ask her to show you some of the books she has on the subject. When I get home, I'll dig around for some of the ones my parents got me when I went through my circus phase."

"Yeah, I'll read those in my spare time," Devon mocked. "In the meantime, complicating the circus theory is how Wisconsin is one of only a handful of states allowing residents to keep almost any animal they want as a pet. It's made the state attractive to animal smugglers for decades. There have been backyard exotic animal shows established at different times all over the state, many of them claiming to have one or more primates. Quite a few have had animals escape but it appears all the news articles detailing such incidents claim the animals were found and either recaptured or killed."

"Those are the ones we know about because they admit to the escapes," I said. "Some of these exotic animal farms aren't licensed or legal, so I'm betting they don't advertise it when their animals escape unless they're forced to because they're caught out. I imagine it's particularly true if the escaped animals aren't known to be dangerous."

"Yeah, on that subject," Devon said. "Is a chimp considered dangerous? Could a chimpanzee have inflicted the kind of damage Bodie Erickson suffered?"

"They're a wild animal, Devon, and any wild animal can be dangerous and unpredictable. Do you remember the news story a few years back about the woman who was attacked by the chimpanzee she'd been helping to take care of for years? The animal literally ripped her face off along with one of her hands. No one knows why the chimp turned on her the way it did. The motive behind Erickson's attack is easier to understand. He shot at a pregnant female and the animal attacking him was likely the female chimp's partner. What puzzles me is why there was a male and a female out there. It implies more than a simple one-off escape in the past and begs the question of where they came from."

"Well, back to our circus history," Devon said. "I've saved the best until last. In August of 1910, a passenger train rammed into the back of a Campbell Brothers Circus train in the town of Babcock, Wisconsin, at eight thirty in the morning. One person died, and several animals were killed, some in the crash, others in a resulting fire."

"Yes! I vaguely remember reading about this," I said. "But I don't remember hearing anything about chimps."

"That's because most of the news coverage was about a couple of escaped elephants. They were recaptured, but I dug around in some circus history sites online and uncovered interesting rumors of a cover-up. The official circus report for the crash claimed six camels, six ponies, and two elephants died, while two other elephants escaped and were later recaptured. However, there are claims an earlier report was found that subsequently disappeared, and it included three chimpanzees among the escapees, two females and a male. When a circus official was questioned about it many days later, he claimed it was an error and the chimps should have been listed as having died in the crash. The official report was never amended to fix this error and consequently the chimps don't appear as either escaped or dead. But there were those who believed the chimps escaped and no one realized it for a long time due to all the chaos. By the time anyone did figure it out, the chimps were long gone, and no one wanted to admit to the oversight. As a result, they were never found or caught."

My mind whirled with the possibilities. "You're on to something, Devon. It certainly could explain the presence of chimps here. The Chequamegon-Nicolet National Forest is actually two neighboring but distinct forests and the town of Babcock isn't far from the Nicolet portion. It's also close to a part of the state that's peppered with iron mines."

"What's the relevance of the mines?" Devon asked as I paused to let my brain make the rest of the connections.

"Think about it. The chimps would have needed shelter and a place to hide. Iron mining was a big industry back in the first half of the twentieth century and lots of spots were mined and then abandoned. It would be the perfect place for chimps to hide and get through the Wisconsin winters. It's the next best thing to a cave; in fact, it's probably better than a cave."

"Are you saying you think there could be a whole community of wild chimps living in Wisconsin?"

"It's possible, Devon. I mean, think about it. The original trio could have reproduced over the decades and as their numbers grew, their offspring could have also reproduced. They then might have spread out as territorial natures kicked in." I paused, once again sorting my thoughts. "It's hard to guess how many there might be out there because some of them, in fact, many of them, might have succumbed to weather, disease, predation, or starvation."

"Okay," Devon said thoughtfully. "Wild chimps on the loose helps to explain what happened to this Erickson guy, but it doesn't explain Bigfoot, does it? Chimpanzees aren't as big as a Bigfoot, or as big as most folks claim a Bigfoot to be."

"Chimps can get to be quite large," I said. "They can be as tall as a man and weigh as much as 200 pounds. In fact, if I remember correctly, the one that attacked the woman who lost her face was more than two hundred pounds. And yes, while that's still smaller than what most people report in a Bigfoot sighting, given the tendency people have to exaggerate, the way our memories work when we're excited or afraid, and a degree of confirmation bias stemming from the prevalence of Bigfoot sightings, it's quite possible a large chimp could be seen as a Bigfoot by some. People see what the rumors have prepared them to see, particularly when you add in darkness, fog, heavy trees . . . all the things typically present at these sightings. I should think it would be easy to confuse a chimpanzee for a Bigfoot."

"Okay then," Devon said. "All in all, a good day's work. It seems we've solved one death, but what about the other?"

What about it, indeed? There was still a murderer out there somewhere and I was determined to figure out who it was.

CHAPTER 33

I was certain a human had killed Pete Conrad and also certain it had to have been someone with intimate knowledge of Bodie Erickson's death and injuries. The killer had tried to make it look like the culprit was the same animal that had killed Erickson, but certain clues gave the game away. The medical examiner had noted one of them, though to the killer's credit, the ME hadn't felt strongly enough about the findings with Conrad's wound to officially declare the death a homicide.

Another mistake was the faked footprint, which was, pardon the pun, overkill. It was remotely possible someone else, someone completely unrelated to the murder of Pete Conrad could have arrived at Pine Lake and left behind the footprint as a joke, but the lake was isolated enough, and the time frames narrow enough for me to consider this a highly unlikely scenario. Knowing Conrad had been murdered was useless unless I could figure out *why* he'd been murdered because motive would be key in identifying the culprit.

I leashed up Newt and went back to my suite. After texting Jon the two phone numbers Mrs. Conrad had given me for her no-show callers, I settled in at the table to again sift through all the information in the folders Charlie had left with me. I hoped taking a second look might trigger other connections in my brain that I hadn't made before, much like the burnt wood smell had. Logic dictated that I focus on Conrad's folder and when I came across the picture of the footprint at Pine Lake, I set it aside. Then I took out my phone to look at the pictures I'd taken of the print on Madeline Island yesterday morning. Comparing the two side by side, it was obvious they were different, not only in size but in the angle of the toes, the shape of the overall foot, and the depth of the impression they left.

I felt confident Hans Baumann had made the print on Madeline Island, a task made easier by the softened, muddy ground from the heavy rainfall the night before. Had he also made the one by Pine Lake? Did he have more than one size and shape of foot form he used to salt his sites with prints? I supposed it would lend a level of authenticity to the theory if the prints weren't all identical. If there were giant apemen out there roaming around, the odds of them having the exact same footprint size, shape, and markings were slim to none. But Hans had messed up with the Madeline Island print by using a cast he'd used before in another state. He might have thought he was safe using it again so far away, but he hadn't counted on me being there.

I definitely couldn't put it past Hans to fake the footprints, but why kill Pete Conrad? Was it possible Conrad had provided financial services to Hans Baumann, services that might reveal some less-than-legal financial shenanigans, perhaps? I picked up my phone and sent a quick text to Devon, asking him to check Conrad's laptop for any evidence of an account with, or emails from, Hans Baumann.

There weren't any cameras in the Cheq that I could use to look for Hans Baumann's Land Rover in the forest on the day Conrad died, and I'd already seen how sparse traffic was on the roads out there, so the odds of someone having seen his vehicle were slim. But what about Washburn? Surely a business or two along the main highway had security cameras aimed out toward the road, and any car headed to Pine Lake would have most likely driven through town. Might a camera reveal Hans's vehicle passing by at the right day and time? I made a mental note to run the question past Charlie.

Thoughts of Charlie led me to consider her potential role in this mess. She was certainly vested in the whole Bigfoot conspiracy, but enough so to kill a man and make it look like a Bigfoot had done it? To what end? What did she have to gain? Exoneration? Maybe she *had* pushed her father out of the tree stand on purpose and then made up the Bigfoot story to explain what happened. Yet wouldn't the sighting of a large buck have served the same overall purpose? The Bigfoot story seemed an odd choice, though I suppose a child's whimsical imagination might account for it. I thought it more likely that what Charlie had seen was either a bear or one of the chimpanzees I now knew were living in the forest. To a tired, frightened, little girl, a bear or a large chimp could certainly look like a Bigfoot.

I was on the fence when it came to Charlie. She knew all the nitty-gritty details about Erickson's death well enough to create a copycat scenario. And there was an unnerving intensity to the woman at times. But was she killer material? I wasn't sure enough to rule her out.

Then there was Buck Weaver, an authoritarian bully of a cop who had access to all of the details regarding both Erickson's and Conrad's deaths and who would have been able to fake things enough to mislead investigators. He also made it crystal clear he didn't want me in Bayfield looking into the Bigfoot sightings. Why? What was he afraid I would find? And what might be hiding in his violent work history that hadn't made it into his personnel file?

So many possibilities and my thoughts were still fuzzy from a lack of sleep. I put my arms on the table and set my head down on them for a minute.

I must have dozed off because I startled awake when my phone rang. It was Jon.

"Hey, what have you got for me?"

"Hello to you, too," he chided.

"Sorry. I didn't get much sleep last night and I'm tired. Plus, this case is making me nuts. I'm desperate to figure it out and come home."

"Maybe I can help. I have some news for you about those phone numbers."

"Ooh, you sure know how to get a girl excited." It came out breathless, sensual, and it was met with an uncomfortably long silence. I realized that in trying to make up for my abrupt lack of a greeting I'd likely gone too far, too fast. "What did you find out?" I said, eager to move on.

Jon cleared his throat before speaking. "Turns out those numbers belong to burner phones bought with prepaid minutes loaded onto an SD card already in the phone. That means they were attached to a cell service provider. If the SD card had been bought separately elsewhere, we probably wouldn't be able to track who bought the phones."

"You know who bought them?" I said excitedly. I held my breath, waiting for a revelation, though it didn't quite materialize.

"Not who yet, but we know where and when. Both phones were bought at a super Walmart store in Ashland, Wisconsin, ten days ago. I'm in the process of getting security footage from the store and it would help if you, and especially Charlie, can review the footage to see if you recognize anyone. Unfortunately, the person who knows how to obtain the footage and send it to me won't be available until tomorrow morning, so I likely won't get it until then."

"That's great news. Thank you, Jon. I owe you a big one. I know you were reluctant to look into this."

"Anything for you, Morgan," he teased.

"Have you shared this with Charlie yet?"

"No, but I will. I'll send you both a link to the security footage once I get it."

"That would be great."

"When are you planning on coming home?"

"Tomorrow morning. I'm thinking there isn't much more I can do here now."

"Any thoughts on what you're going to tell Charlie?"

"I'll tell her what's behind the Bigfoot sightings for this area. Most of them anyway."

"I have to say, I still find the whole thing kind of mind boggling."

"I suppose it is and what boggles me now is what to do about it. I'm afraid if they're left alone, they'll eventually be discovered and hunted. I know someone who might be able to help, but in the meantime, there's still Pete Conrad's death to figure out because I don't believe he was attacked and killed by a chimpanzee."

"Let the local cops figure it out," Jon said. "You've fulfilled your role in this. And I'll feel a lot better when you're back home and safely tucked into your apartment again."

Sweet and quaint. I really did like this Jon Flanders fellow. Now if I could just keep from screwing it all up. Once I'd ended my call with him, I placed one to Charlie. It went to voice mail, and I wondered if Jon had called her right after hanging up with me, or if Charlie was simply screening her calls. I left a message, asking her to call me and she did barely a minute later.

"Hi, Morgan. Sorry I missed your call. I was in the bathroom, and I refuse to do the whole phone-call-on-the-toilet thing."

TMI, perhaps, but I felt the same way. "I understand. Have you heard from Jon about the security footage from the Walmart store in Ashland?"

"No. What security footage?"

I filled her in on what Jon had discovered and how he'd be sending us the footage, or a link to it, once he got it, which would likely be sometime tomorrow. Then I asked her about security cameras along the main road through Washburn.

"Yeah, I know of several places with cameras," she said. "And Baumann's vehicle should be easy to identify. Good thinking, Morgan. I'll check on it first thing tomorrow."

"Great. And, Charlie, there's something else I need to tell you."

"Ooo-kay," she said, quickly picking up on my somber tone.

Slowly, carefully, I laid out what I knew and how I knew it. I fully expected her to poo-poo my explanation of her Bigfoot experience but to my surprise and relief, she accepted my version of events as plausible and realistic.

"I suppose it makes sense," she said. "I knew what I saw wasn't a bear because it stood on its hind legs and shook a fist at us. And I suppose a big old hairy chimp could look like a Bigfoot. My father even said the word Bigfoot right before he fell."

I noted her continued narrative of him dying from a fall as opposed to being pushed. Then, as if she'd read my mind, she added, "You know, my mother asked me if I pushed my father out of that tree and made up the whole Bigfoot story. I swore to her it had happened exactly the way I said, but to this day I don't think she believes me. Because to this day, she still thanks me for, as she puts it, 'turning our lives around all those years ago.'"

"Wow. That has to be hard," I said, knowing what it felt like to have other people think you murdered one, or in my case, both of your parents.

"It used to be," she said with a sigh. "But it doesn't bother me anymore. I know I'll never convince her, so it is what it is. However, you have turned my life around, Morgan, by giving me an answer to what I saw all those years ago. Thank you."

"You're not done," I told her. "There's still the matter of who killed Pete Conrad."

"I know, but you've done what I asked you to do. What I needed you to do. As far as I'm concerned, your part in all of this is finished."

Jon had said the same thing to me and I happily agreed. I couldn't wait to get home, to have the security of familiar surroundings, and of the people I cared about: Devon, Rita, and yes, Jon Flanders.

"I'm glad I was able to help solve part of the problem," I told Charlie. "And since there isn't anything more I can do for you here, I'm going to head home first thing tomorrow morning."

"Of course. I'll let Maureen know you're leaving. You can drop your key off at the motel office when you're ready to head out."

"Tell Maureen thank you for letting me stay here on such short notice."

"Hey, she was delighted to have anyone in there after the fire forced them to shut down for so many weeks. You did her a favor."

"Keep me informed with Pete Conrad's case," I said. "I want to know how it all turns out."

"I will. And thanks again, Morgan."

As soon as we ended the call, I started throwing my things together and packing up the car so I'd be ready to go first thing in the morning. Newt, sensing another trip was afoot, followed me around, watching, tail wagging. While I was eager to go home and get back to some semblance of normalcy, contrary to what Charlie had said, I didn't feel like my job in Bayfield was done. Yes, I'd solved the mystery of what had killed Bodie Erickson and ruled out a Bigfoot, but what about Pete Conrad? The perpetrator behind his death—or rather, his murder—remained a mystery and I had a feeling this bit of unfinished business would haunt me even after I went home.

As it turned out, I was correct in this thinking, though in a much deadlier way than I had imagined.

CHAPTER 34

Newt and I were ready to hit the road by eight the next morning and before pulling away from the suite, I sent text messages to Devon, Rita, and Jon to let all of them know I was headed home. My store was closed on Mondays, and I was looking forward to having the place all to myself once I got back.

I was exhausted by the time I pulled around in back of my store a little before three in the afternoon. After driving for more than six hours straight I decided to leave the majority of the unpacking until morning and only removed my suitcase, my laptop, the files Charlie had given me, and Conrad's laptop from my car. I set them on a counter in the bookstore, figuring I could take them upstairs to the apartment later.

Newt needed a walk and a bathroom break, so I leashed him up and we strolled down to the shoreline of Green Bay, where I let him splash around in the water for a while. As I sat watching him, I got a text message from Devon saying he'd found a recent death notice for Anna Perry. He included a link to the obituary and even though my phone battery was nearly dead, I clicked on it.

By the time I finished reading, things had become clearer, though I still had one part to figure out. Excited, I headed back to the store and called Mitch Hollander, the man who had found Pete Conrad's body out at Pine Lake. I was lucky enough to have him answer this time and when I asked my question, what he told me allowed the final piece of the puzzle to drop into place. It also raised another suspicion and after plugging my phone in to charge it, I went outside and retrieved one more item from my car. I knew for sure then.

Took you long enough, Morgan.

I was about to unlock the door to go back inside when I felt a rush of air on my left and turned to see a dark blur of movement beside me.

"Hey!" I hollered and then I felt something hard jab into my side. Inside the store, Newt started barking.

A voice hissed a warning in my ear. "We're going to go inside, and you are going to make that dog shut up and behave or I will shoot it, right before I shoot you."

I turned to look at my attacker, but the person holding what I presumed was a gun had the hood of a sweatshirt pulled down far enough to hide the face. It didn't matter, though; I knew who it was. Even if I hadn't figured it out moments before, I recognized the voice.

"Do you understand me?" my assailant said.

I nodded but then said, "I do," to make sure my answer was clear.

I unlocked the door and pushed it open. Newt rushed toward me, and I stopped him with my legs and hands as I felt the gun jab even harder into my back.

"It's okay, Newt, it's okay." I stroked his massive head while also pushing him back and away from my assailant, who Newt was desperately trying to sniff, a low growl emanating from his throat. "Come on, boy," I said. "Come with me."

I grabbed Newt's collar so I could steer him along as the person wielding the gun stepped inside and let the back door close and lock. With my assailant trailing along close behind, I led Newt into my office beneath the stairs, told him to sit, which he dutifully did, and then told him to stay. This earned me a whimper. He knew something wasn't right and he started to get up and follow me out of the office until I used a sterner, louder voice to repeat my command.

"Newt, stay!" I punctuated the order with a demonstrative pointing of my finger and watched the confused look on my dog's face as I backed out of my office and shut the door, leaving him inside. He barked his objections immediately.

I gave my gun-wielding nemesis a dirty look as I took a few steps down the aisle toward where a mummified Henry stood guard on his wheeled pole.

I whirled around and said, "You've got some nerve, Trip Mann. Why are you doing this?"

He slid the hood off and tipped his head to one side again the way both he and his brother had done before. "It's your fault," he said. "If you'd only minded your own business." He shook his head. "If Charlie had only minded *her* own business," he added with exasperation.

"Murder *is* Charlie's business," I said. "And Bigfoot is mine. If you hadn't faked the footprint out at Pine Lake where Pete Conrad's body was found, I doubt I ever would have gotten involved."

He scowled and shook his head again. "Whatever," he grumbled.

"You're going to shoot me?" I said in disbelief. "You think killing me will solve all your problems?"

"It will solve enough of them," he retorted.

"Really? Did killing Pete Conrad solve any of your problems? Other people besides me know he was murdered by a human, not a Bigfoot. Investigations will be ongoing. And you have other problems, don't you?" I said, nodding toward the cast on his arm. "I'm guessing you didn't injure yourself in a fall, like you told everyone. What happened? Did your college gambling escapades with Kyle grow into a full-blown addiction, one costing you more money than you have? Did you borrow from the wrong people?"

He appeared surprised.

"What will they do to you next time, Trip?"

"Shut up, you nosy bitch."

"Come on, Trip. I figured it out easily enough and if I could do it, anyone else can, too. Killing me isn't going to help you."

As if in agreement with this sentiment, Newt's barking grew in both volume and ferocity. I saw Trip shoot an annoyed look toward my office door and I used the momentary distraction to sidestep a bit closer to Henry.

"I wanted to get rid of you out in the woods," Trip said. "I tracked you out there with that satellite tracking device I slipped into the first aid kit I gave you."

"Clever move, that," I said, guessing he'd used it to track me here, as well.

"Stupid move, that, going out into the woods alone," he countered.

"I wasn't alone."

He chuckled. "Yeah, I gathered as much when I heard the damned dog bark. I was going to do you like I did Conrad, make it look like another animal attack, but I didn't know you had a dog with you."

I recalled the manlike figure I'd seen skulking about in the woods the night I went camping and mentally thanked Newt—who was currently barking and pawing at my office door—for saving my life. Now I was trying to save his.

"It's okay. You did me a favor," Trip said, his gaze drifting over some of the items in my store, taking in skulls, shrunken heads, and taxidermied animals with noticeable distaste. I slid even closer to Henry. "The stuff you have in here is creepy as hell," Trip went on. "I don't think it will surprise anyone to discover you were killed here. A store like this must attract all kinds of creeps."

"No one any creepier than you."

He frowned at me, his brow furrowing even more as he realized I'd managed to increase the distance between us. Then his gaze settled on Henry with obvious repulsion. "I'll take whatever money you have in the till," he said. "That way it will look like a robbery. Much easier than faking another Bigfoot attack."

I knew I needed to keep him talking, to buy as much time as I could. "The medical examiner knows Conrad's death was faked," I told him. This was essentially true, even if the final ME's report didn't state as much.

Trip shot me a look of disbelief. "Bull," he said. "If that's true, why didn't I hear about it from Buck?"

His mention of Buck made me realize how he'd known what to do when he faked the attack on Pete Conrad. It was obvious he and his brother, Lloyd, were good friends with Sheriff Weaver, and the lawman had undoubtedly shared all the gory details of the first death with them. When pressured by Pete Conrad regarding the audit, Trip had brainstormed his Bigfoot idea.

"Buck didn't tell you because I don't think Buck knew," I said. "The report hadn't been officially released yet."

This made Trip look panicked, so I switched gears, trying for some flattery. "Still, I have to say, it was a brilliant scheme. And you know, you almost got away with it. I didn't figure out it was you until just a bit ago."

He tilted his head again, narrowing his eyes at me. "What gave me away?" he asked. I opened my mouth to answer but before I could say a word, he flushed with anger and answered his own question. "It was those stupid burner phones, wasn't it? But how? I didn't think those things could be traced and I blocked the numbers before I made any calls." He shot an irritated glance toward my office door, where Newt was scratching like crazy and growling in between barks. "Does your damned dog ever shut up?" He reached up and massaged his temple with the thumb of the hand holding the gun.

I turned toward my office and yelled. "Newt! Quiet!" It worked, at least for the moment. I looked back at Trip. "The mistake you made was calling an 800 number. The person owning one has to pay for calls coming in and that entitles them to know where those calls are coming from. Blocking doesn't work with those numbers."

"Hunh," Trip said.

"But it wasn't the phones that gave you away. It was the obituary for your mother, Anna Perry. Even then I wasn't sure if it was you or Lloyd who had done the deed, but then I remembered you telling me how you manage all the finances for the stores. I have to say, using your mother's email was a brilliant stroke."

Trip smiled and did a half-hearted shrug. "Kind of an accident, really," he said. "When she handed the reins off to me and Lloyd ten years ago, I took over her email account because it had all the contacts and history. I always meant to set up an email of my own with the company but never got around to it. I guess my procrastination was a good thing, eh?"

"It slowed me down," I admitted, "but then there was the fishing tip you gave to Mitch Hollander, the man who found Conrad's body? I thought it too conveniently coincidental that he got sent out there to Pine Lake when he did. So, I called him and asked what he remembered of the random fellow who had given him the tip. He'd already told us the tipster's name was Jim. He heard the waitress use it when your order was ready. When I saw your mother's obituary and learned your real name was James the Third, I felt certain it was you who'd killed Conrad. When I called Hollander the second time, he described you to a T. And while you and Lloyd look a lot alike, only one of you is sporting a cast on his arm."

Trip cursed and slapped himself on the head with the wrist of his gun-toting hand. The way he held the weapon made me suspect he was right-handed and therefore not used to wielding it in his left hand. Maybe this fact could play in my favor.

"Yeah, I didn't think through the part with the Hollander guy well enough," Trip said irritably. "It was a spur-of-the-moment thing. I figured someone would find the body within a few hours, a day at the most. Then two days went by, and I knew I had to do something. The forecast was calling for thunderstorms to roll through in a day or two and I knew the rain would destroy the footprint I'd made. I needed people to find it and make the obvious connection. And I didn't want the body out there too long before it was found or the wounds I made with the bear claws would get altered by scavengers going at the body."

"Bear claws?" I said.

"We have lots of bear stuff in the store," he said. "Surely you saw the big stuffed bear when you were there?"

I remembered then, the standing bear in the little camping diorama.

"Hunters have brought us lots of bear claws over the years as well as other odd trophies. My mother collected stuff like that. Some guy gave her the Bigfoot mold I used to make the footprint decades ago. The thing's been moldering away in a closet ever since." He paused and looked around the store again. "Come to think of it, she probably would have liked your store."

He turned and stared at a taxidermied deer head on the wall, his expression growing thoughtful for a moment before he made a face like he'd just tasted something horrible. "I'm not much for killing animals," he said.

No, just people.

Then with a sad smile, he added, "Kind of ironic when you consider our stores cater to hunters." He sighed and looked back at me then. "The bear claws came in handy, though using them turned out to be harder than I thought."

I realized the initial neck wound Trip had inflicted on Conrad had been necessary because Trip only had one working hand and needed to incapacitate the other man quickly. Conrad might have easily overpowered him if he hadn't been rapidly bleeding out. I shuddered as I imagined the effort it must have taken for Trip to later stab and rip apart areas of Conrad's dead body with those bear claws. It explained the bear hairs the ME had found on the body and, of course, I now knew why a hair simian in nature had been found on Erickson's body. If only Trip had refrained from making the fake footprint, he might have gotten away with it.

I realized just how crazy Trip had to be and it made my guts feel slippery and cold. He had slit a man's throat, watched him bleed to death, and then tore apart the dead body. Yet he winced at the idea of killing an animal and looked uneasily at Henry. Go figure.

"How did you find out I knew about you?" I asked. "I only made the connection minutes before you showed up."

"Charlie," he said. "She keeps saying she's breaking up with Kyle but then she's constantly calling him and spending time with him." He rolled his eyes. "She tells him everything, which he then tells me, and I've been seeing him more lately because we've been trying to develop a new system to use at the casinos." He paused and looked away for a second or two, squinting as if an idea had just come to him. I took advantage of the moment to slip an arm behind Henry and grab hold of a section of his shirt.

"Anyway," Trip went on, giving a little shake of his head. "Last night, Charlie told Kyle she was going to examine some security footage you had, and she hoped it would reveal who had killed Pete Conrad. She told Kyle about the phones and how you were the one who figured it out and that the security person at Walmart would be sending you the footage today. When Kyle told me that, I knew my only hope was to follow you home and stop you before you can send the footage to Charlie." He looked over at the counter where I'd set both of the laptops. "I'll be taking those with me," he said, gesturing toward the computers.

Imagine my surprise, which I wagered would be small potatoes next to the surprise Trip was about to get. It seemed Charlie hadn't told Kyle *everything*. She'd failed to mention Jon's involvement—to keep Kyle from getting jealous perhaps? Whatever her reason, Trip believed I was the one who had, or would soon have, the security footage. In his panic, he thought stopping me was his only hope. It wasn't like Charlie couldn't get the security footage herself if she wanted to, but maybe Trip thought he could explain it away somehow or convince Charlie to ignore it. Either way, Trip clearly hadn't thought things through very well. Clever as his plan had been, he was obviously no mastermind and now he was panicky, desperate, and flying by the seat of his pants.

"I don't have the security footage," I said quickly. "I never did. But the police do and so does Charlie by now."

Trip eyed me suspiciously, clearly trying to figure out if I was bluffing him. Then he smiled and said, "Live and learn. Or in your case . . ." He raised the gun, pointing it in my direction.

I was about to die.

A loud banging came from the front of the store, someone pounding on the door. I heard yelling outside and when Trip glanced toward the door, I saw my chance.

I shoved Henry toward Trip with all my might. I heard a loud yelp followed by a scream, followed by another bang from the front of the store. Then there was a much louder bang near my right ear as I dove toward the shelves behind Trip and scrambled around the end to the other side. There were animal skulls on display beside me and I grabbed a yak skull, stood, and heaved it at the back of Trip's head before ducking back down. There was a loud ringing in my right ear and while I could still hear, things sounded oddly distant and echoey. Through a small space in the shelving, I could see to the other side and saw Trip's legs were facing away from me, so I grabbed another skull, this one a cow with horns, stood, and prepared to stab him with it. But I froze when I saw another man approaching with a gun.

Jon! He had his gun pointing straight at Trip, who wisely set down his own weapon on the floor and raised his good arm over his head. Behind Jon I saw the white tendrils of Rita's hair, her messy bun a little messier than usual. I had no idea why she was there, but I was mighty glad to see her. I started to go around the shelves to hug her, but she dashed past Trip, kicking his gun aside as she did so, and then bent down to pick up Henry.

"Look what you did!" she said angrily as she righted Henry on his wheeled stand. He had a noticeable bullet hole in his chest and one of his arms was hanging funny. Jon walked up and cuffed Trip.

"You okay?" he asked me over the shelf.

I nodded and tried to slow my breathing. "I'm fine. I need to let Newt out."

"N-n-n-no!" Trip stammered. "It's bad enough that . . . that . . . thing attacked me." He glared at Henry, looking horrified, and a shudder shook him. "Don't let the dog come at me."

"He won't, as long as you behave," I said. I looked questioningly at Jon, who gave me a subtle nod. I went to my office door and opened it. Newt dashed out, sniffing me madly, and then he whirled around and growled at everyone else while standing in front of me. "It's okay, Newt. I'm okay. You're a good boy." I ruffled the fur around his neck and bent down to kiss him on top of his head. It instantly calmed him.

Trip spared us a glance but then quickly turned his attention back to Henry. Based on the way he'd screamed like a girl when Henry came at him, it was obvious he wasn't a fan. As Jon started reciting the Miranda, Trip shook his head and talked over Jon's attempts.

"Yeah, yeah, I got it. Now get me the hell out of this freak fest. This place gives me the creeps."

Ironic words, coming from a cold-blooded murderer.

CHAPTER 35

It was Monday, a week after my showdown with Trip Mann, and I'd invited everyone to dinner so we could compare notes on the case. Jon, Charlie, Devon, Rita, and I sat around my dining room table, all of us looking stuffed and sated after eating a delicious meal Jon had prepared: a Mexican lasagna with homemade cornbread, plus chips, salsa, and sangria. Newt sat beside me, his head mostly under the table so he could watch for any accidentally—or not so accidentally—dropped tidbits. Much to Newt's delight, it seemed everyone at the table was clumsy and accident prone.

"It all came together for me when I saw the obituary you found, Devon," I said. "As soon as I saw Anna Perry was survived by her sons, James the Third and Lloyd, and preceded in death by her husband, James Mann, Jr., it hit me. Namesakes who are the third of their kind are sometimes given the nickname of Trip." I nodded toward Devon. "Then wiz kid over here dug up the history of the Mann Brothers Outfitters. I'll let him tell you that part."

Devon smiled. "Yeah, I discovered the stores were born out of a company in Germany owned by the Perry family going back three generations. The Perrys specialized in the outdoors, camping, and sporting equipment and when Anna Perry met James Mann Jr. in Germany and eventually married him, they decided to move to the United States and open up a branch of the family store here, calling it Perry Outfitters. It did well and when they opened the second store, they combined their names and formed an LLC called Perryman Industries. When her husband died ten years ago, Anna handed the store off to her sons and went back to her homeland in Germany. The sons changed the name of the stores and the LLC registration to Mann Brothers Outfitters, but the company name remained under Perryman Industries with Teach and Springer."

I jumped in at this point. "When Devon told me what he'd found, I knew one or both of the Mann brothers had to be involved in Pete Conrad's death, and while I hadn't ruled Lloyd out, I was leaning toward Trip simply because I knew he dealt with the financial end of things. I remembered how he'd made a big deal out of giving me this complimentary first aid kit and then recalled the figure I later saw in the woods when I went camping. Sure enough, Trip had slipped a satellite tracking device into the bottom of the kit box so he could follow me out into the forest. He concocted some story to explain why the box had been opened but at the time I didn't pay much attention to it. And he used it again to track me back here to the store."

"You're lucky he didn't shoot both you and Newt in the woods," Jon said. "He meant to kill you. He told the police he had a gun on him that night, but he wanted to make your death look like another Bigfoot attack. Shooting you wouldn't have fit with his desired story. Once he realized you had a dog with you, he decided to back off and wait for another opportunity."

"Newt saved the day," I said, giving my dog a pat on the head. He looked disappointed when he discovered my hand was empty but accepted the affection anyway. "Looking back, I realized that the few times I had an encounter with Trip, Newt wasn't with me, and I don't think I ever mentioned him, so Trip had no way of knowing about him. Though he should have figured it out when he broke into my suite and left the note in my suitcase. Newt's dishes were on the floor along with a big bag of dog food."

Charlie, looking a bit abashed, said, "Trip didn't notice those things because it wasn't Trip who left the note. It was Buck. He bullied Maureen into letting him into your suite by saying it was a safety inspection to make sure everything was copacetic after the fire. I'm guessing it was also Buck who left the back window open in case he wanted to pay you another visit."

"I don't get why Buck was so determined to scare me off," I said. "If he wasn't the killer, what was he so worried about?"

"He's been in hot water for some time now," Charlie said. "Heck, for most of his career. There have been issues in the past with excessive violence and doing things he isn't allowed to do, like visiting your suite. He's been written up so many times, he's close to getting fired. One more complaint or infraction and he's done for. He's desperate to hang on because he wants his pension and he figured if you discovered the secret about my dad's death, how I'd claimed I'd seen a Bigfoot and Buck had kept that tidbit to himself, you might share it with his superiors, and it would do him in. I'm convinced he's behind the missing report I had in my file that said the hair found on Erickson's body was simian in nature, though he'd never admit to it."

"A bit of an overreaction if you ask me," I said, unwilling to let him off the hook.

"I know," Charlie said with a grimace. "But he's always been an overreactor. He has his issues but underneath it all he's a good cop and he's been around long enough to have seen a lot."

I wasn't sure I agreed, but since Charlie was possibly going to marry Buck's son one of these days, I decided to let her have her delusions about the man.

"To Buck's credit," Charlie went on, "his gut told him there was something hinky about Pete Conrad's death, but he didn't want to question the warden's findings and call attention to himself. He wanted the whole thing to just go away quietly. As it is, he's in trouble anyway for sharing details about both deaths with the Mann brothers. They've all been good friends for a long time, but Buck still should have known better. His careless oversharing helped Trip commit a nearly perfect murder. Sadly, it may end up being the straw that breaks the camel's back. Buck hasn't been fired yet, but rumors are circulating."

"How is Kyle taking all of this?" I asked.

Charlie beamed. "He's been a real sweetheart to his dad. Even though he's mad as hell at Trip for what he did, he feels a certain amount of responsibility for what happened given that it was his idea to try to come up with a system to use at the casinos back when they were in college. He had no idea Trip was gambling as much as he was—and he lost a *lot*," she said, her eyes growing big. "Lloyd is probably going to end up losing the stores."

"Sounds like you and Kyle are back on again," Rita said. Charlie shot her a look of surprise and Rita shrugged. "There are no secrets here at the store. Plus, I noticed the rock you're wearing on your left hand."

Charlie looked down at the ring as if surprised to find it there. "Kyle and I have an on-again, off-again relationship," she said, blushing. "For the moment it's on again." She shot a glance toward Jon but then quickly looked away.

I looked at Jon and smiled. "And you," I said to him. "You were quite the savior at the last minute."

"Lucky timing," Jon said. "I was heading for your place anyway to surprise you with dinner, knowing you'd be tired from the drive home. When I was on the ferry coming over, Charlie called to tell me she'd recognized Trip on the security video and had tried to find him and couldn't. Then your security camera started dinging on my phone with notifications and, when I checked, I saw someone with a hood come up to you and then shove you inside the store. The ferry had just docked, so I was minutes away, but I had to wait for all the cars ahead of me to offload. I didn't want to have to try to break down your store door so I called Rita, knowing she lived close by, and had her meet me here with her key."

"Thank goodness you were already on the way," I said. "Otherwise, I think my goose would have been cooked."

"Oh, I don't know," Jon said with a wink and a smile. "You had Trip pretty weirded out when you pushed Henry on him."

"Yeah, poor Henry," I said feeling oddly guilty. "I didn't mean to use him that way, but I could tell Trip was creeped out by the store's inventory and Henry in particular. I figured Henry was my best chance at getting away from him."

"How perspicacious of you," Rita said with a wink.

"Good one," I said, smiling.

Charlie looked confused and Jon clarified things for her. "It's this silly game Rita and Morgan play, trying to outdo one another with obscure words." I shot him a wounded look and he added, "Though I have to say it *is* entertaining and I've expanded my vocabulary since I started hanging with them."

Appeased, I smiled and said, "I've hired an extraordinarily talented taxidermist, assuming what I've heard about him isn't . . . rodomontade." I shot Rita a smug look and it was her turn to smile.

"Good one," she admitted. "Nicely obscure."

"Thank you." I did a little head bow. "Anyway, this taxidermist is coming tomorrow to take a look at Henry's wounds to see if he can fix him up."

"Tossing the yak skull was a nice touch," Jon said. "Though you did break it. Can he fix that?"

"I don't think so. But it's not a huge loss."

Devon shook his head. "Man, you guys need to call me the next time you pull stunts like this. I missed out on all the fun."

"You saved the day," I told him. "Without you and your online sleuthing skills, I never would have figured things out."

"Yeah, I should probably get another bonus," he said.

"This younger generation," Rita muttered, shaking her head. "Such entitlement."

Devon grinned at her. Despite the occasional ribbing, those two had grown close. Rita was like a grandmother to Devon.

"What are you going to do about the chimps?" Devon asked, shifting his attention back to me.

"I've contacted a fellow I know who does rehab work with

animals and I'm sponsoring him and his team so they can try to find and catch as many chimps as possible to relocate them. He has contacts with some sanctuaries he thinks they'll adapt well to. But none of you can say anything about it. They're going to work under-cover and keep their efforts as quiet and hidden as possible. If the general public finds out there are wild chimpanzees out there in the forest or in the old, abandoned iron mines, there will be hunters and thrill-seekers tromping around out there shooting at things, injuring themselves and others, and generally causing havoc."

"How many do you think there are?" Jon asked.

I shrugged. "Hard to say. Those original three chimps could have spawned multiple generations by now, assuming they and their offspring survived . . . a big assumption."

"You said those tidy stacks of small animal bones were left by them," Charlie said. "But I didn't realize chimps were carniv-orous."

"They're omnivorous, actually," I explained. "Chimps tend to eat fruits and nuts when they're in their normal habitats, but they also eat insects, particularly ants and termites. Meat eating isn't common but it's not unheard-of and, typically, it's the males that do it. They've been observed in their natural habitats eating bush babies and occasionally indulging in cannibalism when one of their own dies. They've even been known to hunt and eat small antelopes. Who's to say what these wild chimps might have adapted to eating while trying to live in the north woods of Wisconsin?" I paused and shrugged before continuing.

"I think the unusually dry summer this year explains why there were more Bigfoot sightings in Bayfield recently. The area chimps were probably forced to move into populated areas they otherwise would have avoided in search of clean water. And, like bears, they may have discovered the advantages of raiding garbage bins for food."

"There could be a lot of them out there," Jon said.

I shrugged. "Who knows? There are Bigfoot sightings all over Wisconsin, but there are also the crazy impostors like Hans Baumann confusing things. Maybe there are dozens of chimps out there, maybe hundreds. Maybe only a handful. I don't know if what Nathan Hotchkiss saw was the same one I saw, or the same one Erickson shot, or a completely different one altogether. Maybe there's a small nomadic tribe of them. Or maybe it's just people's vivid imaginations."

Silence fell around the table as each person contemplated the possibilities. Then, in a quiet voice, Charlie said, "Or maybe, just maybe, there really is a Bigfoot or two out there somewhere."

I do love plausible existability.

AUTHOR'S NOTE

Wisconsin has an extensive and fascinating circus history, one that honestly surprised me when I learned of it. Baraboo, Wisconsin, which is sometimes called "circus city," is not only famous for serving as home to the Ringling brothers but also for being the winter quarters many a circus retreated to after spending months on the road traveling the country. Ringling Bros. World's Greatest Shows was born there and in 1907 the Ringling brothers bought their largest competitor, the Barnum & Bailey Circus, hailed as the Greatest Show on Earth. The two circuses later merged and became the Ringling Bros. and Barnum & Bailey Circus—Greatest Show on Earth. When they relocated from Baraboo to warmer winter quarters, other circuses moved in, keeping Baraboo firmly embedded in circus history for decades to come.

Circus World, located at the original quarters of the Ringling Bros. Circus in Baraboo, is worth a stop if you're ever in the neighborhood. The museum is filled with circus wagons, posters, artifacts, paintings, photographs, business records . . . basically a fascinating peek into what life was like in circuses from around the world. During the summer they offer a number of family-friendly shows.

Sadly, the plight of circus animals was often heartbreaking during the circuses' heydays, and escapes were not unusual as the animals fled from their abuse for a brief taste of freedom. Most were recaptured. Some were killed. Those are the ones we know about.

Thankfully there are new laws and regulations in place today to protect and prevent some of the cruelties that took place in the past. Even so, we still have far to go when it comes to giving the animals we share this planet with the respect, dignity, and kindness they deserve.

The horrific train accident in Babcock, Wisconsin, that's mentioned in this book did happen and a number of animals died as a result. The two elephants mentioned did escape and were later recaptured. The oversight of not realizing three chimpanzees had also escaped is a bit of fiction. While it's not part of the documented real-life tragedy, it's not beyond reason to think such a thing might have happened as the circuses in those days weren't always quick to admit it when one or more of their animals escaped, fearful of backlash or someone shutting them down.

So, forgive the brief flight of fancy I took for the sake of my story. I hope you enjoyed imagining the possibilities along with me, the plausible existability. And please be kind and respectful to all the animals of the earth, even the human ones.

ACKNOWLEDGMENTS

Heaps of gratitude go to Lynna Martin, Bayfield Conservation Warden extraordinaire and one of the most sharing and helpful people I've ever had the pleasure to work with. Thank you for patiently answering *all* of my questions in such detail, and please excuse the bit of poetic license I've taken with some of the facts for the sake of my fiction. I'm also grateful to Matthew Koshollek, Dane County Conservation Warden, for getting me started on the necessary connections, and Bradley A. Ray, Fisheries Biologist for the Lake Superior Fish Team.

I'd also like to thank the Stoughton, Wisconsin, Police Department for their cooperation with some of my procedural questions and the immensely helpful Citizen's Police Academy they offer. The Academy was not only educational but tons of fun! Please excuse any errors or stretching of the truth I may have committed either accidentally or intentionally.

I owe a "monstrous" debt of gratitude to my agent, Adam Chromy, for all his hard work, excellent insight, and wise guidance. Thank you for everything you do. I wouldn't be able to continue in this career I love so much if not for you (and Jamie).

Thanks, also, to all the wonderful people at Berkley who help to make my books the best they can be, from my brilliant editor, Tom Colgan (I so enjoyed our bonding breakfast at Bouchercon), to the artists, copyeditors, and marketing folks. It's a pleasure and an honor to work with all of you.

Finally, a heartfelt thank-you to my family, friends, and all the readers, both old and new, who have made it possible for me to do what I do. I value your love, encouragement, and support more than you know.

May all the monsters in your lives be kind ones.

Keep reading for an excerpt from Annelise Ryan's
next Monster Hunter Mystery . . .

BEAST
of the
NORTH WOODS

I carefully removed a glass orb from a carton stuffed with wood shavings and held it aloft in one hand, eyeing it in the overhead light of the store.

My employee Rita Bosworth came up behind me in the aisle and peered at the orb over the top of her glasses. "What did you order now, Morgan?"

I noted the light chastising tone in her voice. It was mid-January and with the holidays over, sales in the store would be slow. It wasn't the best time to add inventory, but I hadn't been able to resist.

I glanced from the orb in my hand to Rita and noticed how her typically messy bun of snow-white hair looked surprisingly neat this morning. She was wearing the light blue angora cardigan I'd given her for Christmas, and it really heightened the blue of her eyes.

"It's a crystal ball," I told her, stating the obvious. I reached back into the box with my free hand and pulled out an ornate brass base with two skeletal hands rising up on either side. After shaking loose a few clinging pieces of wood shavings, I set it on a nearby shelf and then carefully nestled the glass ball in between the hands. Once I knew it was secure, I stepped back and eyed it critically, my head tipped to one side.

"What do you think?" I asked, expecting practical Rita to tell me how impractical an item it was and then giving it a week before someone knocked the glass ball loose and broke it. Maybe it was impractical, but I'd bought a crystal ball for my other employee, Devon Thibodeaux, for Christmas knowing one of his Cajun relatives in New Orleans not only had a similar one but operated a successful fortune-telling business centered around it. I'd heard Devon wax on wistfully about the orb on more than one occasion, saying that while he knew the thing possessed no magical powers, he still found it mesmerizing.

Once I saw the one I got for Devon, I realized it was, indeed, mesmerizing and decided then and there to get another for the store. It was precisely the sort of thing my store was known for—that and mystery books. The store name says it all: Odds and Ends. The oddities were what fascinated me the most, whereas the mysteries, in which someone typically comes to their end, fell more in Rita's wheelhouse.

When I turned to look at Rita, I saw she was no longer focused on the crystal ball but instead had her back to me, looking at something, or as it turned out, someone who had been hidden behind her. I eyed a tall—though an inch or two shy of Rita's six feet—slender fellow dressed in a tailored suit and tie beneath a dark gray, herringbone overcoat. He held a briefcase clutched close to his chest, and in contrast to his otherwise neatly pressed self, he had an unruly mop of graying brown hair. The expensive suit and coat and the briefcase suggested he wasn't my typical customer, but my store is located in Door County, a vacation mecca located in Wisconsin, and as such it attracts all types of people. I didn't want to jump to any conclusions. Besides, the store was closed today, and our only sales would be either online or by phone. I wondered how this man had gotten in.

"May I help you?" I asked him, my tone a bit frosty.

"He's with me," Rita said, giving me a tenuous smile. "I let him in through the back door."

That answered one question. I had several more.

"Morgan Carter, meet Roger Bosworth, my brother-in-law," Rita said.

"Technically, I'm a step-brother-in-law," Roger corrected.

"Yeah, okay." Rita turned slightly so that I could see her face and Roger couldn't and she rolled her eyes.

"I didn't know you were having family visit, Rita," I said. "If you need time off, you know it's not a problem. Things are slow this time of year."

This was an understatement. Even though there's plenty of fun stuff to do in Door County in the wintertime, things tend to slow down and freeze up, both figuratively and literally. Lots of local business owners head for warmer climes in the winter, shutting down completely. Others, like me, stay open but with reduced hours and more of a focus on phone and online sales. Thanks to

Devon, I have an excellent online store with displays of some of my more interesting wares.

Roger stepped up beside Rita and she glanced at him briefly before turning her laser stare back my way, clearly trying to communicate something to me. My dog, Newt, sat beside me and he must have been trying to pick up on Rita's nonverbal cues, too, because he tipped his head to one side, then to the other, and let out a little whine as he watched her.

Roger eyed Newt nervously, a common reaction when people meet him for the first time. He's a big dog, and his stare can be intimidating, but that's because he's mostly blind, not because he's a threat. He's a sweet boy and wouldn't hurt a soul unless they were trying to hurt me.

"Well, yes, I might need some time off," Rita said, "but not for the reason you think. Roger wants to hire you."

Something else I should mention: in addition to owning my store, Odds and Ends, I'm a cryptozoologist available for hire. In case you don't know what a cryptozoologist does, let me explain. I hunt for legendary creatures that may or may not exist, like the Loch Ness Monster and Bigfoot. It's not a job in high demand, at least not usually, though things have picked up for me lately. Go figure.

Roger retrieved a business card from his coat pocket and handed it to me. It was made of heavy stock and the name Roger Bosworth, Esq. was embossed on it in thick, black letters. Underneath this, written in gold: *Bosworth & Crown, Attorneys at Law*, and an address in Rhinelander, Wisconsin.

"Roger's a lawyer," Rita said.

"I see that."

Why would an attorney want to hire me? And why did Rita seem so out of sorts? I wondered if I was about to be sued. My paternal grandfather made millions in the Great Lakes shipping business and thanks to his smart investment choices, I'm comfortably situated moneywise after inheriting the family fortune. This can make me a target for lawsuits when certain types find out. I don't advertise my wealth and live a relatively modest lifestyle for the most part, but the Carter family name is well known in the area and word gets around.

"It's my nephew, Andy," Rita said, an odd hitch in her voice. "He's a suspect in a murder case and I'm hoping you can help him."

This only confused me more. "I'm not sure I understand."

Roger clarified. "My son, Andrew, has been arrested for the murder of a young man found in the woods north of Rhinelander. The victim was nearly disemboweled and had severe wounds to his face, neck, and one leg, the latter proving fatal as his femoral artery was severed."

Even spoken in the matter-of-fact, terse, and lawyerly voice of Roger, these facts took me aback. "Oh, my," I said, feeling my throat tighten. My heart picked up its pace and I recognized what was happening right away; I was on the verge of a panic attack. Newt realized it, too, and he immediately thrust his head into my hand, leaning into me. I stroked the fur along the back of his neck and it calmed me. A little.

"Andrew swears the man was killed by a Hodag," Roger continued in a tone one might use to order dessert. "He saw the creature leave the scene."

His claim was absurd, so much so that I felt my tension begin to ease. This had to be a practical joke Rita was playing on me. I tilted my head to one side and smiled at her. "Good one," I said with a sly wink.

Rita opened her mouth to say something, but Roger got there first.

"Rita says you're a renowned cryptid hunter. I need you to prove a Hodag, not my son, killed this man."

I bit my lip while trying to figure out my response to this. After a few seconds, I said, "I don't know how renowned I am, but I'm a serious cryptozoologist who knows the Hodag is a made-up creature."

Roger cocked his head and narrowed his eyes at me. "Is it? Are you one hundred percent sure?" He looked around at my inventory, making a sweeping gesture toward some of the displays. "I see lots of extraordinary things here in your store, some of them real, some of them fake, many of them fascinating and out of the realm of normal. You even have a mummified mascot sitting up front by the door. Rita tells me the fellow was once a forty-niner."

"Henry," Rita tossed out, nervously picking at her skirt. "His name is Henry."

"Mr. Bosworth," I said, "I'm interested in cryptids of all types, but I have to say, the Hodag is at the bottom of my list. The creature was a manufactured hoax perpetrated by a logger back at the turn of the twentieth century. He eventually confessed to the deception."

"While that may be true," Roger said, "the fellow came up with the idea of a Hodag because there were plenty of legends surrounding the creatures already. Who's to say those rumors weren't based on some truth? Tales of similar creatures can be found in folklore all around the world."

Well, he had me there.

He paused and gave me a little smile. "I understand your skepticism, and it's your reputation for thorough and honest research I want. To be honest, if anyone other than my Andrew had come to me claiming a Hodag had killed someone, I would have dismissed it without a second thought. But Andrew is not someone prone to confabulation."

"Even when he's up against a murder charge?" I asked. "Most people are capable of manufacturing all sorts of wild stories under much less life-altering circumstances."

"I get your point," Roger admitted grudgingly. "But I know my son."

"And I know Andy, too," Rita said. "He spent a lot of time with me and George when he was little because Roger lived in Milwaukee until Andy was thirteen. Andy's mother died when he was only two and we often helped Roger with childcare. Andy spent plenty of time in our bookstore and our house. I know him. He's not a killer." She paused and gave me a pleading look before adding, "You have to help him, Morgan. Please."

This pleading version of Rita, so unlike her usual reserved and composed persona, unsettled me.

"At least meet Andrew and talk to him," Roger said. "See what you think. If after you've talked to him you don't want to help, I'll understand."

"I won't," Rita muttered, making me wonder if she'd intended for me to hear her or not.

"Okay," I said. "I'm willing to look into it. But I'm not making any promises."

"Thank you," Rita said, the words coming out in a rushed sigh of relief.

"Help me understand this better," I said. "Why do the police think Andy killed this fellow? Couldn't it have been someone else? Or some*thing* else?"

Rita and Roger exchanged looks before Roger said, "There is some history between Andy and the victim, history that could be interpreted as motive."

Now we were getting into the nitty-gritty, but before I could ask for more details, Roger said, "You'll want to come check out the scene of the crime as soon as possible. They're calling for snow off and on starting in a couple of days and it will alter things. Andy was denied bail, so he's currently housed in the Oneida County Jail, and I assume you'll want to talk to him soon, as well."

"Okay," I said slowly, resisting an urge to slap back at Roger's assumptions.

"I'm coming, too," Rita said. "Devon can manage the store for a bit, can't he?"

This was essentially a rhetorical question. We both knew Devon was more than capable of handling things, especially since we were currently open from Thursday to Sunday, and it was only Monday. I knew he would love the chance to manage things on his own, not to mention the guaranteed hours.

I looked down at Newt and ran a hand over his big head. "Looks like we're taking another road trip," I said. He thumped his tail with happy excitement.

Rita stepped up and wrapped me in an awkward hug, her tall, bony body stiff against mine. "Thank you, Morgan," she whispered. "I won't forget this." When she pulled back, she smiled at Roger. "I told you she'd do it."

"Very good," Roger said. "Thank you. I appreciate your help."

He bowed and it struck me as comically decorous. Then again, everything about Roger was overly formal, from his way of talking to his posture and the clothes he wore. Despite this, I saw hope bloom in his eyes, and it worried me. I didn't want to elevate his expectations, because a big part of me believed this was going to be a fool's errand.

"Don't thank me yet," I said.

"Can you be in Rhinelander tomorrow?" Roger asked, savvily ignoring my caution.

"I suppose." I was starting to feel a bit out of sorts with the speed of it all. "I'll need to find a place to stay."

"Already taken care of," Rita said. "I took the liberty of booking rooms for both of us at a hotel in town. It's nothing fancy, but it's clean and allows dogs."

I arched my brows at her presumptiveness, and she had the good grace to blush and look away.

Roger cleared his throat, said, "I'll see you tomorrow, then," and made a hasty retreat. Seconds later I heard the back door open and close.

Rita said, "I'll drive my own car, in case one of us wants to come back sooner than the other. I left the motel info on the desk in your office. I need to go home and pack." She whirled around and, like Roger, disappeared out the back door moments later.

I looked down at my dog and shook my head. "Looks like we've been played, Newt." He whined back at me but thumped his tail, seeming unsure if he should be worried or happy. "Best get to it, I suppose."

I started to head for my office, a tiny space tucked beneath the stairs that lead to my apartment on the floor above, but detoured and went toward the front door instead. There, seated in a large chair, was Henry, the mummified forty-niner Roger had referred to. The poor fellow had fallen into an ice crevasse during the gold rush and was found by some Native Americans years later. They further preserved his already mummified body and kept him for years at a store on their reservation. My father acquired him back when I was in my late teens, brought him home, stuck an Indiana Jones–style hat onto his head, and named him Henry. He's been something of a store mascot ever since and, along with Newt, he's also my confidante. Henry is a great listener and really good at keeping secrets.

I adjusted his hat to a jauntier angle and then stood back and eyed him critically. He'd suffered some trauma recently, but I'd had him repaired and he looked none the worse for it.

"What do you think, Henry?" I said. "Have I stepped out of the frying pan into the proverbial fire with this one?" He stared back at me. "It's not like I have a choice, really. Rita is like a mother to me. I can't tell her no."

Henry remained reticent. I sighed, turned around, and looked about the store. With everyone gone and the place closed for the day, it was deathly quiet. In retrospect, I probably should have recognized this for the ominous sign it was.

Author photo by H. Claire Photography

Annelise Ryan is the *USA Today* bestselling author of multiple mystery series, including the Mattie Winston Mysteries. A retired ER nurse, she now writes full-time from her Wisconsin home.

VISIT ANNELISE RYAN ONLINE

AnneliseRyan.com
𝕏 Ryan_Annelise
 AuthorAnneliseRyan

Ready to find
your next great read?

Let us help.

Visit prh.com/nextread

Penguin
Random
House